A Knot of Trolls

Also by J.M. Ney-Grimm

Troll-magic

Sarvet's Wanderyar

Livli's Gift

Devouring Light

A Knot of Trolls

SEVEN TALES OF MAGIC AND TROLL-MAGES

ഔഃഔ

by J.M. Ney-Grimm

Wild
Unicorn

ISBN-13: 978-0615977287
ISBN-10: 0615977286

Designed by JMNG

Cover art:
"Medieval Lady" by Vladimir Nikulin / Dreamstime.com
"Woman in an Ancient Corridor" by Jose Antonio Sánchez Reyes / Dreamstime.com

For my readers,
every single one of you,
thank you

Table of Contents

ഇൻയ

A Note About Where

The Troll's Belt takes place in Gosstrand,
a frontier territory of Silmaren.

Crossing the Naiad occurs in Silmaren proper,
near its eastern mountains.

Skies of Navarys starts on an island far off the eastern shore of
Solmondy, but includes two scenes in Cambers.

Resonant Bronze transpires in the mountains west of Gosstrand.

Rainbow's Lodestone has the same location as *Resonant Bronze,*
2000 years later.

Star-drake occurs in the moors west of those western mountains.

Perilous Chance takes place in the northeastern region of Auberon.

Gosstrand

Silmaren

Erice

hathorlynd

fiorish

Meuvessie Sea

Auberon
Pavelle

Cambers

Solmondy

Giralliya

N
W E
S

Istria

Bazinthiad ○

The North-lands

A Knot of Trolls

The Troll's Belt

Brys slammed the door behind him and stomped across his room in fury.

It wasn't fair. It just wasn't fair.

Did Jol have to sweep the floors each afternoon when school let out?

No.

Did Jol have to wash the curing cheese wheels in his motter's dairy?

No.

Did Jol have to help put up vats of kraut when too many cabbages were ready in the garden?

Of course not.

It wasn't fair, it wasn't fair, it wasn't fair!

He banged open the shutters of his bed nook, threw himself down on the mattress, and punched his pillows a few times.

And now he wouldn't get to go to the solstice bonfire either, shun it!

Lars' patter had promised that all the kids old enough could come early and build the fire. Lars said there would be rope-climbing contests, a juggling tournament, and limb-running races.

Shun it! Shun it! Shun it!

Why had he answered back when Patter reminded him of the sweeping chore? He knew it was his responsibility. It was just . . . that he'd thought he'd finished everything.

Pilka and Pehmea, their household reindeer, retrieved from today's herd boy, milked, and settled in the byre.

Cheeses washed, turned, and re-weighted.

Clean laundry fetched from Aunt Mersela and put away.

And the mended chair delivered to Froiken Ildsdotter.

Everything tidy, the chores complete, and his time his own. The schoolmaster had even refrained from setting homework in honor of the evening festival, so the rest of the day was his.

Except then Patter had returned unexpectedly from the mill – something about a caliper-and-chisel set forgotten and needed for one of the men – just as Brys was heading for the entry staircase.

Patter took one look around and said sternly, "Why is there still mud on this floor?"

And Brys had answered, "Because *you* tracked it in."

And that had been that: a nasty shouting match between them, culminating with Patter's decree that Brys spend the afternoon and evening in his room. Not fair!

He gave another punch to his pillows, but it was half-hearted.

I should have just bitten my tongue. Why didn't I?

It wasn't really about the sweeping. It was . . . that Patter seemed to think Brys was trying to skive off without finishing his chores on purpose. Why couldn't he assume the best, instead of the worst? Or have asked . . . something else?

Brys had just forgotten, that was all.

And this wasn't the only instance either. Patter seemed poised for criticism, pouncing on each small fault, convinced Brys wanted to do less than his fair share. And it just wasn't so.

He knew why – besides milking the reindeer, splitting firewood, weeding the garden, and repainting the house stilts with rendered pine sap – he had to do a bunch of other stuff too. Sweep, wash dishes, dust, put away clothes, help put up vegetables and all. It had been him and Patter alone for all his life.

Jol had his motter, Aunt Mersela, to pitch in on all the daily chores.

Now, it was true that Aunt Mersela was known to split firewood when her temper was up, so Jol had to wash dishes on those days. But they had three to do all that needed doing.

He and Patter had just themselves. And Patter did the mill accounts in the evenings at home.

How had Patter managed? Way back when?

Brys could remember that when he was very, very small, he'd spent days with Aunt Mersela and nights at home and hadn't *any* chores. In fact, he'd thought Aunt Mersela his motter (and called her so) until he went to school and learned otherwise.

But Patter must have done everything himself.

No . . . maybe not.

They'd always eaten at Aunt Mersela's and Uncle Karl's table. He remembered that, now he came to think. Even after he started school, they walked across the garden between the two houses every morning for breakfast and every evening for supper. And Aunt Mersela had packed his and Patter's dinner pails. She still did their laundry.

So Patter hadn't had to worry about meals or cleaning up after them. Really he'd organized things pretty well. And Uncle Karl – Patter's younger brother – had been generous with help.

Why couldn't Patter understand now that Brys knew how things were? Knew he needed to pitch in? Knew he had to do his best? Why did Patter assume the worst?

Brys shrugged and slouched moodily over to the window.

He could see most of Glinhult straggling up the hamlet's hill to the clearing at its top surrounded by towering Wych elms. A few folk were still bustling around their homes – most stilt houses like his, a few the old-style tree eyries – putting away hoes and digging forks, locking the doors to the chicken coop, or carrying full milk buckets up to their kitchens. But they'd join the crowd on the hill soon.

I must be the only one who won't be there, he thought savagely.

Not fair! So not fair!

He dragged a low stool over and sat, resting his forearms on the window sill.

There were the Tirillsdotter sisters now securing the byre under their home – where Talja and Syoja were settling for the night – and strolling toward the hilltop. He saw Oskar and Pietur join them. Lars would already be there, undoubtedly arranging the scrap from the lumber mill along with household discards just so, to be sure the bonfire would burn well. Aunt Mersela and Uncle Karl had left early, declaring that if Jol got a holiday from chores (and they'd allowed him that), so did his elders.

A year ago, Patter would have done the same for Brys. Was it something about him turning twelve that had changed everything? But Jol was thirteen, and Uncle Karl was just the same.

Brys gritted his teeth.

Was that a flicker of flame on the hill? A spiral of smoke?

It was hard to tell. Dusk wouldn't arrive until long after the bonfire was started, the days of full summer being so long. He narrowed his eyes.

Yes!

The fire was well and truly started. It must have caught with the first few grinds on the tinder wheel. A good omen, that.

His shoulders sagged.

I'm not there, and I'm not going to be there.

He sighed. Then straightened.

Wait a moment . . . why not? Why not go despite Patter's prohibition?

Brys chewed his lip thoughtfully. So . . . disobey Patter? He generally didn't. But, *generally*, Patter was reasonable. Why seek trouble when it was unnecessary?

But *this* wasn't reasonable.

Miss the solstice fire just because he'd forgotten to sweep the floors?

I won't, he decided. *I don't care. I'm not going to mope here at the window all evening, while everyone else has fun.*

He jumped to his feet, almost knocking over the stool in his haste, crossed the room to the cupboard by his bed nook, and rummaged in its bottom drawer.

There it was: his winter cap.

He'd need to hide his hair, or Patter would spot him, even in the crowd, and Brys didn't intend to return home until he was good and ready. There were other redheads in Glinhult, but they were many years older or younger.

What else could he do to make sure Patter didn't see him and summarily enforce discipline?

I know! I'll borrow Jol's new tunic. He hasn't worn it yet, so Patter won't recognize it. And Jol won't mind. He'd suggest it, if he were here.

Plans settled, Brys hurried from his room, but cast a glance around the gathering area of the house. Yup, sink empty and clean.

Table wiped and clear. Armchairs and settle free of jackets, book bags, and other debris.

He stepped around the bannister to the house entry and pulled up the trap door.

Sias shun it! Patter really had been mad, to close the trap in the month of Joiesse.

Brys hooked it open.

Their stairs down to the ground had been enclosed for as long as he could remember, and they used the trap door only in winter. Even then, if they were expecting guests, they left it open and lit the small tile stove beside the straight door to warm the stair hall.

This door he closed carefully behind him, then galloped through the flower and vegetable garden, in through his cousin's straight door, then up the stairs.

Their trap was open, secured to the wall with a hook, as usual.

He rounded the newel post, heading for the next flight of stairs.

Uncle Karl had built with a bigger family in mind, so Jol's room was one of two tucked under the roof. Brys had always envied his cousin the cozy feeling the slanting ceiling gave to the space and his cushioned window seat in the dormer niche. Its high view made Brys imagine himself a hawk in a tree top, surveying all of Glinhult from the sky.

Ignoring the window for now, he doffed his own tunic and pulled Jol's over his shirt. It was big. Jol had hit a growth spurt after his last name-day, gaining half a head on Brys and adding shoulder width as well. But the tunic wasn't impossible.

Brys lolloped down the stairs again, paused, then tiptoed into Aunt Mersela's bedroom to check himself in her mirror. Would his misdirection with hat and tunic be disguise enough?

Not if he let his jaw-length hair stick out below the hat.

Hmm. What to do, what to do?

He looked over Aunt Mersela's dressing table. Brys' hair wasn't long enough to tie in a horsetail the way Jol did his, but maybe two of his aunt's clips could fasten the front bits to the back of his head. It was only the front bits that were showing.

He wasn't used to hair clips and fumbled them in several too-loose attempts, before achieving something that seemed likely to stay put. He jumped while tossing his head. Nothing shook free.

Time to go!

He'd already missed the lighting, the hymn, and the blessing, but the best was yet to come. He scurried for the hilltop.

His cousin didn't recognize him for a moment, even when Brys came smash up to him.

Jol stared blankly, then laughed. "Brys! What are *you* doing here? Uncle Arn said you weren't coming." He paused, then protested, "Hey! That's my tunic, you thief! Give it back!" He punched Brys in the shoulder, but half-heartedly. Brys shoved him back with equal lack of enthusiasm.

"I needed it, Jol," he insisted. "And you weren't home to ask, now were you?"

Jol smirked. "Day off from chores," he reminded. "So what gives?"

"Patter rated me for not sweeping, and I gave him a flip back answer," Brys admitted.

Jol's jaw dropped a shade. "You back answered Uncle Arn?"

"Um, yeah."

"And you're here? With leave?" Jol closed his mouth, but his eyes widened.

"Without leave."

"Thus my tunic." Jol shook his head. "And your winter hat. Huh."

"Patter's been so grouchy. I can't do anything right," Brys burst out. "I decided I just wasn't going to knuckle under one more time."

"You *are* brave." Jol gave him a curious look, then grinned. "So are you going to sneak around the fringes or be bold and join the fun?"

"Some of each," Brys admitted.

"Are you up for the rope climbing? It's about to start!" Jol bounced on his heels.

"Who's judging?"

"Old Matts."

"He won't notice anything," Brys asserted. "He hardly sees well enough to greet me in the street at high noon. Come on! Let's go!"

He actually won second place in the rope climbing, which triumph gave him courage to enter the limb racing.

Patter subbed in for Herr Olson as judge halfway through the heats, but seemed to notice nothing amiss with the contestant in the black hat and crisp, new clothing.

It was probably a good thing Brys came in seventh. Likely none of the runners were very visible as they raced along the branches high above the ground, dodging twigs and leaf clumps. But Brys doubted his disguise would have passed muster, if Patter had handed him one of the carved boomerangs being passed out as prizes.

The rest of the evening was equally satisfactory.

Playing tag as the shadows deepened. Watching the last round of the juggling contest where the winner lofted twenty-five balls into the air and kept them up in a flashing, elongated arc stretching as high as the flames of the bonfire. Scarfing down sweet nut pastries.

And finally settling around the fire as it burned down to tell haunt stories and jokes or to just tip his head back to look at the stars.

I'm glad I came, he thought.

That was before he arrived home sometime after midnight.

Patter was sitting at the table, waiting, when Brys climbed the stairs and emerged through the trap.

For a moment, they simply looked at one another, Patter grim and angry, Brys with a sinking sensation in his stomach.

"So." Patter's voice was even, but held a disturbing undertone. "You chose to leave the house, when I bade you keep within it. No doubt your reason seemed good to you." His eyes were flat.

Brys swallowed, trying to recapture his bravado.

It eluded him, but a spark of his earlier indignation straightened his spine. He lifted his chin.

"You weren't fair. I'd made a mistake, and you were hoping for it."

"This isn't about sweeping the floor, Brys." Not even a hint of understanding warmed Patter's face, which stayed cold and implacable. "You disobeyed me. In a sneaky and underhanded way. In your actions, you lied. You broke the trust between us."

That internal spark struck tinder, and Brys was furious, although the chill in his middle still ate at his courage. How dare Patter speak so!

"You broke it first, shun you!"

"Enough!"

Patter rose to his feet, controlled, but with menace in his movement.

"You made pretense of obedience, then once my back was turned, you dropped an inconvenient loyalty and used disguise and my absence to flout me. How dare you accuse *me* of broken trust! How have *I* ever deceived you?"

Patter trod deliberately closer.

Brys stood his ground and swallowed, deeper anger thrusting apprehension aside.

"Never, shun you!" he spat. "You broke my trust when you started hunting up my mistakes, when you forgot that errors merit teaching and forgiveness, not punishment!"

Patter's hand came up. Brys struggled to stay put, not to flinch. He glared upward, refusing to cower.

With effort, Patter lowered his arm to his side.

"Go. To. Your. Room." His chest rose and fell as though he'd just felled a tree. "Now."

Brys glared a moment more, nodded jerkily, and turned on his heel. He carefully *didn't* slam his door.

On the other side of it, he leaned against its thick panels in shaken reaction.

Sias in Sanember!

He'd never seem Patter like that before. Was his forbidden participation in the solstice really so bad? He didn't think so, despite Patter's frigid fury. Some thing else must be wrong.

I am not the problem, he insisted to himself. Something's changed, and Patter is . . . worried?

What an odd conclusion to draw.

He shook his head, stooping to remove his shoes.

Patter might be worried – was worried, insisted his intuition – but dang if he knew why.

I'll observe him, Brys decided, *and see if I can't notice something. And* – he made another resolution – *I'll double check everything I do.* No mistakes on the morrow.

This decision allowed him to sleep, hoping the morning would be better.

It was, but not much.

Patter's rage had subsided into a false calm, marked by even courtesy and no warmth.

It was the sevenday, so no school awaited Brys. He milked Pehmea and Pilka, then took them to Diri, who had herd duty for the day. Then he mucked out the byre, washed his hands and saw to the cheeses, and picked a bushel of fresh greens.

He and Patter had intended to put up a cask of gundru, as well as starting a batch of kjaeldermelk, but Brys suspected their plans had changed. Hoped so. Working side by side with the distant stranger Patter had become would be worse punishment than missing a half-dozen festivals.

Patter met him at the trap, considerately took the bushel basket from him, and gestured at the table. "Go sit," he instructed.

Brys did as he was told, watching as Patter dumped the greens in the filled sink, swished them around to remove any sand and dirt clinging to the leaves, then ladled them into an oversized colander to drain. He check the vast kettle where the milk was heating, covered it, and removed it from the stove.

Then he joined Brys at the table, selecting the seat at Brys' right, rather than the one around the corner.

Brys turned his head warily and inched himself to the far edge of his seat.

What was Patter up to?

The gentleness with which he'd taken the bushel basket and his choice to sit side-by-side seemed to indicate forgiveness, even kindliness. But the lack of light in Patter's eyes, the sternness about his mouth, contradicted any such softening.

Brys didn't know what to expect.

Patter clasped his hands together on the table, simulating an ease belied by his hard voice.

"You're right," he began abruptly. "I've been harsh of late. But you don't seem to realize your own contribution to my displeasure. You're often careless, and almost always leave some portion of your duties undone."

Brys didn't think so, but there would be no benefit in arguing. He listened.

"You're getting old enough that you should be able to fulfill your responsibilities unsupervised. I will not speak more of this now."

Brys glanced down at the table, then looked back at Patter.

So, maybe it is that I'm twelve?

It still didn't seem like Patter – not the companionable, easy, and affectionate man he was used to.

"It's your transgression of last night that I want to address. Sneaking disobedience is utterly unacceptable, Brys. Do you understand?"

Brys nodded.

"Yes, Patter."

His voice sounded high and childish in his ears.

"Good. If I can't trust you, can't rely on you when you are not under my eye, then our life together as patter and son cannot work. I'll have to ask your Uncle Karl if he can take you. Or send you back east to your motter's sister – your Aunt Matilde."

Shock deprived Brys of utterance for a moment.

Then he stuttered, "B-but . . . w-we've always been together. I th-thought we always would be. P-partners."

Patter looked at him expressionlessly.

"I thought so too. But without trust, we cannot be."

His lips tightened. "Brys, I am not willing to embark on a course in which you disobey and I punish, and you disobey and I punish again."

The weight of Patter's gaze felt unbearable. Brys' eyes fell once more, stayed fixed on the table.

Patter's voice sharpened. "Do you understand, Brys? Your next disobedience, your next dishonesty, means you go."

His eyes flicked upward, seeking some sign of caring in Patter's face. There was none, only graveness and judgement.

"I understand," he responded huskily.

Patter said nothing, waiting for something more.

"I'm sorry, Patter," Brys mustered. And he was sorry, just not as sorry as Patter wanted him to be. "There won't be a next."

"Good. Good." Now Patter's face was lightening. "I believe you."

Miracles: was that actually a smile tugging at Patter's mouth?

"But, Brys, you know there must be a consequence." Warmth had returned to Patter's voice.

"Yes, I know," Brys agreed reluctantly.

"Very well. Are you ready to hear it?"

Finally, Patter was returning to the usual script they followed when Brys did something wrong.

"What is it, Patter?"

"You'll spend today and the next three sevendays hunting deadfall in the forest. You may have Jol's company, if you can persuade him to the task, but you'll take the hand cart immediately you've finished morning chores and return only when it's time for evening ones. Understood?"

Brys nodded.

Yes, he understood. And . . . it wasn't *so* bad, if only it hadn't been *four* sevendays. A whole month without leapfrog or hide-and-bide or ring toss or any of the other games he and Jol and Lars and the others enjoyed on the rest day.

He repressed a sigh.

At least Patter was normal again. The tension had left his voice, his face, and his movement.

He met Brys' gaze normally when he offered: "I'll pack your dinner pail while you step over to your aunt's, if you wish to talk with Jol."

Luckily, Jol was willing to join him in deadfall scrounging. The day would not be nearly so lonely and boring.

Brys scampered to pull the hand cart out from under the stairs and add a drop of oil to the left axle. The left wheel had started to squeal the last time the cart was used, and he didn't want to listen to it all day.

Jol was ready by the time Brys returned the oil can to its shelf.

They headed north into the forest. Glinhult had been built within a grove of Wych elms, but the boys soon passed into the endless stretches of pines that supplied the timber claim granted by the Queen to Patter and Uncle Karl.

The going was easy, since the land was flat around Glinhult's hill. Small thickets of rowan and juniper dotted the forest floor where enough sunlight trickled through, but deep shade cloaked most of the space under the evergreen canopy. The ferns and reindeer moss that thrived in it created little barrier to the hand cart's passage.

Brys found a small sapling gnawed down by beaver before they'd gone far, but he knew that the nearer reaches would be largely bare. Too many other Glinhulters scavenged near the hamlet for wood.

He broke the branches off the trunk, then knelt to saw pieces from one end, while Jol sawed at the other.

"You alright?" questioned his cousin.

"Yeah." *Why wouldn't he be?*

"You said you'd never seen Uncle Arn so . . . grim and flat . . . and . . ." Jol trailed off, then made another effort. "Scrounging deadfall seems pretty mild. I thought . . ." This time he didn't continue.

"Patter didn't take a stick to me, if that's what you mean."

By Jol's flush as he tossed pieces of sapling into the cart, that *was* what he'd meant. Brys added his wood to the cart, grabbed the pulling handle, and moved off. Jol fell in beside him.

"So, you scrounge deadfall for a day and that's it? My patter would do more than that, if I pulled what you did last night." Jol sounded envious.

"No," corrected Brys. "Every sevenday for the next month."

"Oh." Jol looked mollified. "Yeah. That's more like it."

Now Brys was indignant. "It would be, if that was all, but it's not."

Jol just looked at him, saying nothing.

"If I do anything like it again, Patter'll send me away, back east, to Aunt Matilde," Brys blurted.

"He wouldn't!" Jol looked disbelieving.

"I believed him. When he said it." Brys shivered at the memory. "You would too, if you'd seen him. Heard him. He was . . ." Brys didn't want to admit aloud just how scary Patter had been.

"Huh." Jol walked in silence for a while. "So, you gonna test him?"

"Patter won't give me another chance."

"Huh."

Jol said nothing more, and neither did Brys. He didn't really want to think about it. Patter was . . . kind again . . . ordinary, and Brys would take good care not to provoke him another time. He never wanted to see that unyielding expression on Patter's face, that was sure.

Jol interrupted his unspoken decisions with a smart rap on the forearm and a dash ahead. "Race you to the Alten Pool," he called.

"Hey! I've got the cart! How could I possibly beat you?"

Jol snickered and kept going, tossing over his shoulder, "Giving up without trying, mill rat?"

Brys rose to the bait. "I'm no more a mill rat than you, wood beetle!" But he gripped the hand cart more firmly and began to run while dragging it through the soft clutch of the ferns and lichens.

Jol got there first, of course, but Brys achieved his own victory when he succeeded in pining his cousin in an arm lock during the impromptu wrestling match that followed.

"I give! I give!" yelled Jol. "Don't break it!"

"Hah!" gasped Brys, and let him up. It was rare that he could beat his cousin. Jol's taller inches and broader shoulders gave him a decided advantage.

There were a lot of beaver-felled trees all around the Alten Pool and upstream along the rivulet that fed it, more than enough to fill the cart several times over. In undiscussed agreement, they completed the wood-gathering before lunch, then lingered by the water after eating. No point in bringing *two* cart loads, when one would satisfy Patter. And snatching half a sevenday with Jol would be almost better than a full one with Lars and the gang.

They tried leapfrog, but that wasn't so good with just two. And hide-and-bide got boring for the same reason. But swimming and ducking one another was fun, as was racing to see who could shimmy fastest to the top of a pair of twin Bythean pines.

It was during a second round of hide-and-bide (more satisfactory now, when they wanted something quieter) that he found it.

Jol was the seeker, and Bryce the bider. He'd gone downstream to the Alten Pool and past it, then upstream along a minute tributary to a smaller smidgeon of still water. It looked like some other Glinhult foragers must have been through, although why they'd left a scattering of sawn logs behind puzzled him.

But one of them had lost something even more precious.

It gleamed deep, deep blue in the reindeer moss – the color of the highest arch of the sky just after the evening star shone out at dusk. Small sparkles of gold against the smooth leather drew Brys' attention.

He picked it up.

It was a belt, finely crafted with double buckles, also of gold, and a gold keeper. The metallic scintillas in the leather were actually gold stars attached with rivets. The back of the belt was wide, nearly a full hand's span, while the front narrowed to two fingers' width.

Without thinking, Brys pulled his tunic up and strapped the belt around his waist over his shirt.

Ow! Each one of the riveted stars felt like a small pin-prick in the skin of his waist.

But the rest of him felt . . . different, strange.

He pulled his tunic down and jumped to reach the lowest branch of a large, old birch with multiple trunks.

He seemed to spring higher more easily than ever, and his hands caught their grip more securely. He hauled himself onto the branch as lightly as he might have pulled a mischievous kitten out of a basket of yarn. His arms and legs felt refreshed, full of energy. His torso felt ready for a hundred sit-ups. He climbed to the topmost branch that could bear his weight with scarcely more effort than he might have climbed the stairs at home.

It's a belt of strength, he marveled. *I've found a magic belt, just like in the legends of old!*

Jol eventually wandered into view below.

He checked under the trunk of a fallen pine, behind a tumble of boulders, within a rowan thicket, and beyond the cascade feeding the diminutive spring. Finally, being no stranger to hide-and-bide in the woods, he looked up.

"Hah! You hide, I ride, and now you're spied!"

Brys laughed and came out of the tree in a controlled tumble.

While Jol's eyes widened at this sample of daring, Brys charged him in an exuberant tackle. His cousin's automatic hook behind the ankle and twist while falling brought Jol down uppermost. In the past, the move resulted in Brys' defeat.

Not this time.

Brys dug his heels in beneath himself, gave a mighty heave, and flipped Jol into the pine needle duff.

Jol's surprised eyes widened still more. "What'd you do?" he gasped, and then tapped out as Brys completed a head lock.

"I'm stronger! I'm stronger! I'm stronger!" crowed Brys, letting his cousin up.

"You are not!" yelled Jol, stung and missing his meaning. "I've pinned you any day since solstice last, and you know it, you mingy mill rat!"

(They were all mill rats, really. Most of Glinhult's felled logs had to be milled into planks before the wagons hauled them east. That's why the hamlet existed.)

But Jol was used to winning, and losing twice in one day did not sit well. Yet Brys didn't mean he was stronger than *Jol.* Although . . . he was *now,* wasn't he?

"Lift this log!" he challenged.

It was a massive thing, suited to be the heart of a winter solstice fire, likely weighing eight stone or more.

"You can't lift that." Jol looked shocked and a touch confused.

"Can too! Can too!" Brys bubbled with the assurance that he *could* lift "that."

"My patter couldn't even lift it," insisted Jol.

Brys bent, gripped a protruding root at its base, wriggled his other hand into a crevice at the other end, tightened his belly, and shoved upward with his legs. Like a dog pulled from a bog, the log came glueily upward. Brys stood balanced for a moment, then, in a further boast of his prowess, tossed his burden some five paces away. He glanced, pantingly triumphant, at his cousin.

Jol's face had whitened, and he was backing away.

"Well?" demanded Brys.

Jol shook his head. "You're bewitched. Or accursed. Or something worse. I don't know, but you're not –" he broke off, then concluded, swallowing some other word, "yourself."

Brys' ebullience ebbed. *Was* the belt accursed? Was *he* accursed, wearing it? In the excitement of discovery, he'd not considered . . . anything. But . . . *accursed*?

"Am not! Am too!" he countered Jol. "You just can't stand losing *twice*."

Jol licked his upper lip. "Brys, wait."

"Hah! I won! I won!" Brys crowed again. "You're weak! You're weak!"

"You did not either win, you skunk!" Jol's qualms, whatever they were, evaporated under Brys' continued trumpeting. "You cheated! Just like you cheated last night!" Jol's face was red now, not white.

"I did not either cheat! I won that second place fair and square!"

"But you wouldn't have won anything, if you hadn't cheated my

Uncle Arn! You tricked your way into that rope climbing contest. So there! And I don't blame Uncle for threatening to send you away east. Who'd want to be step-motter to *you*? Liar!"

What? What was Jol talking about?

Well, lying, for one thing. Now Brys could feel his own face reddening in rage.

"I've never lied in my life! You mucky midden rat!" (A much nastier insult than the common "mill rat.") "Not even when Aunt Mersela asked me about Lars' broken toe. She thought it was *your* fault, but I confessed it was mine. You – you – troll-witch!"

His cousin narrowed his eyes, and Brys felt his stomach lurch at his own words. He was angry, yes, but . . . troll-witch was worse than an insult. It implied a serious crime. He shouldn't have said it, no matter what.

Jol's voice leveled in exactly the horrid way that Patter's had last night. "I'm no troll-witch, but you just might be. Listen to yourself." Scorn crossed his face. "Enemies don't accuse each other like that, let alone friends and cousins. No wonder Uncle Arn is worried. Why would Briet Sigrunsdotter want *you* as a step-son?"

Jol turned his back abruptly and stalked off.

Brys felt his jaw drop.

He'd had fights with his cousin before. Of course. But mostly they were teasing taken too far. Or, if it were serious, they worked it out. Or let it go, turning real anger to mock fisticuffs. This – Jol simply walking off after serious censure – had never happened.

I think I really went too far.

Or was it the belt? Wanting to look at it again, he pulled his tunic off over his head, tossing the garment to the ground.

He stroked the belt's smooth leather. It was as deeply blue as he remembered. The buckles, keeper, and riveted stars as richly golden.

But was the uncomfortable prickle of pins and needles around his waist stronger? Maybe.

A raspy, old man's voice interrupted Brys' investigations. "So, young un, was that dark-headed fella an old enemy or an old friend?"

Brys started and turned toward the speaker.

He was short, nearly a hand span shorter than Brys, but he wasn't a boy. His hair was a grizzled gray and grew in a wild mane around his face. His beard was equally wild, but thin. His voice had sounded genial, almost friendly, but his watery, pale blue eyes held a mad glitter. And his nose was long, his ears overlarge.

Was he, could he be, a troll?

Brys had never seen one . . . but this grandpatter – if he were one – bore the signs Brys had learned at school.

"A friend," he muttered in answer to the old man's question.

"I'd say he won't be a friend much longer, lessen you do some good groveling."

How much had this geezer heard? The whole stupid interchange?

"I know," Brys replied glumly. "We've been friends since we were babies. His motter – my aunt – was my wet nurse."

"Might be worth some grovelling then," concluded the stranger.

Was he a troll?

He seemed pretty normal, aside from his odd appearance, not crazy like trolls were said to be.

"I doubt grovelling'll be enough." Brys sighed. "I'm an idiot! Just an idiot! Gah!"

"Come take a cuppa tea with me, young un. I've seen a heap o' troubles worsen yourn, and I might have a few suggestions."

Brys eyed him suspiciously. *Was* he a troll?

"Or not." The old man seated himself on the log Brys had

tossed. "M' name's Ryndal. Ryndal Vensson, but plain Ryndal's good enough."

"I'm Brys, Brys Arnsson." The courtesy came unthinkingly, but absently. His real worry carried more vehemence. "Do you really know how I can make things right with Jol?"

"Yer cousin, eh?" Ryndal tilted his head to one side and scrutinized Brys with his twinkling eyes. Maybe they weren't mad, just merry? "Well . . . lettin' some time go by afore you try is usually good. Let the other fella cool off, maybe even miss ye a bit. I bet yer already missin' Jol some."

"Yeah."

Brys shifted uncomfortably. He was missing Jol. But that wasn't why he was wriggling. The prickles around his waist *were* growing stronger. He wished he could just take the belt off, but it seemed rude to simply undress in front of Ryndal.

"Do you think Jol's missing me?" he asked.

"Maybe. Maybe not. Who was in the wrong, just now?"

Brys felt his face flush in embarrassment. "Me. I was boasting. And I just kept on, even after Jol made it plain he was sick of it." Brys shook his head. "It's just . . . even when we were younger and closer in size, I only beat him sometimes. And almost never since he turned thirteen. I was so excited this time." His voice sounded forlorn in his ears. "And it wasn't even true."

"What wasn't?" Ryndal looked puzzled.

"Beating him. It wasn't me. It was . . ." Brys didn't know why he hesitated, suddenly uneasy. "It was just luck," he finished.

"Hmm." Ryndal stood, sprightly despite his apparent age. "Well, Brys Arnsson, I'm headed home. I want that cuppa, even if you don't. But yer welcome to join me. Or not, as ye choose."

Brys surveyed his new acquaintance.

His suspicion was beginning to feel silly. *Ryndal's shorter and skinnier than me. Why am I afraid of him?*

"Is it far?" he asked.

"Just a quarter hour's walk."

Not far then.

"I'll come, Ryndal. Thanks."

The way lay farther upstream along the tributary that joined the outflow from the Alten Pool. Ryndal followed its winding course along the flat forest floor, nipping agilely over small boulders, detouring occasionally to go around rowan and juniper thickets.

Brys trailed him, not really marking the route, increasingly preoccupied by the needles circling his waist.

Ow! Ow! Ow!

Finally it dawned on him: now was the time to take the *shunning* belt off. *Ryndal's got his back to me. He'll never notice.*

Sias! The relief of it, once the leather dangled from his hand, was exquisite. But the pain had been more than mere discomfort. His shirt was dotted with blood where each star rivet had touched. *Huh!*

He wrapped the belt into a compact coil, but it was still too bulky to fit in the pocket of his trews, so he held it in one hand.

A few moments later, they rounded a stand of rowan, and Brys saw Ryndal's abode. It was nothing like the tree houses and stilt homes of Glinhult. A massive hunk of granite – seemingly plunked down in the forest by a cloud giant – rose steeply amidst a grove of aspens. A neat, shingled wall with a door and a window in it filled what must once have been a simple opening to a natural cave at the base of the stone hill. A stove pipe protruded from the hillcot's front wall, and a bird feeder topped a pole in the clearing.

Ryndal skipped to his front door, beckoning. "Welcome to Stenstuga, Brys. Do come in."

Inside, although the floor had been leveled and flagged, the rough cavern walls and ceiling remained in their natural state. But it was furnished like a normal home.

A tile stove squatted between the door and window. A round table and two chairs occupied the center of the space, while a freestanding cupboard – pushed against a side wall – held Ryndal's bed nook.

The back wall featured a massive riverstone hearth with a bread oven over the low fireplace. Niches corralled kindling and logs, and in-built shelves stocked jars of tea, honey, flour, and other staples.

A door quilt hung to one side of the hearth. Maybe covering a passage to a cellar?

Ryndal spooned loose tea into a teapot, then poured hot water into it from the kettle bubbling on the hearth. He gestured Brys to one of the chairs. "Honey?"

Brys sat and nodded. "Yes, please. Just one spoonful, though." He'd learned that most grownups assumed kids had a sweet tooth. And he did, but not for tea.

Ryndal replaced the kettle on its hook and took a pair of mugs down from his shelves. Grotesque imp faces peered out from around their handles. Brys couldn't decide if they were funny or scary. A bit of both, perhaps.

Where should he put his belt?

It'll just fall to the floor, if I set it on my lap.

He shrugged and set it on the table. It certainly wasn't going back on *him* anytime soon. He could feel the small wounds around his waist scabbing over, but the entire band of skin was tender.

Ryndal poured from the teapot into the mugs and pushed Brys' toward him along with a spoon to stir the honey well in.

"So, yer the younger cousin, are ye?" began his host.

"Yeah." Brys sipped his tea. It was scalding hot, but tasted just the same as Aunt Mersela's mint blend from her garden.

Was Ryndal watching him extra closely?

No, he decided. The old man was just awaiting more of an answer. "But it doesn't usually matter. Really, it never mattered." He gripped the table edge in sudden inspiration. "We always used to joke, Jol and me, that we were like Nils and Jan, the brothers in the Langladan Saga."

Ryndal frowned and shook his head slightly, so Brys explained.

"You know, when Jan attempted the glass hill to challenge the griffon at the top, Nils was his stirrup man. And after Nils dueled the wild unicorn in the faerie wood, Jan dunked him in the magic spring when he lay dying. They watched each other's back."

"You and Jol were always on the same side." Ryndal nodded.

Brys sighed. "I think we still are, except . . ."

"Except what?"

"Except this." Brys pointed to the coiled belt resting beside his tea mug.

"Mm?" Ryndal tilted his head, birdlike.

Did the glitter of his eyes grow more pronounced? *Was* that glint merriment? Or . . . something else?

"I found it in the forest," Brys confessed, prodding the leather with a finger.

"So, it's not truly yourn." A tiny smile curved Ryndal's lips.

"No," Brys agreed. "But that's not really the problem. It's . . ." He hesitated, then rushed on: "It's that I really *was* cheating. It's a belt of strength, and I couldn't have beat Jol right then without it. He had me fair and square. It was the belt that let me flip him and pin him."

He looked imploringly at Ryndal. Somehow, if this stranger understood and forgave him, then maybe Jol would too.

"Would you like me to examine it?"

Huh? That wasn't what Brys had been angling for. Aside from making Brys' cheating possible, the nature of the belt wasn't at issue. He stared at Ryndal, puzzled.

The old man perched at the front of his chair, eager, and the gleam in his eye *was* stronger.

Brys shrank back in his own chair, feeling the slight alarm provoked by this new friend – *was he a friend?* – edging toward . . . fear?

"What does the belt have to do with Jol forgiving me?" he asked warily.

"I think it might have something to do with it." Ryndal's bushy eyebrows were raised.

Oh.

Oh! Of course. Maybe it wasn't just a belt of strength. Maybe it was also a belt of lying or a belt of . . . of . . . corruption. Or something like that.

Brys straightened and leaned forward.

"Really? Could you check it? Find out if the *belt* made me act like such a . . . such a donkey?"

"Do you want me to?" Ryndal's eyes grew grave, but still held an unsettling gleam in their depths.

"Yes!"

"Very well. Hand it to me, please."

Brys complied.

Ryndal slowly uncoiled the blue leather and let it hang from one hand. He looked intently at Brys, a strange quirk to his mouth – mocking?

Then he pulled the belt behind his back, held it straight, seeming almost reluctant to clasp it round himself, took a deep breath, and quickly buckled it closed. A suppressed hiss of pain escaped him.

"I'm sorry! I should have warned you. It hurts, doesn't it?"

Ryndal, still with the odd look on his face, nodded slowly. "Yes. It stings."

Then he squared his shoulders, hopped briskly to the door and lowered the bar. Turning, he paused to contemplate Brys.

"What is it?"

The brightness in Ryndal's eyes rekindled and spread across the rest of his features.

"I'm hungry, young un." His tone was mild, but his hands reached out clawlike.

Brys' stomach felt sickly hollow.

Surely Ryndal couldn't mean . . . what he seemed to mean.

Brys' body assessed the situation much faster than his stunned thoughts. While his mind yet debated Ryndal's words in astonishment, his arms shoved him away from the table violently – knocking his chair over with a clatter – and his legs leapt toward the door quilt.

Please, please, please be a back door, a secret passage, a way out, any way out.

His frantic hands swept the fabric aside.

Not a door.

The quilt had hidden a *cage*, about the heighth and width of a door, equally deep, and fashioned from stout sapling trunks.

Brys spun to dash for the barred door, but Ryndal was on him: hairy, bony, and impossibly heavy.

Brys crashed to the floor.

Ryndal's breath stank. And the thrashing of his old man body as he blocked each of Brys' panicked bids for freedom was nauseatingly loathsome.

Brys made a final effort to squirm out from under his captor and then submitted as he felt Ryndal seize his head and twist. He went limp.

"That's better," purred Ryndal. "A shame to snap a brave lad's neck untimely."

Brys suppressed the shudder that tried to run through him.

Oh, Sias! He is *a troll. I should've known, should've guessed, should've run. When I first saw him.*

The weight pinning his shoulders down released him suddenly. Then a quick jerk dragged him up headfirst by the hair and flung him inside the cage.

Gasping from the force with which his ribs hit the flagstones, he saw Ryndal stretch to reach something out of sight while holding the barred door closed.

The item proved to be a heavy padlock.

The troll placed it around the first bar of the door and the adjacent bar of the cage, then guided the hasp home with a metallic click.

Brys was dazed. It had all happened so fast. His scalp burned from the yank to his hair, and his ribs felt bruised. *I should say something. Ask something. Persuade . . . somehow.* But no utterance came to him.

Ryndal was standing outside the cage staring in. Also without words, panting a little, and even yet with that odd brightness in his face. He nodded, turned on his heel, unbarred the hillcot door, and went out.

Released from Ryndal's stare, Brys found himself able to move. He pushed upright and scooted to lean against the hearthside bars of the cage.

Oh, Sias, what a mess I'm in!

How was it that he'd not known Ryndal was a troll? Every child in Silmaren learned the signs: elongated nose, enlarged ears, sagging skin, watery eyes, bent body. Ryndal had all those marks upon him. Somehow the reality was different from the picture Brys had formed in his mind.

And Ryndal was so short. And brisk. And friendly.

I didn't see it. Didn't see it at all. Not til he said . . . *that.* Now the repressed shudder shook him.

I'm hungry, young un.

What was Ryndal hungry for? A pet? A servant? Maybe just a whipping post?

Brys didn't want to admit he knew. The gross memory of the troll's stinking breath and heavy weight burgeoned and cloyed.

Brys scrubbed his hands across his face. Whatever Ryndal wanted, Brys *had* to escape.

He levered himself to his feet. Yes, he could stand – no bones broken – but his knees wobbled.

He checked the padlock. Its hasp was firmly seated in the locking mechanism. At the other side of the door, iron chains, welded closed into loops, served as hinges.

He grasped the bars and shook.

Everything rattled; no fine joinery here. But it was sturdy. And the door was tight enough that he couldn't squeeze through a gap between it and its frame.

He sank back to the floor, wrapping his arms around his shins, leaning his forehead on his knees. He shivered, even though this spot next to the hearth was overly warm. His thoughts circled wildly: have to escape, no escape, must escape, no escape.

A sound outside in the clearing brought his head up.

What was that? Was Ryndal returning? He shot to his feet and craned his neck, trying for a view through the window.

He could see the bird feeder – a trio of chaffinches clustered on its perches – and beyond it to the gap in the woods through which he and Ryndal approached the troll's hillcot. The portions of the clearing at the far sides were hidden from him, but . . . the chaffinches would have flown to safety, if a visitor – or his troll "host" – were present. Come to think, that abrupt crack, followed by a swishing rush and soft thump, tended to accompany the fall of a weak limb from a tree.

This exercise of logic restored him to sense.

So, he couldn't escape, but it was possible he didn't need to. Patter would come looking for him when Brys didn't arrive home for evening chores. Which – he gauged the shadows creeping across the clearing – would be soon.

The light would last a long while yet, but milking Pilka and Pehmea, washing the cheeses, and eating supper didn't wait on nightfall. Especially in high summer.

He envisioned Patter rounding up Uncle Karl and Lars' patter and some others.

They'd bring lanterns just in case the search went on after dark. And they'd know where to look. Jol could tell them where he and Brys had been gathering deadfall. Surely they'd fan out from the Alten Pool. And Ryndal's home wasn't far.

They'd find him. Of course, they'd find him.

He drew a breath of relief. They might even arrive before Ryndal got back from wherever he'd gone.

Brys uncurled his body, crossed his legs tailor fashion, and stretched his arms overhead. He'd grown cramped without realizing it. He was also . . . hungry.

The word chilled him.

I'm hungry, young un.

Ryndal's matter-of-fact tone had carried an awfulness in its very moderation.

Brys shook himself as though he were a retriever drying off after a dip in a lake. He wouldn't think about it. Patter or Uncle Karl would be here soon, and then all would be well.

Or would it?

Suppose Patter *didn't* organize a search party? What if he decided Brys were playing truant?

Oh, Sias, no!

But it seemed all too possible. Patter would think Brys was disobeying once more. Repeating the disobedience of last night to shave today's punishment. Oh, Sias, yes!

A footfall outside arrested his descent into frozen panic.

This time it was Ryndal. He carried an armful of sticks in through the door, nodded companionably to Brys, deposited his load in one of the hearth nooks, and went back out for a second and then a third load.

After dusting his clothes of bark pieces and sawdust, the troll started supper preparations, adding some charcoal to the fire, grinding hazel nuts with a mortar and pestle. He added water and the paste to a pot, then stirred the nut porridge over the heat of the hearth.

Watching these homely tasks, some of Brys' tension waned. When Ryndal pushed a bowl of porridge under the cage door – it barely slid through – he plucked up enough courage to ask, "Couldn't you just let me go home?"

Ryndal looked startled, almost as though the porridge pot had grown mouth and tongue to speak. He scratched his head. "Why would I do that, young un?"

"Because I want it. Because I've never done you any harm. Because it would be right." *Maybe I can talk my way out of this.*

Ryndal shook his head. *Maybe not.*

"But ye have harmed me."

What?

"Ye stole me belt." Ryndal was still wearing it, although smudges of the blood it drew stained his tunic at the lower edge of the leather.

The troll seated himself at the table and began to eat.

"It's yours?"

"Yep. I usually take it off between bouts o' wood choppin'. It does sting, ye know."

Yes, he knew. But! "Why didn't you say? I would have given it back!"

Ryndal looked at him shrewdly. "Would ye now?"

Brys blushed.

Would he?

He *thought* so, but he wouldn't have wanted to. And maybe . . . unfortunately . . . he would have claimed finders-keepers. Or worse, pretended to disbelieve Ryndal.

"Uh huh." The troll's voice was knowing. "Hard to give up power once ye've held it in yer hand."

"But I didn't know. And I *didn't* steal it. You have it back now. With my own hand, I put it into yours. Oh, please, let me go! Why wouldn't it be right?"

"Because I'm not wishin' to starve, young un. Nut porridge isn't enough to keep a man. It takes a bit o' meat, now and again."

Brys stared at the troll. He sat there quite calmly, spooning supper into his mouth. *Divine Mother.* Neither pet nor servant nor scapegoat. Ryndal wanted *dinner*.

Brys felt sick. He put his own spoon back into his full bowl, unable to contemplate swallowing.

"You can't mean that," he asserted, knowing Ryndal *did* mean that.

"Why not? Me bread oven's big enough. I just need to chop a bit more wood. Make sure I've got enough to get it good and hot. And keep it good and hot while ye roast."

Sias within! Brys inched himself backwards, fetching up against the rear bars of the cage.

"Eat up, young un. I'll want to wash that bowl afore I turn in. But ye've a while to do it, if yer not hungry yet."

Ryndal hopped to his feet, collected the porridge pot from the floor where he'd placed it to cool, and took it outside with his own empty bowl. Evidently he did his washing in the stream.

I'm hungry, young un.

Brys tried to drag his thoughts away from Ryndal's words as they echoed in his memory. *I have to stop thinking about that. I need to think about what I can do.*

But what could he do?

He was in the presence of a troll. Even could he escape his cage, how could he defeat Ryndal's terrible strength, augmented as it was by the enchanted belt? And even if Ryndal eventually took that off – it *was* painful to wear – how could Brys withstand the potent troll-magic that Ryndal surely commanded?

How did *I miss his troll-hood?*

The answer – an unwelcome one – popped abruptly into his thoughts.

I didn't miss it. Not really.

He'd known something was wrong. Felt that Ryndal was not to be trusted. He'd almost not answered Ryndal's first question.

Almost declined his invitation to tea. Almost stayed silent about the belt. Almost . . . listened to that inner whisper of peril, of prudence. Almost, but not quite.

I wanted a magic solution, he admitted.

An easy way to repair things with Jol. A shortcut to physical strength. A sure way to make Patter . . . always be Patter.

And he'd sensed that Ryndal had the power to give him all these wishes. Likely a troll *could*. But never *would*.

Brys gritted his teeth.

He'd been a fool. Maybe a few things in life came free, dropped like magic into a day. But the best things – a friend's trust, useful skills, a patter's love – didn't work that way. You got more than you'd actually earned, yes, but you still had to do your part.

With Jol, he needed to apologize. And really mean it. And trust that Jol's friendship was strong enough that the shower of obnoxiousness from Brys hadn't withered it. Which it was. Not that he meant to abuse that loyalty, but he trusted Jol all the way down to the ground.

Jol would never betray him.

As for physical prowess . . . well, that would come with time and growing. Patter was physically strong. Likely Brys would be too. And he was getting cleverer at wrestling. Jol was bigger, but wrestling wasn't all muscle might. Brys had won a few matches in the past, and he'd likely win more in the future.

If he had a future.

He glanced at the window. Had Ryndal gone off to chop more wood? Left the dishes to dry in the slight breeze?

Brys looked at his own nut porridge again.

I should eat. I'll think better, if my stomach's not empty.

True, but he still felt sick.

Just try one bite, he urged himself.

It was good. Ryndal had cooked a savory version, adding salt and umami herbs. Brys' nausea vanished as his very real hunger bloomed.

He scraped the bowl clean just as Ryndal arrived with, indeed, more logs. *Those remnants I thought other Glinhulters left must have been his – Ryndal's.* Huh.

The troll saw Brys' empty bowl. "Good job, young un." He scooped it out of the cage and took it outside, returning shortly with the other dishes as well, all clean. "Do ye want a pillow? I've got an extra."

"I guess."

Did he want one? It hardly seemed to matter. He didn't plan on sleeping.

He'd try chewing his way out, if he had to!

Wait a moment. Chewing? He wouldn't need to chew.

Ryndal hadn't checked Brys' pockets. Which meant . . . his pocket knife should still be there! He almost moved his hand to check.

Not now, you fool! He's looking at you!

"Oh, I'll not be roasting ye til the morrow." Ryndal reassured him.

Sias!

The troll continued: "I'll start building me fire afore the dawn, o' course, but ye may as well rest comfortable tonight."

Brys didn't want to hear these plans, but he supposed it was good to know that he *did* have time in which to effect his escape. He accepted the pillow that Ryndal pulled from the drawer below his bed nook and stuffed through the cage bars.

"The hearth'll keep ye warm, but if ye did want a blanket, I can spare one."

Brys nodded. He didn't need a blanket either, but perhaps he might use it to muffle the sounds of the whittling he hoped to do once Ryndal slept.

He longed to slip his fingers into his trews pocket.

Was the knife there? He couldn't remember pocketing it this morning, but why would he not have? He carried it always. You never knew when a sharp blade might come in handy. Like now!

Ryndal maneuvered the blanket into the cage, then fetched a canister from a shelf along with a pipe, and began preparing a smoke. Once the pipe was filled, he went back into the open air. Brys could see the troll's back through the window. There was a bench under it, he remembered.

Ryndal blew a few smoke rings.

Brys shoved a hand in his pocket.

Yes!

Sias be praised! He could escape. Or try to.

No, I will. I'll get out of this cage. I'll get out of this hillcot. And I'll get home. I'll stab him, if I have to.

But not now.

Ryndal would simply take the knife away, if he saw it. Brys moved his hand away from his pocket. It was hard to do nothing. Waiting, just waiting, for a troll to roast you alive – no!

I'm not waiting for roasting. I'm waiting for Ryndal to sleep.

Which gave him an idea.

It might be futile, or just unnecessary, but why not give Ryndal the impression that Brys had given up? Likely the troll was too shrewd, but still. Brys spread the blanket on the floor of the cage, placed the pillow to one side – away from the hearth – and lay down.

The cage was too small to permit him to straighten, but the softness of the blanket atop the flagstones was a relief. He closed his eyes. It would fool no one, but he didn't want to see this place anyway.

I'll plan my escape.

How would he accomplish it?

Wait till Ryndal goes to bed, then wait a while longer. Whittle through one of the bars encircled by the padlock. Ease the padlock through the gap, and open the door. Tiptoe to the hillcot door and unbar it. Open it and slip out. Walk softly until he was far enough away that he couldn't be heard. Yes!

Would that really work? Could he be quiet enough? Would Ryndal wake up amidst it all?

He shook his head.

I'll just do my best.

He opened his eyes again. The light was beginning to go. The clearing outside was wholly in shadow. The sky above the treetops glowed golden.

Inside, the dim radiance from the dying fire flickered.

Ryndal still sat on his bench in the open air, staring at nothing, and taking the occasional puff of his pipe.

Brys sat up and stretched. Then stood and stretched some more.

It wasn't enough.

He wanted to climb a tree, wrestle a friend, or run races with Lars and the gang.

Sitting still, lying still, standing still was getting old.

But when he heard Ryndal at the door, he sat abruptly and dove for his pillow.

"Asleep, lad?" Ryndal's voice sounded kind, except for that note of . . . hunger . . . that underlay it.

"Mmm," answered Brys.

Dusk had arrived, and the fire was nearly out. The corner holding his cage was very dark. He doubted Ryndal could see that he didn't look sleepy at all.

"I'll wake ye when it's time. Sleep deep, Brys."

Sias! As though he'd be getting up for morning chores!

He cracked his eyes open.

Ryndal was rummaging in the drawer under his bed nook. Evidently the troll wanted extra covers for himself. Blanket in hand, he drew open one shutter, nipped up onto the mattress, and pulled the shutter closed. A snick of metal told Brys that that the troll had some sort of lock inside.

Good. A bit of delay, if Ryndal *did* wake up.

Another sound hushed from the bed nook: an internal curtain? Better and better.

Brys squinted, trying to see more clearly in the growing dark. Were the bed shutters solid? Not louvered? He hadn't noticed earlier, and now he couldn't tell, but he thought . . . *not!*

Sneaking away began to seem more practical.

His hand itched to pull out his pocket knife.

Wait, he counseled himself. You've got to give Ryndal a chance to go to sleep.

He turned onto his back with his feet flat and his knees poking up.

There was still a chance Patter would arrive with a search party. But he wasn't going to wait on rescue from others. He would rescue himself. Because, even if the Glinhulters were out in force, would they find Ryndal's cot? And Brys inside it? They'd missed this place for all the time Ryndal had lived here. They might miss it now also.

He shivered. Not from any chill.

I won't be waiting for Patter, he reassured himself.

Reaching for bravado, he added: if he *is* searching for me, *I'll* find *him* in the forest on my way home.

Although . . . if? *If!* Of course Patter would be searching. Even if he did think Brys were playing truant.

How had he ever believed Patter might abandon him to a night in Gosstrand's vast forest?

A memory of the time when he was very small and had gotten stuck up in a tree swirled through his thoughts. It had been daytime, but Patter had somehow known something was wrong, even before Aunt Mersela – who was watching him – realized Brys was missing.

Patter turned the mill over to the foreman and left in a hurry.

And searched the entire hamlet, until he found Brys, paralyzed with fright in the branches of the tallest Wych elm on the hill.

Patter had climbed up to him so swiftly and gripped him so securely in the circle of one arm. They were back on firm ground moments later, and Patter spent the rest of the day home, comforting Brys.

And then insisted he climb another tree – a shorter one!

Brys felt himself grinning.

Suddenly he knew that Patter's threat to send him east to Aunt Matilde was just that: a threat. Despite his surface calm, Patter had still been mad enough to spit wood chips. And . . . Brys had to admit his sneaking out to the solstice was but the last of a series of transgressions.

His turn watching the Glinhult reindeer, he'd left the herd untended when he found he'd forgotten his dinner pail. And Patter had merely cautioned him reasonably when he encountered Brys running home at noontide.

Then he and Jol locked Lars in the garden storage. They were playing brigands and soldiers, and the garden storage made an excellent castle dungeon. But then Einar went by on his new stilts, and he and Jol ran after him and stayed watching his antics, forgetting all about Lars.

Patter heard thumping when he got home from the mill.

And let Lars out.

He'd been reasonable about that too. And again when Brys shirked house chores the entire week before the school promotion exams. It hadn't been the shirking, Patter explained, but the not communicating that was the problem.

I'm still behaving like a child, he realized. As though the rules are there to break or get around, and doing the minimum to get by is enough.

It wasn't that he slacked a lot. Or avoided chores often. Mostly, he did do . . . his fair share. Sometimes even more.

It was his attitude that needed work.

He needed to stop treating . . . not life, but other people . . . like players in a game where there were points to be won or lost. He'd been winning. Collecting points by doing his chores and his homework and helping the widow next door.

But he needed to do those things, because . . . because . . . it was good to help others. And to be helped in turn.

It was part of being human – *not* being a troll – to live in community, to give, to cooperate. No wonder Patter had been so angry. It wasn't just the disobedience.

A faint sound from the troll's bed nook reached him. Was that a snore?

It came again.

Yes! Ryndal was sleeping.

Brys felt for his knife, drew it out, and unfolded the blade.

His cage was largely dark, but the glow of coals from the hearth illumined the front bars. He touched the door edge, then its frame. The frame felt thinner. He shifted the padlock out of the way and started digging with his blade.

The wood was tougher than he'd suspected, and the whittling made noise. Not a lot, but it wasn't silent. It sounded like a mouse gnawing at wainscoting.

But Ryndal's faint snores continued unabating.

With his fingertips, Brys investigated the notch he was creating.

Still small, but this *was* working. And he need not be so precise as if he were carving an owl or a hawk or a chaffinch. Big, ragged chunks were just fine for his purpose.

He started in again, pausing occasionally to push the shavings under his blanket.

Scrape, scrape. Scrape, scrape.

Ryndal's snores stopped when Brys was halfway through the frame bar.

He dropped to the blanket-padded floor, hiding his knife under his pillow.

But the troll stayed behind his bed shutters and eventually slept again. Perhaps he'd never really awoken, just changed position. But the resumed snores were reassuring.

Brys made it the rest of the way through the bar, and the snores were still sounding. The padlock slid through the tight gap just as he'd imagined, a steady pressure and then a sudden "thunk" as it sprang loose.

He eased the barred door open and slipped out, keeping his open knife gripped in his right hand.

He crept toward the front door, setting his feet down toe first as he stepped.

Maybe he should have taken his boots off.

Sneaking would be easier in stocking feet. But he wanted to be able to run once he was outside. If he needed to.

He rounded the table and saw that Ryndal had not barred the front door.

Excellent.

A flicker of movement caught the corner of Brys' vision.

What?!

No, not the bed cupboard.

Something outside.

He moved to the window to look. And saw Jol looking in, wild eyed, with most of his curling hair escaped from the tie that usually corralled it in a bushy horsetail down his back.

Brys jerked his finger to his lips in a frantic gesture for silence, but Jol wasn't looking any more.

"Brys! Why didn't you come home? Sias within!"

Then his cousin was tumbling through that unbarred door at the same moment that Ryndal tumbled out of his bed cupboard.

Brys leapt for Jol, trying to push him outside, but succeeded only in knocking him over.

"Run, Jol!" he yelled, miraculously keeping his own feet, trying to pull Jol back to his. "It's a troll!"

A bony thumb and forefinger clamped onto his ear. Brys jerked his head, feeling the thumbnail gouging deeply as he shook it off.

He stumbled forward, dragging Jol with him.

He was outside!

But Jol remained snarled in a heap on the threshold.

Brys bent to get a better grip on his cousin's arm. And met Ryndal, stooping for the same purpose.

"Ah, ah, ah," chastised the troll, smirking. "I wouldn't."

Brys ignored him, levering Jol up.

And Ryndal let go! Yes!

But the troll didn't back away as Brys somehow expected.

Jol found his balance, and Brys grabbed his hand, taking his first running step.

Then he heard Ryndal's shout behind them: "Stop, halt, be still! Flee not, my will! Wait late in my hill! Heat meat for my fill!"

A flash of acrid, orange light confused his vision.

Then his legs stiffened, abruptly immobile.

This time, he fell, and Jol with him.

He swept his knife arm aside – thank Sias he could move that – frantically trying to avoid stabbing his cousin in their tangled topple.

Could he hide the knife before Ryndal saw it?

Pressing it closed against his thigh, he slid it into *Jol's* pocket and let go the haft.

Ryndal approached, more menacing than he'd been before.

Brys struggled to rise, *run*, but his legs wouldn't move.

Ryndal loomed above him. The troll looked pleased.

"Never known me larder to be so full. Excellent!" Then his face lowered. "But running away. Sneaking! Ah, ah, ah. That won't do." He sounded querulous, like a sleepy grandpatter scolding an errant grandson. "Up with ye now."

Brys found himself climbing to his feet and shuffling back into Ryndal's hillcot. It felt natural, as though Patter had caught him slipping out for a moonlit ramble, except for the corner of his mind shouting: *Turn and run, fool!* Jol came with him, Ryndal chivying behind.

The troll ran his gnarled hands over the broken bar of the cage, and the wood healed under his touch. Next he brushed his fingertips across all the unbroken bars.

Did they change color?

It was hard to tell in the dim glow from the quiescent coals in the hearth.

"In ye go, lads."

Following Jol, Brys filed obediently through the door frame into the cramped space.

Ryndal drew a key from the pocket of his nightshirt – evidently he'd changed within his bed nook, although the blue belt still encircled his waist – unlocked the padlock, repositioned it around the cage door and frame, and fastened the hasp once again.

Then he gestured sharply with one hand, and Brys felt his limbs become his own to command.

His legs nearly buckled, and he clutched the cage bars to avoid falling. Jol was less fortunate, slithering abruptly down to the blanket with a thump.

"That's better." Ryndal nodded. "But no more mischief, young uns. Ye'd best get a good night's sleep afore sunup. It's not far off."

Brys shivered and gritted his teeth.

If only he'd been just a bit faster. Made it outside before Jol arrived. Or even gotten to the window quick enough to signal before Jol called out.

He'd *almost* escaped.

But almost only counted in games. This was no game.

And now Jol was also headed toward the bread oven. Brys glared at Ryndal, who seemed oblivious to his hostility.

The troll glanced at the dark clearing through the window behind him.

"I suppose it's not so bad ye woke me. Time to be heatin' the oven about now. And I can get a nap afore it's time to add a second serving o' logs to the fire."

He bent to stir the coals, then began placing kindling atop them. As the light grew brighter from the hearth, Brys could see blood stains wetting Ryndal's nightshirt at the lower edge of the charmed belt. The wounds inflicted by its enchantment must continue to worsen the longer it was worn.

Would Ryndal take it off for some relief?

Even if he did, could Brys and Jol prevail against his normal strength? The troll looked spindly, but even were he as puny as he appeared, his magic was invincible.

Brys could feel Jol shivering against his legs, crouched there on the cage floor, but he didn't look down.

I'll deal with Jol after I've seen Ryndal retire to his nap.

He realized that he didn't feel daunted, even though he should. *I haven't given up.* And he wouldn't.

Once the fire was truly blazing, sparks snapping and flames leaping, Ryndal moved another armful of logs from their niche and stacked them on the floor, ready for immediate use. Then he paused, scrutinized the results of his labor, looked fixedly at Brys, and said, "That'll do."

He rummaged in the drawer under his bed nook and pulled out a clean nightshirt.

Brys looked down at Jol.

His cousin had stopped shivering, although it probably wasn't because of the heat rolling off the hearth, but he still huddled his arms around his legs and body.

He's shocked just like I was when Ryndal first captured me. Wishing he'd wake from this horrific nightmare.

Brys pressed his lips together. He still didn't know how he was going to defeat Ryndal. It seemed impossible. But he felt renewed determination to try. And a nudge, a hint, a wink – something – made him feel it was possible.

He looked up again. Ryndal was finally removing the belt of strength and hanging it on a nail to the left of the hearth. Was it within reach? Brys didn't think so, but didn't give it much thought.

Ryndal's nightshirt was sodden where the belt had lain, soaked with blood. Yet he'd given no sign of the pain it must have caused.

He still evinced no symptoms of incapacity.

Instead he hopped into his bed nook, drew the inner curtain, rustled about behind it, threw the dirty nightshirt onto the flagstones, thrust out an arm to pull the bed shutter closed, and – apparently – lay down.

Jol looked up, lips opening for comment.

Brys put a finger to his own lips and shook his head. *Wait.*

This time Jol saw and nodded.

Good.

Brys couldn't understand why their captor did so little to prevent his prisoners from attempting escape – well, overwhelming power might be why the troll wasn't worried, didn't want to bother – but it still seemed prudent not to announce their intention.

He tapped Jol's shoulder and made gestures showing his desire to sit. His cousin scooted over to make room, and Brys sank down, putting a finger to his lips again.

He almost fell asleep before Ryndal's snores indicated the troll was enjoying his intended nap.

Brys' eyes snapped open.

Jol was staring at him wide-eyed, no doubt incredulous that he could doze. He smiled. *I don't feel like a victim,* he realized. Although he had during his first sojourn in the cage.

Keeping his voice to a low murmur, he moved his head right up to Jol's ear and said, "I put my knife in your pocket. Can I have it?"

Jol's wide eyes went wider, but he produced the knife.

Brys tested it on a cage bar. Nope. Ryndal had done something to the wood, and it was tougher than before. His blade could score the bark, but not carve even the smallest chip from it. The cage was secure.

He stood and eeled an arm out out between two of the bars. If he could just reach that belt, it mightn't give him strength enough to breach the cage, but it could permit him to stun Ryndal once outside of it.

Nope.

His fingertips just missed brushing the blue leather.

But . . . what about his knife arm?

He wriggled his left hand back inside the bars, then tried to maneuver his right out through them. It couldn't be clenched, fist-like, around his knife, no. But pinning the knife between thumb and flattened palm got his hand through the gap, and then he could rearrange his grip with the help of his other hand.

He pressed his torso sideways against the cage, forcing his arm through narrowness to his shoulder.

Almost . . . almost . . . there!

His knife tip barely touched the leather.

He leaned a little harder, and the metal sank into the cobalt surface. He dragged his hand downward – still outstretched – and a ragged line of undyed suede followed the progress of his blade.

The cage bars were digging uncomfortably into his upper arm. His fingers felt numb and a little tingly. He tightened his grip and tried to continue his damage to the enchanted belt.

The knife slipped from his fingers and fell – click – on the floor.

He sagged against the cage, then straightened and retrieved his arm. Ryndal's snores buzzed without interruption.

"Will he notice?" Jol murmured. "The troll?"

Brys nodded. "Yeah. I'll try and reach it when my arm stops tingling. I think my knife fell a little closer, because of the angle I was cutting."

He massaged his shoulder, rotated it, then let it hang. Feeling was returning.

He motioned Jol to the rear of the cage while he knelt at its front and inserted his arm between the bars once again. After his hand and forearm were through, he maneuvered himself flatter to the floor, then walked his fingers toward the knife.

Closer, closer.

And, yes, it was just within reach.

Delicately he pushed the haft toward him, then folded it in his palm and drew it inside the cage.

"Do you want to try and stab him? When he gets us out? Or would you rather I did?" Brys asked his cousin.

"Uh." Jol looked nonplussed. "You seem like you know what you're doing. You keep it."

Brys folded it and put it back in his own pocket.

So: cage tested, belt damaged, and knife retrieved. What else should he be doing?

I'm ready. But Jol isn't.

That should be next then. But how? Just exhorting a friend to be brave wouldn't make him so.

He turned to face his cousin.

Jol was just as disheveled from his night time passage through the woods as he was when he appeared at Ryndal's window: hair wild with twigs, clothes torn, eyes strained. And – critically – lacking the confidence that usually backed his gaze. How to restore it?

"I owe you," Brys began, voice low.

Jol's brow wrinkled.

"I *was* a rat. Earlier."

Now Jol looked exasperated.

Better.

"Never mind that!" He aimed an elbow at Brys' ribs, but pulled it before contact. Likely worried about the noise a scuffle might produce. "I was a rat myself. What are we going to do about this?" He gestured at the cage, then the bed nook. "About him? I don't want to be some troll's breakfast."

That was supposed to be flippant, but the quaver at the end spoiled it. At least Jol was trying.

"Me neither."

"You got a plan? 'Cause I sure don't." His cousin sounded pugnacious now. Even better.

"I think this is one of those times when a plan doesn't help much. Patter says you just have to be ready for opportunity. But you have to be *ready*. Or the moment'll pass you by." He glanced sharply at Jol. "Are you ready, Jol Karlson? 'Cause I am. And I need you to be."

A slight smile curled Jol's mouth. "That's Uncle Arn's line, alright. I can just hear him." He drew a slow breath. "I suppose I was a useless goof when I got here."

"You weren't expecting a troll. Who would be?"

"No, but I didn't have to make a racket and wake him up. And then shrivel into a sniveling baby when he spelled me." Jol shook his head and pressed his lips together. "I think *I* owe *you*. You'd have gotten away, if I hadn't yelled."

"Maybe."

"Next time – well, I hope there isn't a next time! Not like this. But I aim to do more looking before I leap – or yell – if we get out of this, shun it!"

"Look, Jol, done is done. Just –"

"Don't do it again," interrupted Jol. "And I won't. But, Brys, I *will* be ready. If all I can do is be furious, then I'll be furious. But if his troll-magic leaves me any room for a punch or a kick or . . . or a chair smashed over his head, I'll fight."

"Then we're ready."

"As we can be." Jol wrinkled his nose. "Why'd you scratch that belt? What good will it do? Besides make him mad?"

"Might not do anything, but I figure any hurt to his stuff might give us . . . well, not an edge, but something."

"Huh."

"Was anyone besides you searching for me, Jol?"

"Oh, Sias! Only all of Glinhult!"

"Really?"

"Just about. Even my motter and Froiken Singrunsdotter insisted on joining the party. If there's anything to find in the forest, they'll find it." Jol shook his head. "Course they'll be just that extra mad when they do find us."

"I'll take any kind of mad, if they'd only walk through Ryndal's front door right about . . . now!"

"Me too. But they won't. Most went upstream, a few down. And the rest are combing the stretch between the stream and the hamlet."

"Then we'll find them."

"Yup."

They sat in silence for a bit, listening to the troll's snores.

Brys noticed a slight grayness at the window, a lightening to the dark sky. Dawn was approaching.

He yawned, wriggled all over to be sure he wasn't too stiff, and glanced at Jol.

"What did you say his name was?" Jol asked.

Before Brys could answer, Ryndal swept his nook curtain aside, pushed the pillow-end shutter open, and hopped out.

"Rise and shine, young uns. Morning's here."

Brys climbed to his feet, Jol following.

Ryndal paused in front of the cage. "I doubt I can fit ye both in the oven at once. Who wants to go first?" he queried, for all the world as though he were proposing a treat!

"I'll go first," Brys volunteered sturdily, remembering that he was the one with the pocket knife. What *had* happened to Jol's? Not that it mattered. He didn't have it.

"Alright then. That's settled." Ryndal carried on with refueling the fire. "We'll just let that heat the bricks a tad more, perhaps have tea" – he swung the kettle closer to the flames – "and get on with things."

Brys stiffened, anticipating Ryndal's move to open the cage. But the troll didn't. Instead, he disappeared back into his bed nook to dress, then gathered his blood-stained nightshirts and yesterday's clothes, and stuffed the garments into a basket hamper. "I don't suppose ye'll behave, if I just invite ye to the table, will ye?"

Brys said nothing, but Ryndal answered his own question. "O' course not."

He sighed and raised his left hand. "So." Then in a weary voice: "Sit still, do my will. Be not shrill, no thrill. Drink tea with me. Then look, and cook."

A brief flicker of orange light flared from the troll's palm, but Brys felt nothing.

He tensed again, could sense Jol shifting his weight forward onto the balls of his feet. And now Ryndal did unlock the cage and swing its door open.

Brys lunged.

Except he didn't.

Nothing resulted except a mild step toward the table, followed by another.

His heart hammered as he sought control of his limbs, but his feet simply marched him to a chair, where he sat. Jol did the same at the other chair, while Ryndal pulled up a three-legged stool for his own perch.

The troll fixed tea, pouring out three mugs.

Outside, the clearing grew fully visible in the gray light presaging the sun's leap above the horizon. Brys sipped, mouth and fingers calm, thoughts and feeling anything but.

Shun it!

The relaxation of his muscles told his mind that all was well. Which felt so very odd. His mind kept wanting to believe his body, but it shouldn't.

Death was a moment away – unless he got that opportunity Patter spoke of in his exhortations to be ready.

Brys sipped again, glancing at Jol. His cousin looked equally relaxed, but with a similar horror lurking in his eyes.

Ryndal drained half his mug, then set it down and stood.

"The oven should be about ready."

He moved to the hearth and opened the iron hatch above the fireplace.

Heat rolled out of it, making the already too-warm room more so.

"Yep." He closed the hatch, paused with his head tilted to one side, looking at Brys, then took the blue belt from its nail. "I reckon I'll need extra strength to boost ye up to it."

Brys tried another lunge – this time up from his chair – and again did not succeed.

Shun it! I'm about to be roasted alive without lifting a finger to stop it.

Had Jol attempted an abortive attack also? And failed? His face was pale enough.

Ryndal stood with his enchanted belt held straight behind his back as he had the day before. This time Brys knew why. The troll's waist must be a band of scabbed skin. It would more than sting when the star rivets made contact.

And it did.

Ryndal hissed and closed his eyes as the belt tongue slid home through its keeper. Then he staggered, as though his entire left side had gone numb.

He didn't have time to do more.

The unnatural relaxation that gripped Brys (and Jol) fled on the instant.

Brys shot to his feet, and his pent readiness did all that Patter had promised. It was as though he and his cousin had planned and practiced all through the dark hours before dawn.

Jol flew to the oven hatch and yanked it open, while Brys rocketed into the teetering troll, knocking him flat.

The next thing Brys knew, Jol was at his side, and they were boosting Ryndal up together, bundling him into the scorching maw of the oven, and slamming its hatch shut.

Brys leapt for the hillcot door, dragging Jol with him – except that Jol seemed to be leaping and dragging Brys – fully expecting Ryndal to burst out of the oven spouting death-defying troll-magic.

Front door.

Front steps.

Bird feeder and clearing – suddenly dappled golden as the sun rose and shone through the trees.

It all rushed by in a confused, panicky blur.

But no avenging troll-mage chased on their heels.

Brys kept running, even when the stitch in his side grew knife-like. He didn't notice Jol slowing either.

Finally, when they reached the Alten Pool, he tripped and went sprawling.

The ground came up hard, knocking the wind out of him.

He lay, cheek down, struggling for breath.

When he caught it, he burst into wracking sobs which lasted only three heartbeats, and then pushed himself upright.

Jol was returning from where his unreasoning legs had carried him. "You alright? Break anything?"

Brys wriggled his feet, shifted his shoulders. He felt bruised all over, but everything moved.

"Nah. Yeah. You?"

"Think so. Come on!" He grabbed Brys' arm and hauled him up. "We need to find somebody."

They walked, listening for sounds of pursuit. Or sounds of Glinhult searchers. But none came.

"Where is everybody?" complained Jol.

"Probably looking west when they didn't find me east. Or" – Brys felt a grin stretching his cracked lips – "they're just now entering Ryndal's hillcot. Hah!"

"Ryndal was his name?"

"Yeah."

But Brys wasn't thinking about the troll.

He would, he knew. Troll insanity was . . . a whole 'nother deal, not a thing like reading about it in a school book. And his memory of the feel of Ryndal's spindly body – so different from its hairy weight when augmented by the enchanted belt – as he and Jol lifted the troll up to his death sickened him in a way wholly different from Ryndal's brutal capture of himself.

But he would sort that out later. *At least* I'm *alive. And that's good!*

Right now he wanted to know something else.

"Does my patter really want to marry Briet?"

Jol laughed, surprised.

"Yeah, I think so. I heard him talking with Motter and Patter when they thought I was asleep. Do you mind?"

"Are you kidding? When we were all nursery babies being taught by her in our first schooling year, everybody kept thinking she was my motter. And she still gives me presents on my name-day and for winter solstice."

He wouldn't mention that he reciprocated. No need for Jol to know . . . well . . . everything.

"Huh."

"Huh, yourself!"

And Brys aimed a friendly punch at his cousin's ribs.

Crossing the Naiad

She stood looking across the bridge, feeling the cool breeze and . . . something wrong.

The bridge was old – the leached stones worn by weather and time, a structure of ancient Silmaren.

But that wasn't it.

Something – sinister? – rose from its broken paving. A miasma of despair and defeat that had nothing to do with its gap-toothed balustrade, the holes in its surface giving wide views of the forested ravine and fast river below, or the crumbling statue of a toga-draped maiden from the past ages of the world.

Kimmer hesitated.

The new bridge, upstream and crossing low to the water rather than high from one steep brink to the other, was flooded and unsafe.

Oga and Chedli and Deas – the goats – had balked. Likely they knew, and . . . only a fool would risk a span immersed in a swift current.

But she had to get home somehow.

She'd been to the far pastures where the grass billowed thick and lush, a day's journey, and spent two nights.

Mama said the goats were dowly because they needed copper salts. A spell of cropping the cocksfoot in the foothills beyond the river would put them right.

And it seemed she was correct.

Oga pranced perkily behind her. Kimmer could hear her hoofs clicking on the apron of the bridge, while her mother – brown Chedli – whickered softly. Only the matriarch of the trip – gray Deas – stood still, gazing sternly ahead.

Did she feel it too: the dread emanation from the bridge?

They'd left the uplands of the foothills at dawn, following the track that wound west through the valleys, skirting ruins of ancient places: towers, spring basins, and even a burial cenotaph.

The streams were full. Had it rained in the mountains?

Descending into the ravine of the Gweltspaen, she'd been worried.

The trees hid the river from view on the steep, hairpin approach, but surely the water flowed high. And the bridge was low. Would it be possible to cross?

It wasn't.

She'd retraced her steps, leading the goats, climbing back out of the ravine and searching for the abandoned track to this alternate crossing.

The ground was rocky here on the eastern rim and the track overgrown only by mosses and lichens and a few stubborn tufts of grass. Finding her way had been more a matter of discerning the true route amidst many false possibilities than uncovering league stones buried by rank scrub.

As she turned off the main track for this old one, she noticed movement on the cliff of a near hill.

Someone traversed the path where it looped across the steep bluff, cut into the limestone. A girl?

Kimmer squinted.

None of the other girls in her hamlet – either friends or enemies – were visiting the foothills. Their families could afford the yarrow pastilles supplying the copper salts missing from the herbage around Beyholt.

Besides . . . this girl didn't have goats . . . and was dressed strangely.

Kimmer shaded her eyes with her hand, and compared her own garments with those of the distant stranger. Was she Hammarleeding?

Kimmer had never seen one, but she'd heard stories from some who had.

Elias, nasty bully that he was, claimed they wore the shapes of beasts when they traveled. But this girl wore red, a tunic perhaps, and leggings and a fleece cloak with the hood drawn up. Was her hair dark? She was too far away to be sure.

I think she is Hammarleeding.

Certainly her garb was nothing like Kimmer's striped skirt of grass green and cream, her black woolen stockings, her sage bodice and white blouse, and her woven cape of dark pine hue.

Half-tempted to wait for the traveler to descend the cliff – wouldn't it be interesting to meet one of the fabled Hammar-folk? – Kimmer shook her head, scraped a strand of blond hair back from her face, and stepped onto the old track.

The detour would cost her time. If she lingered for every curiosity, she'd be hiking long past dark.

She quickened her stride and clucked to the goats, encouraging them along the unfamiliar route.

And now she'd reached the river crossing and paused.

I've got to get home, she told herself, attempting to override the reluctance rooting her to the spot.

The Gweltspaen in spate was nothing she could ford. This was her only option.

I've got to cross.

She stepped onto the bridge.

Leaped back.

What *was* that? Sharp, foreboding, aggressive.

With her half-boots firmly planted back on the mixture of gravel, rock, and moss that formed the bridge apron, the feeling faded, but a lingering sense of dread and loss fed her qualms.

I can't do it.

She had to, but she couldn't.

A sharp yapping broke her indecision.

Aani! Ugh! It wanted only that.

The small white terrier broke from the fringe of trees behind her, racing toward Kimmer's ankles, ready to nip.

The feisty little dog, nuisance enough, was the least of it. Where Aani pounced, Elias couldn't be far behind.

Clucking to the goats, Kimmer took to her heels.

And the bridge seized her.

ഇൗരു

When Elias noticed the storm clouds dumping rain far to the east on the mountains, he'd worried and done some quick private calculations. Yep. The storm surge would be hitting the low bridge right about when Kimmer did.

He dithered.

She didn't like him. He knew that.

Heck, she had reason. He blushed remembering all the names he'd called her when she started instruction under their hamlet's keyholder.

Why couldn't he have just said what bothered him?

Keyholder Pavana was such a fusty old thing: never bathing, never washing her faded old skirt, and speaking in that strange northern accent through toothless gums.

She was a gifted magicker, yes.

She'd pulled his own motter back from the brink of death when that nasty grippe hit last winter. Kimmer would learn under her, no question.

But . . . what *else* would she learn?

Would *Kimmer* get fusty and musty and stooped? Fresh young Kimmer with her clear eyes and slow-blooming smile?

He hated that idea.

So he'd chanted that stupid rhyme invented by Beyholt's bullies and called her cheese licker and wheyface.

Then she'd caught him beating Torluk (the supposed model of all a boy should be) to a pulp behind the smithy. How could she know that Torluk has said worse things behind her back? *He'd* never tell her. Those words were too foul to repeat.

So she hated him. He admitted that now. And hated him with reason.

But he was worried. Also with reason.

So he'd set out the next morning to check the low bridge, Aani at his heels, and been unsurprised to find it flooded.

But now he had to hurry.

Why hadn't he set out at first light?

Going upstream to the forbidden crossing of flat rocks – forbidden because it lay above the falls – and then back down river too was going to take some time. There was no path. He'd be bushwhacking all the way.

And he didn't want to miss Kimmer.

Who knew what she'd do when she found the bridge impassible?

If only young Naaja hadn't gotten sick in the night, vomiting again and again and scaring Motter half silly. He'd run for Pavana, snuffy old Pavana, and sat with Naaja, holding her hand. And overslept himself in the morning.

So now he hurried.

And found Kimmer's tracks along with a few goat droppings leading to the old bridge.

Oh, goddess, no!

He began to run.

Didn't she know? Hadn't she heard the stories? Did she not believe them? Or did she think her nascent keyholding skills would protect her?

Aani dashed ahead of him at the last, barking with frantic urgency, but even Aani was just too late.

₧₳

If cold stone could flow like water, this stone was running like the racing Gweltspaen far below.

If time-worn paving could sear like glacial ice, this paving burned.

If ancient bridgeworks could come alive, this bridge was waking.

Darkness, unseen by the naked eye, but real and palpable in the mind's eye – the keyholding eye – rose up from the broken balustrades and arched over to enclose Kimmer in a tunnel of shadow and hunger.

A chill current – inexorable like glacial ice, yet fluid as the summer rain – pulled her ankles.

And a hatred, mean as the Reindeer People's Deathwind Woman, shoved her shoulders.

A voice, grating, yet soundless, spoke to her. *Die. Fall and die, and feed my lady.*

No. Oh, no. No.

Kimmer was crying and running – dodging the gaping holes in the span, yes – but dashing forward, her goats brawling and skittering ahead of her, when she wanted to turn back.

No. Oh, no. No!

Her attempt to resist failed utterly.

She approached the halfway point.

Could she surrender? Give in to the force buffeting her like a storm wind and let it carry her fast and furious out of danger? Forward and off the bridge?

"Go!" she called. "Chedli, go!"

The goats *did* go, flashing past the midpoint in panic, wild and stumbling, but headed for safety.

Kimmer did not.

Faster and faster her feet that were not hers carried her.

Leaping a fallen baluster.

Skirting a smithy-sized gap to the abyss.

Right up to the brink . . . and over.

She was falling.

೮)ೞ

Elias hit the bridge before Kimmer ran ten paces, but he couldn't catch her.

He was caught himself.

Cold and black and bitter, the magic of the stones engulfed him, sped his pumping legs ever faster, but not fast enough.

Kimmer reached the brink first, and then he followed, tossed into the air like a pebble kicked by a giant.

Falling, he remembered every tale he'd ever heard about the fabulous works of the ancient Silmarish . . . and the perversions wrought by the trolls who came after them.

The marble satyrs from a grand fountain sculpted for a queen fled their playful water battle to fight in earnest at the bidding of the troll lord Carbraes: stone fists like warhammers, stone horns like lances.

The ghosts of a forgotten triumphal arch stripped Ghriana warriors marching under the crumbling porphyry of their souls, laying bare their bodies in the shadow, faces horror-struck.

A haunted remnant of road, isolated on its fragment of embankment, grew hungry and swallowed travelers whole.

He smacked the Gweltspaen feet first, plunging deep and gripped by the water's cold strength.

Down and down.

Chill and black and numbing.

He felt frozen, like the statuary satyrs of the queen before their dreadful freedom.

Green-black immobility congealed around him, then abruptly blinked blacker.

Green black.

Blacker black.

Where was he? This was not water that surrounded him, but stone.

Faien. The stone groaned. *Faien.*

No longer drowning. No longer himself. He could feel the wrongness in this body: spine hunched and aching, knees and elbows knobby and pained, nose elongated and blistered.

He was a troll.

But how? And where?

ᘛ)ᘓ

On the approach to the bridge, Hammarleeding Sarvet skidded in her haste, hair twists flying, fleece cloak lost along the trail, red tunic whipped by the speed of her passage.

"Don't!" she screamed. "Don't!"

It was far too late for that. The girl – the one she'd seen from the bluff – splashed down violently, arms akimbo, head smacked by the water's surface, then sucked beneath the white-frothed current. The boy, midair, screamed – "Kimmer! Kimmer!" – before the river claimed him.

Sarvet slid to a halt.

She'd learned to swim this spring, preparing for her wanderyar, but could she swim well enough for this?

Then she felt the stones beneath her feet stir: awakened, grasping, and hungry.

"Oh, Sias, no!"

This wasn't *duoja* – too sorcerous and dark.

Could it be *incantatio*? The forbidden magic of the trolls?

Sias, no.

The pair in the river needed more than swimming to survive. Was she the one to provide it?

Her thoughts flashed back to her first sighting of the girl, a lowlander. The first lowlander Sarvet would meet.

How exciting!

This was what she'd longed for, prepared for, hoped for.

She'd lived all her life in an isolated enclave among Hammarleedings, wishing she could have a wanderyar like the boys did. Girls didn't get them, but now they did.

Because of her.

I made it happen.

Made it happen because she wanted to travel the wide world seeing wonders: new places – cities even – new ways and new faces. And here she was, the first of many Hammarleeding sisters who would venture out of their mother-lodges.

She'd been hiking all morning after breaking camp on the lower mountain slopes, following a track through the foothills, noting the tallness of the pines, unstunted by winds at this lower elevation, and the abundance of the streams. Listening to the fluting of birds. Amazed by the differences arriving so quickly.

And pondering her readiness.

She'd learned so much in the ramble class: not only swimming and survival skills, but safe methods for approaching strangers and even special *duoja* – a *duoja* of light – for travelers. Other cultures had *duoja*, but they named it differently. The Giralliyans said antiphony. The people of Auberon called it patterning. The Silmarish – this boy and girl were likely Silmarish – called it keyholding.

Whatever its name, it was power; a power of the mind and spirit fueled by the body's roots. And she, Sarvet, wielded it as a mere novitiate. Would it be enough?

Shun it, I don't care!

A girl and a boy were drowning, and she couldn't let them go unaided.

Still catching her balance from her sudden stop, barely halted, she sprinted onto the bridge and felt its evil seize her: black and gelid, yet speeding her footsteps somehow faster, aimed for the brink.

ഇ౧ಚ

The water was cold, cold and deep.

Kimmer hung there, suspended and dizzy, vision black.

Had she hit her head? She couldn't remember.

Her lungs began to ache.

I need to breathe.

I need to.

Now.

But her limbs seemed detached from her will.

Go up, she told herself.

Swim.

But nothing happened.

She felt the water, chill and implacable, stinging her nostrils and caressing her lips.

Take a breath.

There was no air here in the green-black of the river's depths.

Take a breath.

Instead, she reached for the still point within her.

Pavana trained me well.

She reached, felt it, her own anchoring, her serenity.

Silver sparked between her keys, tracing arcs from crown to brow to throat, then to heart and out her fingers. Silver turned to aqua where the energy met the water and then bubbled upward.

The ache in her lungs eased.

I am breathing. My keys breathe for me.

But still she could not move.

The river moved.

She could feel the turbulence of the water, sweeping her unresisting downstream, unable to surface, unable to seek the west bank or the east.

She reached through her keys for more.

The silver arcs thickened and brightened.

She moved her fingers – yes! – and nearly inhaled from the pain of it, sharp and sudden.

Bearing a sense of malice.

You are mine. My food. Mine.

It was a whisper without sound.

Mine. All mine.

With the words came pain again, an invasion, a bruising probe toward her keys.

Give me.

No.

Yes. You will give.

Kimmer reached within once more.

Chartreuse light glimmered along her inner links, fountained out from her feet and palms, enveloped her wrists and ankles.

Her pain melted under its advance, from elbows and knees, from belly and heart. That was better.

What next?

ℬℭ

Elias tried to ease his joints, to move. The stone held him.

Then the black of his prison released. He flailed in water once more, greenish and cold, but fluid and translucent, not obdurate and opaque.

He kicked out, scrabbling for the surface, for air.

And found it: a brief snatch of breath – air – then water again, then air.

The river tumbled him, the current wild and eddied in its upper reaches.

He fought the liquid tumult, thrashing.

A boulder smacked his ribs and spun him around.

He went under again, then bobbed up, gasping.

Was the river a live beast, determined to consume him?

He fought to see, but couldn't, his eyes submerged more often than not and blinded by froth when not. Was the river's white turbulence endless?

A moment later, he wished it were. Stone gripped him again.

Faien, whispered the silence.

And images bloomed in his thoughts.

It was a battle, he was sure, but a battle like none he'd ever imagined.

No swords, no shields. No armor-denting blows.

The lady was fair, tall and queenly, and gowned in slender green. How many knights of old had vowed their victories to her honor?

The man was short and knobby, his kindly face twisted by rage and grief both, and by something else.

Bagging eyes, elongated nose, sagging chin.

He was a troll. How many hangmen had looped a noose for his neck?

The weapons were gouts of light and thunder: piercing silver cast by the lady toward the troll; sizzling orange hurled back by her foe.

The lady was beautiful, but she scared him.

The troll should scare him, but Elias wasn't scared, not of him.

Why not?

It was their faces: the lady, cold and hating and . . . hungry – *feed my lady* – the words whispered in his mind; the troll, diseased, yes, but . . . humane.

Who were they?

Why did they contest so fierily within this trap of cold stone?

⋚⋛

Kimmer could see a hand – gauzy and translucent in the water, nearly unseen, but there – encircling her own wrist, drawing her into a presence: alien and cool with no good purpose.

A pale female face coalesced.

The spirit of the river? A naiad?

Her lightless eyes focused on Kimmer. *Come*, she hissed soundlessly.

Kimmer yanked her arm.

In plain air she would be free. Here, submerged and entangled, her intended vigor transmuted into a gliding dance.

The grip on her wrist tightened and pierced the chartreuse light summoned by her keyholding.

Aching, bruising pain bloomed in the joint.

A different current flowed, an inner tide of hurt drawn from Kimmer's bones.

She felt strength leaving her body and jerked again at the grasp holding her.

The stream of departing energy intensified.

For an interval, she struggled futilely . . . then relaxed.

Physical resistance would not free her.

She reached inside herself through her keys: there the *energea* surged limitlessly. She channeled it, saw the chartreuse of her keyholder's armor brighten, and felt the drain by the river spirit lessen.

The naiad's face tightened.

Mine.

She attacked again.

This time Kimmer knew how to defend.

Her energetic shield edged toward citron.

They balanced there, held in the water's current, besieger and besieged, predator and prey.

"Who are you?" Kimmer mouthed.

The naiad smiled, but not in answer, not in comprehension. She anticipated her next onslaught, potent and penetrating.

Suddenly Kimmer was angry, no longer reacting and protecting.

Take that, you fiend!

She cast a net of sparkling silver toward her foe.

An attack?

Not exactly.

Kimmer had learned none of a magical nature. Keyholding aimed to build and create and heal. But it was time to push out. So she pushed.

The naiad's face registered surprise, then shock.

And Kimmer found herself immersed in memories not her own: the loss of something precious, more precious than coin or sovereignty, more longed for than beauty or love.

The queen had lost a child, and her hunger sharpened by the year.

ℰ❍ℭ

Sarvet plunged into the river feet first, over her head in both water and memory, the memories of the queen Faien.

Grieving and empty, she glided through her marble palace.

Furious and famished, she excoriated her chancellor.

Aghast and angry, *he* castigated *her*.

Their difference was simple: deprived of a daughter, the queen sought power; deprived of a princess, the chancellor sought magic.

And each considered the other wrong.

Their emotions tumbled Sarvet's mind and heart even as the river tumbled her body.

"You risk *incantatio*" – the perilous magic of trolls – "and troll-disease!" accused the queen.

"You risk cruelty and tyranny!" countered her adviser, Theon.

And, in the end, both were right: she, an embittered mourner who leapt to her death in the raging torrent; he, a troll whose *incantatio* killed him when he extended it to save (and fail) his sovereign.

Sarvet's feet struck bottom, the scoured rock of the river bed.

Holding her breath, she kicked to plunge upward.

I can swim, she reminded herself. *I can.*

But this river was rougher by far than the calm lake where she'd learned, and the buffeting of thoughts not her own broke her concentration.

The dead – Faien, cold and covetous; Theon, rigid and despairing – were not the only souls drowning.

Sarvet sensed the pair she'd seen fall – the girl and the boy, both young – also fighting the river's strength.

I know this, she realized slowly.

And she did. She'd fought her clan's customs and lost. She'd fought her mother's fear. And lost. She'd fought her own fear. And lost.

But then . . . she'd surrendered and won.

Her head popped to the water's surface, its white froth swirling and racing, but less tumultuous than the stretch immediately under the bridge.

She allowed her legs to swing around and surged feet first downstream.

She opened her mind, inviting the intruders in.

"Be here," she whispered. "Be now."

ଔଔ

Kimmer felt the arrival of the newcomer within the net of communication she'd woven.

Oh! She is *Hammarleeding.*

"Be here, be now," enjoined the girl from the bluff. *Sarvet*. Her name was Sarvet. How unusual!

The water-queen's lips thinned. "The river entraps me. How should I be elsewhere?"

Sarvet answered her: "Are you sure? Is there no consent for imprisonment within you?"

Faien's reply was oblique and terrifying. "You shall feed me, too."

"I think not."

Kimmer hoped that were true, but how could it be?

Without her consent, the Gweltspaen's current held her fast, while the queen's antagonism prevented her from seeking the surface and shore.

But even were Sarvet wrong, at least she was on the right side.

Kimmer added her voice to the argument: "Please, you have other choices."

Did she?

Did Kimmer herself?

Keyholder Pavana always said so, when Kimmer's choice was inept.

Another presence arrived, and then another: both male, one strange, the other . . . not.

Elias!

So he had been close on Aani's terrier heels.

"Let her go!" demanded the bully.

"My lady must sup," declared the stranger.

"This hurts you as well," insisted Sarvet. "I should know."

"How can you know anything of me and mine?" The queen was contemptuous.

Her male advocate, derisive. "How could you know?"

Kimmer had a feeling Sarvet *did* know, young as she was, perhaps a year or two older than Kimmer herself. But what would she say?

"My losses were my own, not yours. Yes. But they were real."

Silence from the queen and her companion – Faien and . . . Theon – at this pronouncement.

Sarvet continued: "Others hurt me, but the hurts I dealt myself in the struggle were the worst ones. The ones hardest to heal from."

"There is no healing for me," said Faien.

"Then, let go," Sarvet urged.

The queen's face – the only one Kimmer could see, despite the incorporeal presence of the others – tightened, and her lips drew back. "Never."

Kimmer felt the deep pain of Faien's draining recommence, stronger this time, penetrating the keyholding shield even as Kimmer renewed her defense. Her joints throbbed; her bones ached.

You have another choice. The words from memory echoed.

No! How could defeat be a real choice? Be a freedom? Surely those words were for the queen, not for Kimmer.

Not defeat: surrender. No memory, this time. Sarvet? And what could she mean?

Find the current. Align your will to it and . . . push. Or pull.

Kimmer didn't want to.

And yet . . . she was weakening. Another interval of resisting this draining and her hold on her own keys would fade.

Would she drown first? Or would Faien empty her sooner? Either would be defeat indeed.

She let go.

The chartreuse light of her armor flashed yellow, then ceased. The tide of *energea* leaving her quickened. And the silver lattice connecting all five swimmers brightened.

Faien . . . screamed.

And let go.

What? Then Kimmer saw through the queen's eyes.

A shepherd girl lay in the water, the calming water, pale and dying, blond hair loosed from its braids and fanned by the river. She was lovely, her fading life lovelier still. Come back! Oh, come back!

What was there in this to conjure Faien's scream?

Another child: a girl-child, younger and sweet, her short curls drifting among Kimmer's long locks.

"My baby!" The queen's voice was harsh. "My child!"

And now Sarvet was there. "She could be yours. Will you kill her?"

Faien sobbed, her mouth agonized. Had she never come close to her victims before? Never touched their humanity? Never seen herself or her daughter within them?

"So much pain," moaned the queen. "I hurt."

"Yes," whispered Sarvet.

"Help me."

"If I can." A reaching hand, Sarvet's hand, swept through Kimmer's vision.

"Please," groaned Faien.

"Let it in."

"I cannot."

"You can."

"I'm afraid."

"Yes."

With that affirmation, the queen's face relaxed. Her translucence gained, grew transparent, became water and a rush of bubbles.

Kimmer seemed to follow them upward, watching them break the river's surface as a mist, rising skyward into pale sunlight.

She returned to herself, enervated and bleached.

I must swim.

She hung suspended. Drowning?

Then a hand gripped the back of her bodice and yanked.

She broke air coughing, hearing Elias' yells in her ear. "I'll kill you if you drown!"

She laughed and choked and gasped all the way to the bank, dragged by the bully's frantic determination.

ॐ

When Elias tumbled once more from stone into water – calmer water this time – Kimmer's listless body hung below him.

Dear Sias, he was late! Too late?

He dove, reaching for her, snagging the fabric of her dress, and hauled her to the surface.

Air; she needs air.

Next moment she was coughing and . . . laughing? Thank the goddess, she breathed.

He shifted his grip and stroked toward shore, relieved and thinking.

What had happened just now in the stone?

He'd felt himself to *be* Theon, the troll counselor to a queen of old. Theon's twisted body had become his for a time. Theon's thoughts tangled with his.

Sarvet – the girl Kimmer knew, but he didn't – said: "Be here, be now."

And Elias – no, *Theon* – thought: *We are here, young optimist. Drowned here. Forever here. And my lady must sup.*

"This hurts you," came Sarvet's observation.

Any prison galls. The one you create yourself . . . ravages and consumes. My lady must sup.

"The hurts I dealt myself were the worst."

Oh, yes. Yes. This I dealt myself . . . and to my lady. My magic lacked strength enough to save or to heal. My magic could only destroy.

"There is no healing for me" – Faien's words.

Heed her, heed her! Theon was begging.

"Never!"

Ah, Faien.

"You have another choice." Kimmer! Not drowned yet!

Ah, the shepherd girl, the youngest of us all.

So strange to be Theon and Elias combined.

Sarvet again: "Find the current. Align your will."

Stubborn resistance from Faien.

Please, my lady, heed her. Heed her and free us all. My incantatio must break.

Came . . . something. Had the queen surrendered? Had Kimmer?

An agonized scream.

My lady! My lady!

And then Elias was himself alone.

As he tumbled into water, a fleeting vision lingered before his mind's eye: the troll Theon emerging from the bridge stone as marble, the statue of a troll, then crumbling to dust – a dust that sifted on the breeze and spiraled upward, dissolving in the sun.

Elias' stroking hand brushed the pebbled river bottom. He pulled his feet under him, rising and bringing Kimmer up too.

&⁊Cʒ

Sarvet came ashore just downstream of the two lowlanders – Elias and Kimmer, she reminded herself.

Her dripping tunic dragged heavily against her thighs. Her hair twists, more resistant to moisture, shed water down her back.

Thank Sias she'd lost her cape on the trail and tossed her pack just before she hit the bridge. They'd have taken her down never to rise, if she'd retained them in the river.

She glanced upward once more.

The ascending mist of the dead queen was gone, likewise the spiraling dust of her loyal chancellor.

Had she truly seen winged translucence – pegasi? – accompanying the lost souls as warm Sias gathered them home? If so, they were gone as well.

Sarvet's feet stumbled on the shifting pebbles underfoot, and she looked down to catch her balance. Elias and Kimmer were hugging and jabbering at one another, but they turned as Sarvet approached.

"Goddess! The queen's ghost would have devoured us without you! Thank you!" the boy – Elias – exclaimed.

The girl was quieter. "Were they trapped in the bridge all that time? Centuries?" She shuddered.

Sarvet nodded. "The bridge and the river, I think. You freed them."

"Me?" Kimmer's eyes widened. "You did it, not me!" She shivered, and Elias slung an arm over her shoulders in a futile attempt to warm her.

Sarvet shook her head and smiled, but didn't argue. "Let's go hunt up my pack. It's got blankets. And my cape is warm, too. If we can find it."

The wool of her tunic, despite its wetness, was gathering her body heat the way wool tended to do. But the linens worn by the lowlanders wouldn't do the same. And they all needed to get dry, even though the spring afternoon was mild.

"We're on the wrong side of the river," Elias pointed out as they crossed the shingle toward the slope of the ravine.

"The bridge should be safe." Sarvet gestured. Its stone arch was visible over the trees, white in the sunlight, just around the bend upstream.

Elias nodded and reached for Kimmer's hand.

℘ℭℬ

Later, quite a bit later, they gathered around a fire on the bridge's western apron.

Kimmer had crossed the span unharmed – twice – to help retrieve Sarvet's belongings.

They'd scavenged kindling and a dead branch; doffed their clothes, wrung them out, and draped them on a few convenient, sunlit boulders; then wrapped up in the makings of Sarvet's bedroll while the goats grazed nearby on the verge.

The Hammarleeding girl shared out dried pears from her pack.

Kimmer chewed. Umm. Softer and sweeter than the Silmarish version. And with a stronger spicing as well.

"So, you're on a . . . a wanderyar?" Kimmer asked. What was a wanderyar anyway?

Sarvet explained that Hammarleeding boys had always traveled for a year or two when they turned sixteen or seventeen.

"Usually from father-lodge to father-lodge, but a few leave the mountains. I'm the first girl to try it." Her eyes glowed. "I never dreamed it would be like this!" She waved at the bridge behind them. "But I'm so glad I met you. You're . . . you're amazing!"

Kimmer felt herself blushing.

Elias interrupted whatever Sarvet was going to say next. Was he embarrassed too?

"We're glad you came along. You saved us, you know," he insisted.

Sarvet tilted her head. "You needed help," she agreed. "But . . . I think Kimmer's willingness to let the queen in is what saved us. I was caught also," she added.

"Were you?" Evidently Elias hadn't realized that.

Kimmer pulled her blanket closer, brushed a spark that snapped from the fire off the wool. Ow! Hot!

She hadn't realized either that Sarvet was caught. "It was so sad, the queen grieving and grieving for hundreds of years."

"More likely thousands," put in Sarvet.

"But I was too scared to feel sad for her." Kimmer nibbled on a second slice of dried pear. "I just wanted her to go, leave me be, let me live."

Elias shifted uncomfortably in his blanket. "Kimmer . . ."

Kimmer frowned. Why was he unhappy? They were safe. And they'd made a new friend.

"Kimmer, I'm really sorry about . . ."

Oh, he was thinking further back than the events of this afternoon.

Kimmer felt her lips curving up. Somehow she'd forgotten Elias was a bully. Getting pulled from drowning by someone did that to a person. "For calling me cheese licker and wool grubber and who knows what else?" Her voice had a saucy note to it.

"Wheyface," he confessed. "I mean – no! I –"

Kimmer laughed, but asked, "Why did you?"

He looked down. "It seems pretty stupid, but – I guess I was jealous."

"Jealous?! Of me?"

"Jealous of – of Pavana," he hurried on at what must be the surprise in her face, "because Pavana got your attention. And jealous of you, because you get Pavana's teaching. I wish" – he shook his head – "I wish I could learn keyholding too."

"Oh!" She would never have guessed that.

Elias continued, "I'd really like it if – we could be friends." He ducked his head again.

Kimmer reached out to touch his wrist.

When he looked up, she said, "Of course I'd like to be friends. We are friends. I think you saved my life, dragging me out of the river there at the end."

Elias fell silent, but his eyes beamed. Then he added, looking at Sarvet, "Will you be our friend too? Even after you travel onward?"

Sarvet smiled.

"Kimmer's right. We did something amazing there in the water, and it connects us. But you're right too. Because we have a choice about what we'll do with our connection." She nodded. "I'd love to be friends. No matter where I am. Forever."

Kimmer let her breath go in satisfaction. Feeling relaxed. Feeling happy. Feeling . . . *right*.

ഇൻഈ

Skies of Navarys

The tale is usually told with the great Palujon Clisto as rogue and thief, and the legendary Zandro Mytris as hero and savior. But one mother of ancient Navarys knows the truth.

She was there on the fabulous airship *Subindo*, the only one of the fleet to ride untouched through the storm.

ഇൻഈ

Liliya;h clutched the back of the divan where she knelt, bounced once, and pressed her face to the slanted window pane of the airship. The glass felt cool against her nose tip.

"Look! Look!" she exclaimed. "It's Eirene! Going to the park."

"How can you tell?" Mago's shoulder nudged hers as he peered downward. "We're way too high to tell who's who."

"She always goes now. Besides, I just know. It *is* her." Why did Mago have to doubt everything? He'd been nicer when they were younger. Now it was always "are you sure?" and "why do you think that?" and never just taking her say so. Liliyah gritted her teeth, then refocused on the panorama below.

This was her first time up in the *Subindo*, and seeing home from the air was amazing. The ocean surged vast and blue-gray from horizon to horizon. The island of Navarys, stretching away under the noon sun, showed so many textures of green: dark of pine, bright of meadow, and cool of orchard. And the city tumbled down the western slopes of Mount Sohlon like an infant's set of playing blocks: pierced cubes of colored marble and stucco roofed by verdigris copper or olive tile. *Mother should see this!* She'd be searching through her reticule for paper and stylus the instant the rooftop canvas revealed itself to her, eager to sketch designs for this new dimension.

Liliyah watched her nurse, tiny as an ant at this height, pause in their courtyard by the vivid purple patch – the tubs of balloon flowers – before passing under the gate to the street.

"That *is* my house," Liliyah insisted.

"Yeah. I guess. But how do you know it isn't one of the maids? Or a footman? Or even your mother?" Mago clung to his skepticism.

"'Cause they're bony thin, not plump like Eirene." Liliyah could be stubborn too. She fingered the decorative bronze catch of the window casement. The metal was cool, like the glass, and its scrolling curves soothed her irritation.

Mago puffed out a breath of exasperation, and Liliyah shifted her gaze to his face. His brows contracted slightly over his hazel eyes, and his lips, more usually curved in the hint of a smile, had thinned. "You always jump to conclusions!" he burst out. "With never a smidge of evidence! Why are you always so irrational?"

"I'm not irrational! And I do have evidence! My house, a round figure wearing Eirene's amber head scarf, enjoying the flowers, and leaving at her usual time. How can you be so slow and stupid?" Liliyah felt her own eyes widening in a glare and her chin jutting. "Don't you understand that every last detail needn't be pinned down and labeled in order for you to know something? What d'you have to have? A view through a spyglass with Eirene smack in the middle of the lens?"

"Yes! Exactly!" Mago turned abruptly to sit a small distance away from her on the divan they shared. "Details matter! Precision matters! Fudging the facts can be dangerous."

Liliyah sat back on her calves, her back to the low table of finger foods and the gondola aisle beyond it, her attention fully on her friend. What in the world did he mean? "How could mistaking, oh, Dama Mytris" – his mother – "for Eirene possibly be dangerous?" Her astonishment was cooling her aggravation.

Mago vented an embarrassed laugh. He was calming too. "Well, it couldn't be Mama, of course." His mother sat gossiping with her friend at the far end of the gondola, nibbling on the chilled grapes, and sipping iced coffee. She'd changed seats soon after exchanging stiff greetings with the dark-haired man who took the divan next to hers. "But such a mistake could be risky." Mago straightened his spine."

"How?" Liliyah felt more and more puzzled. Social discomfort, yes. Risk? No. She reached for a grape from the platter behind her, met the bowl of salted nuts instead, and lifted a pecan to her lips. Its barky scent brought her family's front parlor before her mind's eye, a comfortable space where a bowl of in-the-shell nuts always graced the central table.

"What if you mistook an enemy for a friend? What if that weren't Eirene? What if it were someone who hated you putting an *energea* stone in your fountain to make you sick?"

Liliyah shivered and pulled her pelisse more snugly around her shoulders. Inside the airship's gondola was warm, stuffy even. But a casement several panes down from the one she'd been looking through was open, and the breeze from it, chilly. "No one hates me," she asserted. "And *energea* stones are safe. My papa makes sure they're safe." He did, too. Before Liliyah was born, her father and a friend of his had founded a commission to test the *energea* stones and determine safe levels for their powers.

The limited ones used by small crafters – cheesemakers, weavers, potters – to speed and mechanize parts of their work were unlikely to cause harm. But the newer and larger stones being developed for mining and smelting and earth-moving had worried Daymo Lykos, and he'd taken action. Rightly, as it turned out. The old, traditional *energea* stones drew energy from the things and people near them, but in such minute amounts as to be imperceptible. The new stones drew much, much more; sometimes too much. Daymo Lykos' commission had intervened before anyone was hurt. And the Navarean monarch had not only awarded Liliyah's father the Olivine Guerdon in honor of his work, but had created a royal corps that assessed and certified every stone in their island kingdom every year.

"*Energea* stones are safer than they've ever been," Liliyah insisted.

"Except the ones that go untested." Did Mago sound glum?

Liliyah was tired of being patient with him. "There are no untested stones! My father sees to that!" she snapped.

"Oh, yes, there are."

"Do you just enjoy being sad and mad or something? 'Cause I don't! What's wrong with you, Mago?"

"*I* prefer being accurate over illusory happiness" – an unbearably superior tone – "as you clearly don't, Demoselle Lykos. Fine! Be glad and ignorant. I don't care. You're only a baby anyway. With a nurse."

Speechless, Liliyah jerked to her feet. "You, you – crass and loutish boor!"

"Better than a silly goose who wouldn't know logic if it crawled up her nose!" Mago's chin lifted.

Liliyah's chin jutted, but she bit her tongue. *I won't say it. Won't.*

The smooth voice of the man disdained by Dama Mytris interrupted their quarrel. "I think you'd both best aim for a do over." He sounded amused and sympathetic together. "Roll back to when the steward brought refreshments," he advised.

Mago flushed and looked at the carpeting.

Liliyah surveyed the stranger. Unlike her papa, no gray in his hair, but the same faint smile lines at his mouth and a calm intentness behind his gaze. Who was he? Did she know him?

"Palujon Clisto, demoselle," he introduced himself.

Oh! She didn't know him, but she knew *of* him. Daymo Clisto was the most gifted aeromancer on the island, responsible for adjusting the weather along the routes followed by the Navarean merchant fleet. Half the wealth of Navarys depended on his skill.

"Liliyah Lykos," she returned, "and Mago Mytris."

"We've met," muttered Mago. Then, fixedly: "My apologies, Daymo Clisto." He lifted his eyes. Was that desperation in their depths? "But you know I'm right, sir, don't you?"

"Partially." The aeromancer smiled. "Your friend here looks pretty sharp to me." He nodded at Liliyah. "Nothing like a silly goose or an enemy to logic." He winked.

Mago's flush deepened. He turned to Liliyah. "I . . . didn't really mean that, Lili. I – I'm worried, that's all. About someone else who's ignoring . . . possibilities."

Palujon poured three glasses from a carafe of peach juice and raised his in a toast. "To logic, to intuition, to friendship!"

Vivid sweetness from her sip filled Liliyah's mouth. Yum.

"You were once my father's friend," Mago blurted after swallowing.

"I was," Palujon answered. "We served as apprentices under the royal engineer back in the day. Since then our ways have lain apart."

"But more so now," Mago challenged him.

"Yes."

What was Mago wanting? Liliyah studied him. He'd grown away from her these last two years, caught up with lessons and the concerns of the boys' school where he enrolled. His shoulders had broadened, and a light fuzz glimmered on his upper lip. He'd changed. Yet he was the same, too: mostly genial, sociable, and kind. Today's tension was not usual. Anxiety, belligerence, and pleading chased across his expression.

Palujon continued, "Daymo Mytris and I differ on the matter of his latest research, but this is not the place for discussion about it. And you, as his son, are not the person for me to discuss it with."

"I think you are right about my father. I *fear* you are."

Liliyah chewed her lip. Zandro Mytris engineered *energea* stones, the big ones. Her papa often said they were the most efficient for their size of any on the island. And the safest, drawing the least energy for the most output. Zandro and Papa had been friends for decades. Their families met often to dine or ride or attend the opera together. That was why Dama Mytris had invited her on this pleasure expedition in the air. Liliyah peeked out the window bank again. The airship had moved beyond the city and its harbor, hovering over the grand circus where the chariot races were run. She glanced back to where Mago's mother laughed with her friend, oblivious to her son.

Had Papa displayed a coolness toward Daymo Mytris lately?

"Talk with your father," Palujon suggested, "or a family friend. You must know that you should not talk with me, and I cannot talk with you about him."

Mago's lips compressed. "Yes, I know. But – oh, sir, can't you *do* something?"

Palujon shook his head. Not a refusal to act, Liliyah guessed, just a refusal to talk.

What was Daymo Mytris up to? Would Mago tell her? *I'll make him tell,* she decided. *The next time Mama drags me to walk in the park with her when she meets Dama Mytris.*

The rest of the afternoon on the *Subindo* passed pleasantly enough. The airship toured all the notable landmarks – the lighthouse marking the Gorgon's Rocks, the cliff face carved in the likeness of Queen Cybele, the Minotaur's Gorge, and the rest – and Mago relapsed into his more relaxed self as Daymo Clisto guided the conversation into social channels. Had Mago tasted the apricot pastries at the new bakery on Strato Street? What did Liliyah think of the new style for sandals, with the three straps at the ankle? Had either of them seen the new star discovered by the royal astronomers?

The only awkward moment came as they approached the air terminal. The *Subindo* was the largest of the fleet of airships, able to accommodate three gangways rather than the usual one, and it often docked at the main loggia instead of one of the four outlying mooring towers. Liliyah followed Mago and Palujon to the foremost span to disembark. They were just marveling over the frescoed vault of the gallery visible beyond the loggia – an image of Evaia, goddess of the sea, dancing with her sister, Caecia, goddess of the winds – when Dama Mytris joined them, preceded by a drift of her lilac perfume. Liliyah sneezed.

"Bless you, child." Her tone was indulgent until she acknowledged Palujon. She must have noticed that her son and his guest enjoyed the aeromancer's company for the majority of the voyage, but her demeanor belied it. "Surely the center gangway or that aft would be more appropriate?" She sniffed, tilted her head back, and looked down her nose.

Palujon quirked his left eyebrow. "My tenor displeases you, Dama?" His tone conveyed irony.

"Your mere presence suffices," she snapped.

Mago interposed uneasily, "Daymo Clisto has been most kind all afternoon, Mama."

"Let him dispense children's entertainment to others than Zandro Mytris' progeny then." His mother sniffed again, and her dark eyes flashed. "You dare too much, Daymo!"

"Indeed, you are correct, Dama. I'll relieve you of my daring."

Liliyah wrinkled her forehead. Was he apologizing for social effrontery or insulting Dama Mytris for her dislike of boldness?

Palujon touched Liliyah's shoulder. "'Twas a pleasure to meet you, demoselle. Your father and I" – was there a touch of emphasis on your? – "have grown busy in our separate professions, but we remain friends. I hope to encounter you again." Then he was gone, stepping from the gangway's heel and vanishing in the crowd.

Liliyah never got her opportunity to grill Mago about his father.

That evening she accompanied her parents to the Grand Exhibition Hall. The Corps of Royal Engineers were holding a gala reception at the unveiling of their proposal for a rail line to connect the copper mines to the shipyards. The arcade just inside the quadruple portals was jammed with notable guests. Dama Jeno, one of Mama's cronies, swept out of the crush to greet them. "Persis, my dear! Daymo Lykos! It's just too amazing! My husband declares it will ruin our green countryside, but I think the device is clever. Have you seen it?"

Liliyah's papa bowed. Her mama laughed, a ripple of pleasant sound. "How should I? We've just arrived, Zephyra. Where is the miniature?"

"Just beyond the columns." Dama Jeno waved a careless hand. "But you must meet Daymo Eryx first. He's longing to compare notes with you and your husband. And you'd best doff your wraps." She fluttered her fan, puffing the scent of roses through the warm air with its silver-encrusted panels.

Liliyah had already shrugged out of her pelisse. The thin silk of her frock, too light for the chill of the night air, was welcome in this overheated gathering space. Its pale turquoise folds felt cool and smooth against her body. She craned her neck, trying to see around Dama Jeno to where the "clever device" stood on display, but the crowd was too dense.

They edged past a matron displaying purple feathers in her headdress and flashing diamonds around her throat, nibbling dainties of sweet almond paste, and talking nonstop with an excited acquaintance. They were not the only pair so animated, rather than fashionably bored. A buzz of enthusiasm pervaded the space. Liliyah's parents paused again for more meeting and greeting. Their progress remained slow, and Dama Jeno eventually peeled away before they reached the man she intended to present to them.

Daymo Eryx proved to be one of the civil engineers who devised the engine that would travel on the new railway. "With just a slight change in the gearing ratios, we can make it work with the old *energea* stones," he was declaring seriously to Liliyah's papa. "The lever to disengage the flywheel is probably a good idea even when the power source is not continuously supplying power the way these newfangled lodestones do."

Daymo Lykos nodded genially. "I reviewed your schema a few days ago and was pleased to note your variants. Truly excellent, proactive work, Daymo. I wish all inventors would pursue a branching strategy."

The engineer's eyes lit with enthusiasm. "Are you a fellow devotee of systematic thought?"

"A mere smatterer, I'm afraid." Papa's voice sounded regretful. "But the systems approach yields multiple solutions before they are needed, which prevents incidents like the Heremias disaster. A narrow, focused approach may be efficient, but prompts investment and commitment prematurely."

Eryx shook his head. "A sad loss of life."

"Which we'll avoid with this project. The commission will test the lodestone before it's installed, of course. The date's set for an eight-day from now. But the small prototypes were proven safe, and the working stones are likely to be no different."

The two men plunged into a discussion of the esoteric details.

Liliyah noticed that her mama's attention wandered. Daymo Eryx had planted himself beside a charming mosaic mural, one of Mama's, in fact. It depicted a pebble strewn rivulet flanked by watercress and wild iris. Actual river stones combined with fragments of vivid glass and larger painted tiles. Liliyah reached out her hand to touch the metallic sheen of a minnow. Its scales felt strangely warm. She sent a startled glance at her mother.

"I used chips of galena," Mama mused. "I wonder if I should try a creation entirely of metals; copper, tin, bronze, and lead. Could be an interesting composition . . ." Mama wasn't really paying her daughter any heed.

Liliyah closed her eyes and exhaled slowly, attempting to open her awareness to *energea*. Did a faint hum, that wasn't really a hum, but would be if *energea* were perceived through the ears instead of the mind, permeate the exhibition hall? She inhaled in preparation for another easy breath out. The aroma of sautéed fish croquettes threaded through the dominant florals of the perfumes and colognes worn by Navarys' wealthy and powerful, distracting Liliyah's focus. She was new to manipulating and perceiving *energea*. Like most children, her lessons in it had started soon after her celebration of her thirteenth natal day. Relax, she told herself. Yes, what was almost the lazy drone of a bumblebee lay on the air.

"Lili?" Papa's question interrupted her probing.

Liliyah's eyelids flew open.

"Let's go see the miniature." He touched her shoulder and gestured to an opening in the crowd. She stepped forward.

The island of Navarys lay before her once again, this time at waist height on a tabletop stretching from the reflecting pool at one end of the hall to the sculpture of dolphins playing at the other. Comparing the diminutive landscape built by model enthusiasts to the real thing, she wondered if they too had experienced flight in one of the five Navarean airships. Navarys in miniature was so like Navarys from the air. Merely lacking the haziness provided by five hundred feet of air or the vivid brightness imparted by sunlight. She reached out to brush the spinning sails of a tiny windmill. *How –?* Oh! An *energea* stone – matte black and pebble-sized – capped its twirling roof, which propelled the drive shaft moving the sails.

"Ingenious, no?" came Papa's voice.

"But where is the fabrimancer operating the stone?" she wondered aloud.

"This is one of the new stones Daymo Mytris has been working on, the lodestones. They draw *energea* without the prompting of a human handler."

Liliyah felt her eyes widening. She turned away from the little miracle presented by the windmill to assess her father's feelings about it. His brows lifted slightly, and the corners of his mouth turned up. So this was for real. She thought immediately of her friend with the silk shop. Would the small crafters like Dama Omys have access to these lodestones? Imagine if a spinner could set one at the hub of her spinning wheel. Or a potter use one to move his potter's wheel. "Is it safe?" she blurted.

Papa's mouth straightened, not in tension, but in seriousness. "Yes. I tested it myself."

Liliyah's breath puffed out in a sigh of relief. Mago was wrong. His papa wasn't courting risky possibilities. She turned back to the miniature landscape. The gate to the model of the monarch's country palace had been mechanized with another of these lodestones, and its bronze filigree swung open and closed. Beyond the palace on another hillside, a tram drawing three carriages filled with nuggets of copper ratcheted along geared rails. This was the engine and the railway prompting this exhibition and reception. Going by the excitement of the public here tonight, the proposal would receive a quick approval.

Liliyah moved on around the table's edge, eager to see more of the intricate work of the modelers. Daymo Jeno was right. It *was* clever.

Closer to the city lay the aerodrome with the vaulted loggia where she'd disembarked just this afternoon and the four mooring towers, from one of which she'd crossed onto the *Subindo*. Instead of the spiral stair giving access to its top balcony and moveable gangway, a lift moved up and down the needle-nosed structure. Daymo Mytris would like that! She'd complained that climbing a hundred steps to get up to the airship was hard on her poor knees.

Sudden shadow fell across the aerodrome. *What?* Liliyah tilted her head toward the ceiling. Oh!

The model of an airship – not the *Subindo*, but the smaller *Ganador*, its silken covering vivid with magenta and royal blue stripes – drifted slowly down from overhead, controlled by yet another lodestone fastened to the bottom of its forward gondola. A thin, almost transparent guideline controlled the route the *Ganador* followed. Evidently its lodestone provided merely motive power to the propellers whirring on the side nacelles, not steering. Liliyah vented a quiet giggle. This was *energea*, after all, not fantasy!

Papa rested his hand on her shoulder, solid and comforting. "Pretty amazing, isn't it?"

Liliyah nodded. "And Daymo Mytris invented them? The lodestones?"

"He did, indeed. I'm proud to know him." Papa smiled at her quick glance. "And glad to live now. We're at a cusp of history, Lili. Our lives will change, probably unimaginably so. Can you guess what might be different?"

She couldn't, but found herself gazing across the miniature landscape to where Daymo Mytris stood receiving congratulations from a long line of guests eager to meet the great man. Dama Mytris posed at his side, gracious and welcoming, a nice counterpoint to her husband's slightly triumphant air. Where was Mago? Liliyah wondered uneasily. Surely his father would have liked him to participate in this celebration. *Papa can't be wrong.* But what if Mago was right? What if there were something to worry about?

She looked at Daymo Mytris again. Was his nose . . . different somehow? His color pale, compared to all the flushed and overheated people around him? She shook her head. *Papa's not wrong. He's never wrong.*

Next morning, Eirene woke her late.

"Wha' time izzit?" she murmured sleepily.

"Time for me to go to Dama Zario. She's joining a walking group today."

"Mmm?" Liliyah blinked and snuggled deeper into the silk of her quilts. The sun had warmed her bedchamber; she was seeking darkness, not escape from some long-gone dawn chill.

"Her physician told her the baby would be fine without her for an hour or two, but that she wouldn't be fine if she didn't get out of the house a little more and stretch her limbs." Liliyah could hear the smile in her old nurse's voice. "I must say I'm looking forward to having the little one to myself for a spell." Yes, Eirene did love babies.

Mago's words from yesterday came back to her. "You're only a baby anyway. With a nurse."

Liliyah sat up abruptly, snorting. She loved Eirene, but she didn't need her anymore. And even Mama couldn't bear to part with her. She'd become part of the family during all those years while Liliyah was little. And moped even amidst her pride when Liliyah outgrew the nursery and her nurse. Everyone was relieved when Dama Zario, a few doors down the hill, inquired whether Eirene could give her the mornings to help with the new baby. Win, win, win all round.

"I'm up," Liliyah announced, slithering out from under the net canopy that sheltered her bed.

The gauze of the window curtains tinted her room golden. It must be well past breakfast, if the sun had moved around the corner of the house that typically shaded her windows. She started scrambling out of her nightdress, rifling through the gowns on the wall pegs for something casual and comfortable.

"Now, sweetling, that's no way to go." Eirene's hand checked hers. "Your governess has indeed arrived in the schoolroom, but you've time to dress properly and eat." She gestured toward a tray resting on the low bench by the door. A bowl of berries, a pitcher of raisin kvass, and skewers of roast mutton sent tantalizing aromas into the air. Liliyah sniffed appreciatively – umm, she could almost taste the savory roasted meat – and slowed down enough to allow Eirene to tie her sash.

"Kiss the baby for me," she told her nurse as Eirene whisked herself away.

Lessons were ordinary, but interesting. The new math – algebra – was much more fun than mere calculation, and she'd always liked history, but studying *energea* – also new – was her current favorite. Her governess said that Liliyah was an aural practitioner, because she perceived the *energea* as sound. She couldn't imagine what it must be like for visual or kinesthetic fabrimancers. The musical tones resounding in her mind's ear felt so natural, so easy to compose the extensions that controlled their physical results. How would those who saw lattices of colored light or felt pressure on their limbs manipulate their *energea*? Her friend Cressy claimed to be a visual practitioner, but still. Liliyah tilted her head in puzzlement. People were so *different*! It was fascinating.

The afternoon found her in Cressy's shop. Liliyah had tried to persuade her mother to call on Dama Mytris. She still wanted to question Mago in private. But Mama had her own plans.

"No, Lili. I'm walking with Hyacinthe, and looking forward to it, too. She's found a way to infuse essential lavender into clay tiles and promises to share the secret with me." Mama paused, scrutinizing Liliyah, then reaching out to tip her daughter's chin up. "You usually shirk formal visits, love. Why the sudden interest?" Her left eyebrow quirked up.

Liliyah felt her face heating and worked to meet her mother's curious gaze. "I wanted to ask Mago something."

Mama's eyes widened slightly. "Truly?" Her voice registered a teasing suggestiveness.

"He's an old friend, and yesterday reminded me that I missed him." Liliyah heard defensiveness in her own voice. But, really, how embarrassing that Mama thought she might like Mago *that* way. She didn't like anyone that way. Although Mago's newly broader shoulders had felt . . . nice against hers on the divan in the *Subindo*. She shivered, not in cold, but . . . unease.

"Well, Ione's busy entertaining the engineers from last night's gala in any case. We'll pay her a call in a few days." Mama's hand released Liliyah's chin to pat her cheek. "If you do indeed wish to see Mago."

Liliyah had acquiesced to the delay and headed out on her own more typical afternoon activity: visiting the shop owners on Neander Row. She'd started the habit young, asking questions of the clerks while in tow behind her nurse or her mother when they ran errands. The adults had laughed because her curiosity wasn't aimed at the sweet smells in the parfumiers, the music of the chimes in the garden shop, or the bright colors in the silk shop. She'd wanted to know how many units they kept in stock, what they paid to their suppliers compared to what they charged their customers, and all the other details of running a business. By the time she turned ten, Mama and Papa not only accepted her unusual interest, but encouraged it.

"She's got a gift for commerce," Papa declared. "Let her pursue it."

Now, at age thirteen, her afternoon interviews were commonplace.

The silk shop was one of her favorite stops. Its heavy, musky smell – exuded by the ornate brocades and the middle-weight velvets and the light gauzes alike – was associated with the ultimate pleasure in Liliyah's experience. Dama Omys had accepted Liliyah in some sort as a protégée and begun teaching her all the business savvy at her command. Liliyah got to inspect the financial records, the inventory lists, and the back storeroom. Plus Dama Omys had a young assistant who took to Liliyah the instant the girls were introduced. Cressy, three years older than Liliyah, possessed an equal fascination with commerce. She was intrigued by the possibilities of the new lodestones.

"Can you imagine putting one on the spooler that unwinds the filament from the silk cocoon? Instead of one fabrimancer per machine, you could have one per *six* machines! And he wouldn't have to use *energea* most of the time." Cressy bounced on her toes. "Every Navarean on the island will be rich!" she exclaimed.

"We're already rich," Liliyah insisted. "Compared to the mainlanders."

"Oh, mainlanders," scoffed Cressy. "Without *energea* . . ." her face sobered. "Dama Omys says their poor go hungry every winter. And it gets cold there!"

"I'm glad I was born here." Liliyah tried to imagine the chill of an ice-house continuing on for hours or days or months and failed. Visiting the underground space during a hot summer day felt good. It was less comfortable on that cool autumn morning last year, but she'd warmed up fast upon emerging with the ice chips she'd fetched to soothe her burnt tongue.

"I'd like to visit Imsterfeldt, though," mused Cressy. "Dama Omys says it has canals passing right through the city and town houses four and five stories tall!"

They'd moved on to talking about Liliyah's voyage on the *Subindo* and making plans to visit the dyer's manufactory next revel-day when shouting erupted in the allée outside, followed by running feet.

Liliyah broke off what she was saying to frown at Cressy, who frowned back. "What is it?" her friend worried.

Dama Omys was waiting on a customer purchasing vast amounts of heavy turquoise damask to curtain her drawing room windows. She looked up briefly to instruct the girls. "Go see what that's about, will you, please?"

Of the handful of passersby – early afternoon saw few shoppers – it was hard to get anyone to stop. One fat woman bustled up the stairs just above the shop's doorway, whimpering, "Oh, no! Oh, no!" under her breath, while three errand boys ran downhill, yelling, "Hurry! Hurry! Or you'll lose your place to the next fellow on the list!"

Liliyah turned to Cressy, eyes wide. "I don't know," Cressy answered her unspoken question. "It can't be good."

No, it felt bad. Which was scary and strange amidst the normal sensations of a spring day: sun warm on her cheek, cobblestones firm beneath her slippers, scent of almond flowers on the breeze. But something dreadful had happened, and something worse was coming.

❧◈◆

His mother wasn't listening.

Mago gritted his teeth in frustration.

First Mater had explained that Pater was short on sleep. Next she'd insisted that he always sneezed in the spring, his lungs irritated by the pollens of orange blossom and almond. With all the seasonal chafing, of course his nose swelled.

"There's really no reason to worry, my dear," she repeated for the fourth time, and reached for the vial of nail enamel she'd set on the fountain coping beside her. Uncorking the diminutive vessel, she dipped a minute brush through the narrow neck, withdrew it carefully, and painted a broad stripe of emerald green on her thumbnail. She wrinkled her nose. The pine tar in its formula smelled unpleasantly.

Mago unclenched his jaw and looked away.

His father *had* been staying up late and rising early, frantically finishing last details on the massive loadstone that would power the engine transporting copper ore from the mines to the harbor. But Pater was experienced with deadlines. His temper had never grown quite so short-fused and volcanic for deadlines past. Why now? And his nose was more than swollen. It was changing shape. Something was wrong. Very wrong.

The breeze gusted strongly for an instant. Spray from the fountain misted his face, evaporating and cooling, then drying as the warmth of the sun prevailed. Mago stared at the horizon where sea met sky. Their house, just like its neighbors, fronted on a sloping allée punctuated by steps at the steepest stretches. But the walled courtyard behind the domicile occupied a slight bluff, giving him a more expansive view of the shore cliffs, rows of palms, and the tumble of mansions climbing this reach of Mount Sohlon. He sighed.

Was there any point in continuing this discussion? Mater would just defend Pater, no matter what he said, without answering his real question. He looked back to his mother, sitting on the wide curve of sandstone a little removed from him and concentrating on her grooming. Her hair gleamed blue black, and the skin of her throat emerged smooth from the upper drapery of her gown. She always seemed more poised than his friends' mothers. But right now the corners of her mouth crimped closed, and faint lines spread from the corners of her eyes. Two deeper lines marked the space between her brows.

She's worried, too, realized Mago. She's defending Pater from *her* accusations, not mine.

"Will he be normal again in the summer?" He hadn't meant to speak that fear aloud.

She set her nail brush back on its tray, re-corked the vial and clenched her fingers around it. "No. He won't."

Evaia below. Now he had her admission, he didn't want it. Wanted her false reassurance back. "What will we do?" he whispered.

Before she could answer, loud sobs broke from the open casements of the scullery. Shouts echoed in the allée. Their steward emerged from the house, his tread steady and majestic as always, despite the disturbance, as he crossed the sandstone flags of the courtyard. He stopped before Mago's mother. "Dama, there is news." His tone was even, his words unhurried. Why did Mago's stomach drop once more, falling again from the nadir produced by Mater's judgment of Pater?

"What is it?" Mater's tone was sharp.

"The sea bed shrugs its shoulders. Our monarch's own geomancer divines it."

Mater hunched as though punched in the gut. "Merciful deeps," she murmured. "It's the wave?"

"Yes, Dama."

"Mago! Come! We must get to the quay. Your father has sway with Daymo Zario. One of his galleys will carry us to safety." She started to her feet.

"There is time, Dama. And a governance."

"A governance? What governance? And how *much* time?"

"Eight turns of the glass. And a place by lot on a sea vessel or an airship."

"By lot?" Mater's nose pinched in, white, and her chin jerked up, outraged. "My husband is friend to the monarch and holds a seat in the first circle of merchants! How dare anyone deny his family by something so fickle as lot!"

Mago moved to grip his mother's forearm. She couldn't, she really mustn't, strike old Phyllos. He'd been with them from before Mago was born, and his dignity wouldn't stand the affront. Mater shook off her son's hand, recollecting herself.

"You have a place on Daymo Theniar's caravel, along with Daymo Mytris, Dama."

"And my son?" She looked haughty now, rather than alarmed.

"All children under fifteen years have a place, Dama." Did Phyllos' words possess a sardonic tinge?

Mater tossed her head. "Well, then, we must pack." Her brows knit. "Who has not a place?"

Phyllos bowed. "Our monarch has refused to depart until the last of his subjects is boarded. And . . . not all will board." The steward fell silent on the heels of this utterance, his demeanor stern.

No! Mater's mouth shaped the word. Mago felt his own do the same. But no sound issued forth.

Phyllos continued, "There are not places for all."

"No. There wouldn't be." Mater murmured, subdued. Then she rallied. "Mago, you will go to the quay now, while I direct the servants in their duties. Phyllos will accompany you." Her decision suffered a check. "Do *you* have a place, Phyllos?"

"Yes, Dama. I do, but –"

Mater looked shocked and relieved at once. "Good! Do you send a footman to Daymo Mytris and yourself take Mago to the caravel.

Oh! And have another footman pull the travel trunks from storage. I'll start the maids to folding garments and swathing the heirloom china in padding –"

"Dama." Phyllo interrupted her. "The children are to be evacuated by airship, and Mago's place is on one of them. The *Subindo*."

Mago felt Mater's arm grope round his shoulders, trembling, while her lips shaped another silent no. Why did his presence on the *Subindo* appall her? If the coming wave were so huge as to threaten all of Navarys, the seagoing vessels would also be threatened. The airships provided the safest berths. Thus their reservation for the island's children. Mago followed that logic perfectly. What was Mater thinking?

"I shan't part from my son!" she declared.

Phyllos' mouth quirked. "I fear you have little choice," he told her.

❧ ❦ ☙

Liliyah paused in the atrium of her home.

Trunks, packing cases, and portmanteaus littered the marble floor. The servants' sandals slapped loudly as they hurried about their tasks. They barely noticed her, the daughter of the house, so focused were they on gathering valuables and stowing them. The head veil worn by one of the maids brushed Liliyah's cheek – an unwitting silken caress – as the young woman rushed by.

Mama appeared in the doorway to the front parlor. She stood straight, her eyes distant. Was she calculating what to leave and what to bring? Then she saw Liliyah. Her gaze warmed, and she surged forward to take Liliyah's hands. "You've heard? You know?"

Liliyah nodded, unspeaking. The messenger bearing the news had emerged from the shop next to Dama Omys' just as she and Cressy turned to go back inside.

"Mama . . . must we truly leave? Can a wave reach so high? All the way to the top of Mount Sohlon?"

Her mother's arm slipped over her shoulders, guiding her into the parlor, away from the bustle of the atrium. They sank onto the divan under the windows into the courtyard.

"We'll be safe, Liliyah. The ships will carry us away from danger. And we'll make new homes on the continent."

"Why can't we come back to Navarys? Back home. After the wave has passed?"

Mama sighed. "Our flocks and orchards will be swept away, love. How would we feed ourselves?"

Liliyah shrank into Mama's embrace. She'd been imagining massive ocean breakers overwhelming the quays, flooding the low-lying harbor streets. This new picture in her mind – trees uprooted and churned, goats and chickens submerged and drowned, a wave so immense as to be a mountain itself – presented disaster on another scale altogether.

"I'm scared," she whispered, then blushed. She should be strong, helping Mama choose and pack and get ready, not quivering like a baby and seeking comfort.

"It's a scary thing," agreed her mother. "Imagine if we had no geomancers." Liliyah shuddered. "But we do have them. And Navareans are wealthy. Even the poorest of us have resources enough to make a new start in Cambers or Solmondy. It will be an adventure!"

Liliyah felt her eyes widening. "Mama, you can't be looking forward to this!" Could she?

Mama managed a chuckle. "Well, no. But since we *must* do this, better to embrace it than resist it." She gave another squeeze to Liliyah's shoulders, then took her hands again. "Now. Can you choose your favorite trinkets and scrolls? I've packed my wardrobe, and I'd like to do my studio next. Do you need help?"

Liliyah bit her lip. Could she manage by herself? "No, I can do it," she decided. "I'll fold my gowns, too," she offered, "and wrap my sandals."

Mama patted her hand, hesitated, then forged ahead. "The weather's cooler on the continent. Pack all your warmer clothes, but only as many as will fit of your lightest gauzes and voiles. I've had two trunks placed in your chamber. One for clothing, one for toiletries and miscellany."

Liliyah clutched her mother's hand in sudden distress. "Dama Omys! Her silks! She can't possibly pack them all. Can I go help her? Will there be room on the ships for shop inventory?" The messenger had listed off baggage allowances and other practicalities, hadn't he? But she hadn't been listening, too confounded by his news, and Dama Omys had insisted she return home at once, before the messenger finished declaring all his tidings.

"The cargo holds are capacious enough," Mama answered. "It's time and –" Mama visibly swallowed . . . something "– it's time we lack."

"Please?"

Mama looked exasperated. "I'd rather you stay close." Her lips straightened. "Close to me."

"The Row's not far!"

"Lili." Mama's shoulders settled, and her voice chided.

Liliyah flushed.

Well, it wasn't far. Not really. Just three allées over and halfway down the hill. Of course it wasn't close either. But not clear across the city or down by the harbor.

"Liliyah." Mama sighed. "The city won't be . . . as safe as usual. When people are scared, they get angry. Sometimes violent. I want you close," she repeated.

Was that all? The tightness in Liliyah's chest eased. "One of the footmen could accompany me."

Mama tilted her head. Was she weakening?

"The hurly burly amongst the latecomers will be dangerous. The sooner we depart" – Mama's voice wobbled on that last word, then grew crisp – "the better."

"Will we go the instant your studio's packed?" Liliyah probed.

Mama's breath puffed out on a small laugh laugh. "I'm a fast packer. I'll be helping Hyacinthe as soon as I've finished here. Which . . . won't be long."

Ha! I've got her now. "If you're helping your friend, why can't I help mine?"

Mama's torso lost some of its rigidity. She reached out a hand and pinched Liliyah's chin. "Alright. Once you've packed your own things, you may help Dama Omys. But only two turns of the glass, mind." Her hand turned to cup Liliyah's cheek, cool and smooth and comforting. "And come straight home. Don't go to the aerodrome. Hear?"

What? Liliyah felt her forehead wrinkling. What did the aerodrome have to do with it?

"No, I won't. But . . . won't we go down to the harbor?"

"Oh!" Mama looked stricken. "Didn't the messenger say?"

Yet more anxiety fluttered Liliyah's stomach. Was there no end to the way dread piled atop dread piled atop dread?

"What is it?" Why had she asked? She didn't want to know.

"You're on the *Subindo*, love. All the children are. On the airships high above the wave and safe."

"Mama, no! I won't! I'll go with you and Papa. On the sea. Please!"

Mama bent and kissed her brow. "Go pack!"

☙ϋβ

Mago stood uneasily before the lodestone.

It was matte black, a flattened oval nearly the size of his own head, and resting on a limestone pedestal. Did an air current flow off it? No, but there was something. Mago closed his eyes.

The fluting of a single bird floated through the open windows of the workshop, accompanied by the wafting perfume of the clematis vine. Mago extended his arms along with his sense of *energea*. He was a kinesthetic practitioner – a beginning one – and felt this invisible power through touch and pressure. Was the tide off the lodestone *energea*? It surely wasn't air.

Ah! Energea, indeed!

The hairs on his forearms rose. A heaviness pressed against the whole front of his body, even while an ache awakened in his bones and surged up through his skin, a stinging prickle, passing outward to the lodestone. Mago gasped.

"Get away from there!" Swift, hard footsteps followed the shout, and then his father's angry grip jerked Mago backward. He stumbled, working to get his feet under him, and overbalanced into Pater's chest. Together they slammed into something, and Mago's eyes flew open. He grabbed for the work table's edge, missed, and plummeted. The grasp on his shoulder brought him to an abrupt halt just above the floor, nose to brick. Apparently Pater had kept his feet.

Next instant, Mago had his feet, too, hauled upright by Daymo Mytris.

"How dare you jeopardize my genius? My workshop is not your play patch! What are you doing here?" Pater's face darkened with rage.

Mago opened his mouth to reply. Closed it again. This made no sense. He'd often watched his father work before. Always been welcome in his workshop. His mind flashed to his question – asked just one turn of the glass ago – and to Mater's answer. *Will he be normal again? No.* This was not normal.

"I could help you pack up your tools," Mago suggested.

Pater's brows drew down farther. "Unnecessary." Which was true. One need merely lock the latches to the chests, and footman could carry them to the caravel's cargo hold. "You'll go to your mother and do as she tells you. Now."

But Mater wouldn't be at home. She'd departed for the palace, determined to pester the monarch for a place for her son by her side on the sea-going caravel. She'd sent him to help his father. Who was sending him back. But now was no time to argue. Mago saw that clearly enough.

"What do you wait for?" demanded Pater. "Get out!"

Mago got.

The allée outside the workshop traversed a particularly steep slope of the mountain. It was all steps and landings, too precipitate for a ramped roadway. Pair after pair of liveried footmen tramped down the stairs with heavy trunks. Pater was not the only tenant moving the contents of his workshop to the harbor. Mago descended a dozen steps, then dodged aside to allow a bulky packing crate manhandled by six porters to pass before him. He glanced back at the workshop door to see Palujon Clisto knocking on its panels. What?

The door opened swiftly, Daymo Clisto stepped inside, and the door closed behind him.

Huh! Mago started to follow in the wake of the massive packing crate, then stepped back into the nook where he'd squeezed himself out of the way.

Why was Palujon Clisto seeking out Mago's father, someone he deliberately avoided? And why had Pater admitted him inside the workshop?

Mago paused a moment longer, then turned uphill rather than down.

I'm going to find out.

He climbed beyond the workshop door, then turned into a narrow passage between buildings, worming around a forgotten trash bin and then under a low drainpipe. Through an ell bend, down one step, jump over a cellar opening, and then up three steps. Around the next corner lay the courtyard adjacent to Pater's workshop. Mago slowed and edged along the wall toward the nearest open window. He stopped beside the lattice supporting the clematis. No need to get closer. Neither Pater nor Clisto was keeping his voice low.

"You spurn me when my research suffers few results and now court me when it prospers. Why would you expect my welcome under such circumstances?" Pater sounded scornful.

Clisto's reply remained moderate. "This is not about me. Or about you. I speak on behalf of our children. Your son and his friends. My nieces and nephews. All the young ones of Navarys."

"Mere diversion," scoffed Pater. "You seek to steal my work, my ideas! I know your sort: unable to devise your own creations, parasitic on those of others. Surely your cunning suggested better avenues than approaching me directly!"

Did Palujon sigh? If so, the puff of breath huffed too softly for Mago to hear it. "I intend no deception, Daymo Mytris. My motive and its reason are exactly as I've stated them. I beg you reconsider."

"My victory, my triumph, my hard-won success. You expect me to simply give it to you for the asking? You must be mad!"

"Not to me," urged Palujon. "To posterity and its vulnerable couriers. Our children, Daymo!"

"You have none!"

Was that pause another sigh? Mago crept closer to the window, scrunching his neck forward to avoid the tickling leaves of the clematis vine. He crouched and edged an eye above the low sill. Both men stood tensely, confronting one another over the pedestal where lay the large lodestone. Palujon Clisto held his chin very level and his shoulders straight, as though physical restraint might support verbal moderation. Pater crouched slightly, almost ready for attack? Or . . . as though ill?

Was Pater ill?

Mago scrutinized him: flushed but with a sallow undertone, faint redness to the eyes, a trifling distortion to his features. These were no symptoms Mago had ever heard of. But – *he's sick. I just know he is.* And now he sounded like Liliyah yesterday, just knowing things because. *I'll have to tell her she was right.* Sometimes a person *did* just know. But what could he do for Pater? How could he help him? What was wrong with him?

Palujon reached out his hand, palm up. "Daymo Mytris, for pity's sake." His voice pleaded, rather than commanded.

Pater took the gesture utterly wrong and hit out, knocking Clisto's arm aside, then stepping around the lodestone pedestal to push his visitor roughly toward the exit. "You trespass on my property and good nature alike. Be gone from here!"

Palujon wasn't ready to give up. He stepped away from his attacker, sufficiently nimble to avoid Pater's follow-up swing, but stopped before the door onto the allée. "Daymo, I ask only your small prototypes! And only as a loan! You may keep your . . . your . . . masterpiece" – why did Clisto hesitate over that word? – "entirely within your own purview. Although 'twere better in the deepest depth of the ocean."

Those last words, muttered low, were a mistake. Pater had regained self-control, but he opened the workshop door and coldly bowed Daymo Clisto out. If borrowing the exhibition lodestones were as important as Palujon pretended, he'd failed.

Mago, still crouching, turned, resting his back against the rough stucco of the wall, and slid down to sit on the courtyard flags. Palujon seemed a reasonable man. That was why Mago had sought his opinion yesterday on the *Subindo*. Pater was the unreasonable one. But why *did* Palujon want Pater's lodestones? Especially now, amidst the evacuation of all Navarys? Surely whatever it was could wait. Perhaps Pater was right in assigning nefarious motives to the aeromancer. Perhaps Pater wasn't unreasonable; just irritable because he was ill.

A strong thumb and forefinger pinched Mago's ear, drawing him painfully to his feet. "Go. Home." Pater's anger, chilled under its suppression prior to Clisto's departure, grew icy. "Now."

But Mago possessed no history of fearing his father, and he refused to begin one now. "Pater, why does Daymo Clisto want your lodestones? His concern seemed genuine!"

Pater's rigid jaw relaxed, and he released Mago's ear. "You heard it all?"

"No. Just the last bit. About the evacuating children being in danger."

"They'll be safe enough once they're on the airships. Clisto's seizing this misfortune to test some ideas he's developing for combining aeromancy with my invention. Cold-blooded opportunist!" Pater shook his head. "I can see it now: The *Subindo* and the *Ganador* arrive at Imsterfeldt as planned, while the *Belezea* and the *Magnifikat* go astray somewhere to the south, Istria maybe. And Daymo Clisto is the richer by two lodestones." Pater snorted. "A loan! I think not!"

"He intended to attach the lodestones to the airship engines? In place of the *energea* stones?" probed Mago.

"The engines?" Pater sounded surprised. He paused, then opened the paned door next to the window, and ushered Mago inside. "No, the fins and elevator control surfaces. To increase the stability of the ship before the wind."

Mago felt his eyebrows crinkling.

Pater locked the courtyard door and placed its key on the nearby hook. "Didn't you realize the airships are extremely vulnerable to gusts? They present an enormous area to air movement, like a great sail. They're far more susceptible to weather than sea vessels, you know."

No, Mago hadn't known. But, if that were true, could Palujon's worry be real? "Then shouldn't the children go in the caravels, the adults take the airships?"

"Were we facing a hurricane, indeed yes, but we face a wave, son." Pater's voice gentled, losing all remnants of his chilly anger. "Speaking of which –" he placed a hand on Mago's shoulder and gave it an affectionate jostle "– are you ready to board?"

"Mater sent the footmen with the household crates down to the quay half a glass ago. They'll be here for your tool chests soon, I expect."

"Good. Very good." Pater pulled a small crate next to the pedestal with the lodestone and pried its lid upward. Mago stepped forward to help shift the stone itself, but Pater checked him. "I need no help here. Do you have a satchel packed for the airship? I know the allowance is scant, but you'll need a few items."

Mago nodded.

Pater gripped his forearm. "Then help me thusly: detach the prototype lodestones from their engines in the exhibition hall and pack them in this." He lifted a small wallet with five pockets and a buckled strap securing it closed. "Let your mater place it in her reticule. Can you do that?"

Mago nodded again. He'd done quite a bit of manipulating the small lodestones with Pater before things had gotten so strained between them. *He does trust me. I wonder why . . .* Had it been fear, not anger, that so provoked his father earlier? Mago tucked the wallet into the pocket beneath his belt and moved toward the allée door.

"Mago?"

He paused. Pater's arm wrapped round his shoulders and snugged him in close. Mago glanced up in surprise. Were Pater's eyes the tiniest bit shiny? "The caravels will be some weeks slower than the airships. This is goodbye, for a time."

Mago felt his throat tighten. He turned into his father's embrace and hugged him hard. "I love you, Pater."

Pater's hold strengthened, then let him go. "Tell your mater I'll be along shortly to accompany her to the quay. But don't you wait for me. As soon as you've given her the prototypes, have Phyllos escort you to the aerodrome. No sense in risking the mobs likely to gather later in the day."

The exhibition hall lay on the far side of the city from Pater's workshop, but at nearly the same elevation. Mago climbed two flights of stairs, feeling the pull in his thighs from their tall risers, to a little-travelled lane cutting across the slope of the mountain. Ranks of flowering almond trees generated a speckled shade, pleasantly aromatic, but the usual quietude was missing. Pageboys carrying messages, porters transporting luggage, families locking their front gates and departing, a bachelor delaying to help an elderly relative make sure the curling tongs really were packed at the bottom of a valise: the scene was busy. Although not panicked, or even hectic, Mago noted. The citizenry moved with dispatch, but calm purpose prevailed thus far.

"Mama! Jaffy go boat!" piped a toddler's voice. His wool-stuffed toy giraffe made ocean wave swoops in his hands.

"No, no," corrected his mother. "Jaffy go flying!"

"Ooooh!" squealed her son.

Mago smothered a grin. Pray Evaia the kid was on the *Ganador* or the *Belezea*, not the *Subindo*. Mago didn't want to be present when he discovered neither his mama nor his nurse would be accompanying him into the air. Of course, the *Subindo* would likely have its own complement of crying infants. Phyllos had claimed that each grown woman aboard the airship would have ten or even fifteen young ones under her protection. Most of the kids would be missing their usual caretakers. Mago grimaced. Maybe Mater would succeed in getting him a berth on a sea-going vessel.

Every single one of the many doors into the exhibition hall were locked. *Huh.* What to do next? Return to Pater for a key? Did Pater *have* a key?

Mago checked the attached box office where tickets were sold when an exhibition wasn't free or invitation-only. Not surprisingly, it was empty of the clerk. But the lower sash of the sales window hung open by a hair's width. Mago tested the bronze frame. Loose! He pushed, and the sash slid upward. Ah, ha! Nipping in through the opening, nabbing a key from the several hanging on a rank of hooks, and scrambling back out again took less than two grains falling in the glass. Mago pushed the sash all the way down after his exit, but the catch – inside the glass – perforce stayed unfastened.

He hurried under the hall's portico.

"Mago!" someone called from the allée. Who? He whipped his head around to see.

Liliyah scurried up the portico steps to him, slightly breathless, an even more breathless (and burdened) footman behind her.

"Are you assigned to the *Subindo*? Your house steward said so. I thought we could walk to the aerodrome together." She smiled hopefully.

"Yes, but –" Mago cut himself off. He didn't know that Mater would succeed on her errand to the monarch. "Yes."

"I'm not quite ready. That is, *I'm* ready, but I'm still helping Dama Omys pack up her shop."

Mago frowned. Dama Omys? He dredged his memory. Oh, yes. The proprietor of the silk shop where Liliyah pursued an informal apprenticeship in business practices.

"I'm helping my pater pack up his inventions," he offered in return. Then fitted the key into its lock, turned it, and swung the door open. Liliyah came with him, but her footman, carrying too many parcels, sank onto a bench outside.

It was immediately obvious that something was wrong. No crowds hid the vast table supporting the miniature landscape, where an unnatural absence gaped. The pressure generated by the five lodestones – pressure which Mago, as a kinesthetic fabrimancer, should feel right now – was gone.

"Oh!" exclaimed Liliyah. "The humming! Where is it? It's too quiet!"

Mago looked at her, puzzled.

"I'm an aural practitioner," she explained.

Of course. Just as he should feel the lodestones, she should hear them.

Mago walked forward to examine the denuded landscape, Liliyah in his wake.

He'd expected the gears to the driveshafts to be disengaged. It wouldn't make sense to leave the tram scooting up and down the mountain or the windmill spinning unwatched. Mechanical devices required supervision, even small non-serious ones. But not only were the gears disengaged, the lodestones powering them had been removed, and the model airship, deflated of the gas that kept it aloft, draped its bright silk over one of the mooring masts.

Mago checked the aerodrome lift and the palace gate, and then the shelves in the storage room, but not one lodestone remained on the premises. He turned to Liliyah, still dogging his footsteps and looking as deflated as the airship, as deflated as he felt.

"Someone's stolen them!" It seemed incredible. Who would do such a thing? And why? Surely they had more important things to do now, on the cusp of disaster. His pater's words came back to him. *The* Belezea *and the* Magnifikat *go astray somewhere to the south. And Daymo Clisto is the richer by two lodestones.* Mago reached to grip Liliyah's shoulders. "Daymo Clisto! Pater was right!"

Liliyah drew back, eluding Mago's touch. Her chin jutted. "I liked Palujon," she insisted.

"But he asked Pater for these lodestones. Just now he asked him. Liliyah, he must have taken them. He *begged* Pater to lend them. And Pater said no."

"Why did he want them?"

Mago shook his head. "I have to get them back. They're Pater's life work. And it's not right! Not right that Daymo Clisto uses the disorganization of the evacuation to steal from him." Mago felt his teeth gritting together. "Help me, Lili! Where would I find Clisto?"

Liliyah bit her lip. "Mago . . . I don't know. I'm not sure you're right. Maybe we should be helping Palujon. I still trust him. And I don't –" she stopped. Looked down. Looked back up. "Mago, even you were worried that your pater was making a bad mistake."

He had been. Somehow he wasn't anymore. Pater's irrational anger, familiar across the last year, but previously foreign, should increase his worry. But it hadn't. "My pater is sick," he announced. "Not crazy. And I trust *him*." Would Liliyah understand? Would she agree? Her lips straightened.

"I saw him," she confessed.

Mago leaped on her words. "Clisto? When? Where? Oh, tell me!"

"The tinkers' bazaar. Persuading the vendor of essential oils to unpack one of his crates in order to sell a vial of perfume or something to him. But, Mago, I can't go with you! I have to finish helping Dama Omys." She hesitated, then burst out: "And I'm still not sure you're right!"

They parted then. She to return to Neander Row, while her footman made a trip to the quays. Mago to seek Daymo Clisto in the bazaar, firmly quashing the sense of misgiving that lurked under his certainty.

❧☙

Bidding Mama farewell was hard. *Not* bidding Papa goodbye was harder.

The mood of the streets had changed, from urgent orderly bustle to more turbulent activity tinged with edgy anger. Hurrying pageboys no longer apologized when they jostled elderly matrons. Fathers shepherding families bore frowning faces and a willingness to shove through the crowd. Lengthening afternoon shadows sheltered lurkers with hard, avaricious eyes. Perhaps one of them had stolen Daymo Mytris' lodestones. Liliyah moved closer to her mother, clutching her arm and inhaling comfort from the faint sweetness that clung to Mama's skin, even on the heels of sweaty packing and too many trips up the ladder to their neighbor's attics.

Mama patted Liliyah's hand, but kept her eyes on their surroundings. "Almost there, love."

Reaching the refuge of the air terminal brought relief from the sense of risk, but ushered in a different distress. Infants wailed or sobbed. School-age kids played pranks and started impromptu games of tag. Nursemaids scolded. Worried parents issued last moment instructions or folded their offspring close in anguished embrace. All Navarys parted from their loved ones.

Liliyah stopped dead just inside the great front portal, and the merchant behind her, towing twins, vented a curse, "Evaia below!" before dodging around to one side.

Mama stepped behind a column out of the flow of arriving evacuees. Liliyah reached for her mother's cheek, sculpted and silken under her palm. "Mama, please come with me. Or let me come with you."

Mama drew her in close, bent to touch her forehead to Liliyah's, and smoothed Liliyah's hair. "It's alright. I promise."

"Mama, how can it be alright? Dama Omys says the wave is so huge it will drown Mount Sohlon. Your ship will be crushed!"

Mama's laugh sounded low and encouraging. "The wave grows as the ocean bottom rises to the shallows. Far out to sea, it's very, very broad – many leagues – but so low none of us on shipboard will even notice it."

"Truly?"

"Truly. 'Tis the ships still in harbor that will be lost, and the ones near shore, threatened." Mama squeezed Liliyah's hands. "So. The sooner we get you in the air and me on the water, the better."

The terminal clerks had lists and procedures. The *Belezea*, the *Ganador*, the *Magnifika*, and the *Azulinike* were tethered from the mooring towers, but Liliyah's berth was on the *Subindo*. That largest airship was tied down beside the upper loggia. Had it been it only yesterday she'd disembarked there?

Registered with the clerk tallying evacuees and the one tallying airship assignments, permissions granted by Mama, and her satchel weighed and approved, Liliyah followed the temporary rope handrail to the grand staircase connecting the concourse to the mezzanine, then stopped again. She turned and threw her arms around her mother, felt Mama's arms encircling her. There were no words. Mama's cheek pressed the top of Liliyah's head.

"I love you," Mama murmured.

Liliyah clung tighter.

Mama chuckled. "It's now, sweet."

Liliyah gulped, nodded, and backed up to the first step. "You tell that shipmaster he better do a good job." She thrust her chin forward. "For me!"

Mama laughed – with, not at her. "I've already reminded *Subindo*'s captain that his cargo surpasses the worth of the monarch's treasury a thousand fold." Her face sobered. Her forefinger traced Liliyah's jaw. "Go!"

Liliyah went.

ℰℭ

Mago rebounded off the broad back of a shopkeeper, teetered at the top of half a dozen steps, clutched for the railing that wasn't there, felt wisteria leaves brushing the nape of his neck as he started to fall, and grabbed the twisting bark of its trunk just in time.

"Watch it, you!" he yelled, adding his voice to the shouts of other jostled pedestrians.

The shopkeeper grunted, pulled his hand cart from the narrow side passage, reversed his direction, and trundled over to a ramp adjacent to the the stairs. "Watch your own self," he tossed over his shoulder and turned the corner.

Mago shook his fist, then his head. No point in recriminations. The man was gone, and he wasn't the only one paying less heed to courtesy or care. Any folk who didn't make it to the quays within the next glass or two would find the ships had sailed without them.

"You okay, young 'un?"

Mago let go of the wisteria and swiveled to see a man with a blanket-bundled child cradled against his shoulder with one arm, the other arm reaching to steady Mago. The man's wife, behind and below him on the steps, had a pinched, anxious face and two more children in tow.

"I'm okay," Mago reassured him. He looked up and down the allée. No other family groups in sight. Most mothers and fathers had long since gotten their offspring to the airships and themselves to the caravels. "Are *you* okay?" Maybe *they* needed help. The little boy huddled in the blanket looked sick.

The man jerked his head no. "Calpurnia has a place on the *Subindo* with our son. We'll be alright." His eyes grew stern. "But you're headed the wrong way to the aerodrome, lad. Are you here with leave from your parents?"

Uh, oh. Mago was going to find himself ushered willy nilly home or aboard the *Subindo*, if he couldn't come up with a convincing explanation. This father was clearly the ultra responsible type, ready to see a stranger to safety even amidst his own difficulties.

"I'm fetching my pater's *energea* stones. My pater's Daymo Mytris," he informed the man. Would that work? Most Navareans knew of Mago's father. "One of the engineers took them home from the exhibition hall, and Pater wants to pack them now." There. Almost the truth.

The man's expression lightened. "Don't be too long about it, young 'un. Which ship are you on?"

Mago suppressed a sigh. "The *Subindo*."

"I'll tell 'em you're on your way." He patted Mago's back. "Hurry!"

Mago nodded – "I will" – and strode briskly uphill. The tinker's bazaar lay near the harbor, but he didn't want to follow this family downhill. Daymo "Responsible" might easily change his mind about letting Mago alone. *I'll just cut over to the Athanacles Terrace and walk down that way.*

The bazaar was largely empty, a littered expanse of stone flagging under dim canvas, with one last vendor packing up and another handing four portmanteaus to a footman. The scent of grilled meats lingered, reminding Mago that it was tea time. On any other day, he'd be at home, sipping chilled peach nectar and nibbling cucumber sandwiches. He could almost taste the peaches, feel the crunch of the cucumber under his bite. His stomach stirred. The midday nuncheon was long past.

The footman loaded two of the bags on his shoulders, the straps crisscrossing his torso. He bent to grab the other two with his hands and staggered toward the entrance, the vendor in his wake. Wait! That was the perfume vendor. No wonder the footman lurched as he walked. Four cases full of glass vials must be beyond heavy.

Mago moved to block the bazaar's entrance. "Sir, a moment of your time. Please!"

The vendor frowned. "I don't have a moment, and neither do you," he said.

"I'm trying to find Daymo Clisto. I heard he had purchased a vial of scent from you. Just a glass past."

The vendor snorted. "Glue, not perfume. And I don't know where he went after. Now, scat!"

Mago found himself moving aside since the pair didn't stop. "Please!"

"Try Daymo Ramias, if you must." The vendor frowned harder. "But you'd best wait till you arrive in Imsterfeldt, lad. It's late for doing ought but boarding your airship." And he strode outside, shaking his head.

Daymo Ramias, Daymo Ramias, who? *Oh, I know. He's another aeromancer.* But where . . . ? Basilia Row? Yes. Basilia Row.

Mago sprinted.

The last pull to Daymo Ramias' home was extra steep. Thighs burning, he dropped onto a bench under a flowering almond. The breeze had died, and the tree's aroma hung as a palpable presence on the still air. Mago peered farther up the slope. Which house was it? The one with the lemon stucco? Or the mint stucco? Or – ?

The door to the domicile between the two, more modest in size, but opulent with a limestone facade, opened. And Palujon Clisto stepped out.

Burning muscles not withstanding, Mago leapt from his bench. Up, up, up! Would he catch him? Faster!

But the two men were shaking hands. Clisto passed something very small to his colleague. A lodestone! Then Daymo Ramias went back inside and shut the door. Daymo Clisto departed the front stoop, striding briskly, then breaking into a run. Did he suspect he was followed? Mago attempted more speed, reaching the top of the steep stretch with wobbly legs just as his quarry nipped around a corner. Gah! His command to his own limbs for another sprint produced three faltering steps. Mago subsided to a walk, but kept going. *If I can just keep him in sight.*

The gentle slope up to the intersection felt harder even than the steeper hill prior to it. Mago paused, panting and puffing, feeling droplets of sweat trickling along his temples. He leaned against the stucco of the lemon house. *Must. Keep. On.* No one paid him any heed. Three couriers dashed by him, undeterred by the hill, headed for the palace. They met and sidestepped a gang of wild-looking young men tramping down. One thrust out a foot to trip the rearmost courier, who simply bounded over it.

"What a wuss!" jibed the youth's companion, a puffy-eyed fellow with a nasty leer. "You missed!"

"I'll get the next idiot going up instead of down," replied his friend.

"No you won't."

"Will."

"Na, uh. I will!" sneered the puffy-eyed one.

"Wager you?"

"Done!"

Evaia below. I'm the next idiot going up. Mago staggered away from the lemon stucco propping him, slipped behind the water trough at the corner, and hustled along the level cross way. A couple supervising three porters hurried by, shielding him from the intersection behind. He glanced back. The bullies had passed. But where was Clisto? Mago searched the alleé ahead. A large elderly matron harangued her diminutive husband over a pile of valises and three trunks, while a crone screeched at them to clear the blocked way. Two porters shoved the luggage roughly aside, ignoring the husband's pleas that they add his baggage to their load.

Mago attempted a jog. Yes! His legs could manage that much, at least. He passed the stranded trio, following the curve of the alleé. The street was emptying rapidly, the last laggards heading down toward the harbor and their transport away from Navarys. A smooth head bobbed above the crush at the next intersection. Clisto! Mago sped his heavy feet, then slowed to thread through the clot of people, bags, and a broken crate with spilled household goods surrounding it.

He slowed further in the next deserted stretch of the alleé. A bunch of ruffianly types clustered beside a front stoop. What? Oh! They were wrenching open the bars of a cellar window. Thieves!

Mago stopped altogether. Should he rush forward and yell? Or turn right around and rush away? Did it really matter, given that the absent householder had chosen to abandon whatever was left in the dwelling?

The question became moot when three burly marshals emerged from an adjacent side channel and collared the burglars. Literally. Each law enforcer grabbed two thieves by the hair, banged their heads together, and tossed the culprits toward the next corner with an alleé aimed downhill.

Clisto darted out from a farther side channel, following in the wake of the thwarted housebreakers. Did he have business with them? Mago started forward.

"Hold up, lad." One of the marshals stepped in front of him. "You shouldn't be here."

Mago trotted out his earlier excuse. "I'm on an errand for my pater, Daymo Mytris."

"Then you shouldn't be." The marshal's eyes narrowed. "Nikos, peel off and escort this lad to the aerodrome. The ships will lift soon, but you should just make it in time to get him aboard." His meaty hand felt heavy on Mago's shoulder. "Which airship were you assigned to?"

Mago drew back, but the marshal's grip was firm. "The *Subindo*. But –"

"Nay, lad. I don't want your story."

"But –"

"We've heard them all. Nikos?" And the marshal manhandled him into the grip of his colleague, the said Nikos, returning from the crossway down which they'd dispatched the thieves.

"But a thief stole my pater's *energea* stones. I have to get them back!"

"No time for that, son. Your father'll have to chose between you and his stones. I'm thinking he'd chose you. And if he wouldn't, well, we're here, and he isn't." Nikos tilted his chin up. "Who did you say your father was, son?"

"Daymo Mytris. The famous inventor." Could he persuade these men to help him catch Clisto? "Please! Palujon Clisto covets my father's renown, and it's not fair! These are the *new* stones, the lodestones, and they belong to my father."

"I'd heard . . . something." Nikos grimaced. "Wait a moment . . . He's that aeromancer. The one who advises the monarch." Nikos' grip on Mago's shoulder tightened. "That's quite an accusation, son."

Nikos' supervisor intervened. "Never mind. I'll pass an all-points directive to question Daymo Clisto – *politely* – should he sighted." The man's gaze sharpened. "Which I doubt! Only malefactors left now. Reasonable folk are long gone. Except this boy here who *should* be gone."

Mago squirmed.

"Nikos! Move him along."

And Nikos did.

๛๏๛

Liliyah's legs felt heavy as she climbed the stairs from the concourse to the mezzanine. Head down, she watched the marble treads pass under her reluctant footsteps and wished, *wished*, she could have seen Papa. He'll be safe, she told herself. *Mama said.* He's on the caravel now. *I'll see him in a fortnight.* But she wasn't sure she believed it.

Murmured goodbyes and muffled sobs floated up from the children and parents bidding one another farewell. Shouts from the ground crew outside intruded from the open loggia above. Liliyah could smell the blau gas used to power the auxiliary engines of the airship, volatile and acrid in her nose. Her right foot slapped the top tread of the stairs, her left, the marble floor of the loggia's gallery. She looked up.

Yesterday, the *Subindo* had sailed from a mooring tower, with room for only one gangway connecting the tower's balcony to the airship's gondola. And Liliyah hadn't looked back when she disembarked here at the air terminal. The airship filled the view through the loggia's archways completely. Each arch displayed the polished wood of *Subindo's* gondola and, above that, its varnished canvas of royal blue silk adorned by the monarch's golden heraldry: two unicorns rampant balancing a shooting star on their horns. Three gangways touched the gondola midships, and a short line of children waited at each one. Was that Cressy? Liliyah hurried to the forward gangway.

"Cressy!"

The girl looked toward Liliyah, then looked away again. Not Cressy. Liliyah felt her cheeks heat. Of course. Cressy was just a year too old to ride an airship. She'd be on one of the caravels, sailing west asea. Although the stranger's shiny brown curls were gathered in the exact same topknot as Cressy's, with the exact same twist of green ribbon. There was some excuse for Liliyah's mistake.

A flight attendant stood just inside the gondola doorway with yet another list. She located Liliyah's name on the second page, checked it off, and directed Liliyah to the spiral stair nearer the bow of the gondola. The sitting area – was it really just yesterday she'd perched on that divan? – remained empty of passengers. Likely it would fill later.

The second floor of the gondola featured four gracious dining chambers and a dumbwaiter connecting them to the kitchens located within the skin of the framework holding the airship's gas bags. Harried serving staff ferried platters to noisy eight- and nine-year-olds arguing about whether they liked the food or not. The scent of pea soup made Liliyah swallow. She could see the thick cream swirled over the savory, green liquid. Yum. But a flight attendant motioned her toward another spiral stair. Even with all the extra chairs crowded around the tables, the evacuees would have to eat in shifts.

The third floor of the passenger quarters, with the kitchens aft and the staterooms fore, proved to be Liliyah's destination. She checked the number over the door of the nearest stateroom, thirty-four, and started down that corridor. Thirty-five, thirty-six, thirty-seven – oh! A plump woman backed out of thirty-eight, bounced against Liliyah, and turned abruptly to embrace her.

"Eirene!" It was amazing how good it felt to see a familiar face.

"Sweetling! Oh!" Eirene's arms tightened, then released her. She studied Liliyah's face a moment, then smiled and drew forward a little tot of about three years of age. "Neoma needs to tinkle. Could you take her to the ship's head at the end of the hall?"

Before Liliyah could answer, a cry sounded from within the stateroom. "No! No! No! Mama said it's *mine*. She *gave* it to me! Ow!" Eirene dove back through the door, leaving Neoma staring dubiously at Liliyah.

"I'm Lili," Liliyah introduced herself. Noting Neoma's crossed and twisting legs, she held out her hand and suggested, "Let's go see what *Subindo* has in the way of chamberpots, shall we?"

Neoma stared a moment longer, then grabbed Liliyah's hand, and tugged her forward.

Airship chamberpots turned out to be very sophisticated. A tank above the pot released water through a pipe that cleared the pot after use via a central outlet, the waste disappearing, perhaps to a holding tank. Interesting, and more comfortable than she'd expected. Most of Navarys used sun composting, which wouldn't be practical in the air.

Returning Neoma to stateroom thirty-eight, Liliyah discovered Eirene involved in shepherding three more toddlers waking from their naps. There were only two bunks – tight quarters – but the little ones were small enough to fit with their heads on a pillow at each end. Eirene produced Pago and Juliya puppets on sticks from beneath the lowest bunk, handed them to Liliyah, and left her to it. Three other staterooms full of children, two of whom were infants, lay under Eirene's care. Liliyah, poised for protest, accepted the puppets and nodded. Right. Despite her calm and purposeful demeanor, Liliyah's nurse was flustered. And no wonder! Eirene loved children, but sixteen were too many for anyone, even an expert!

Liliyah raised the Juliya puppet upright and pulled the line that flapped its mouth. She made her voice shrill. "You're a bad boy! Bad! I won't let you hit me!" And she flailed the puppet's arms, lifting the Pago puppet to receive his sister's blows.

⋈〕⋉

Mago glanced aside to a narrow passage blocked by listing rubbish bins. A noisome rankness hung over the cranny, but if he darted in there, he'd just fit between the near bin and the wall, and the marshal – wouldn't.

Nikos' meaty hand, absent for the last hundred paces, descended on Mago's shoulder and gripped. Had he been so obvious?

"No you don't, son. Not worth it. Why are you so set on missing *Subindo's* departure?"

Mago searched the allée ahead. The steep slant of its cobbles punctuated by irregular stairs remained utterly vacant of distractions he could use to escape his escort. Was the entire city empty? That was the idea, he supposed. Withdraw every last Navarean from the island to a caravel or an airship. But hadn't Mater said not all would board? No, that was Phyllos. Was he right? Weren't the other two marshals completing a final pass through the upper alleés, rounding up stragglers, before they sought their own berths at sea? Who could elude them? *I didn't.*

"Mago!"

Mater's voice pealed from the hill behind him. "Marshal Nikos, wait!"

Her tone commanded.

Nikos halted and swung around, his fingers still clamped on Mago's person. "Yes, dama?"

Mago burst into speech. "Mater, he won't let me go! And I've got to go. Pater sent me after the lodestones in the exhibition hall, but Palujon Clisto's stolen them!"

Mater's gaze grew stern. "You know this?"

"I saw him give one to Daymo Ramias."

"Ah!" She shifted her focus to the marshal. "Mago is accurate, daymo. These lodestones belong to my husband. They are valuable, representing many years of research and labor. It is your duty to prevent their theft and restore them to their rightful owner."

Nikos cleared his throat. "Begging your pardon, dama, but my duty belongs to the monarch, and he commands that I push every Navarean I can find onto a boat or an airship as fast as I can manage. No exceptions. They've even dredged up a forgotten derelict to make places for the folk who lost the lottery."

Mater's nose tipped back, and she stared down it. "You tell me, you, a guardian of the law, that you condone thievery and assault? I can't believe my ears!" How did she achieve that regal inflection?

Nikos shuffled his feet and flushed. "I've my orders, dama." The marshal blinked at his uncomfortable sandals, then looked up hopefully. "But we stopped housebreakers upslope without neglecting duty. I reckon we might do the same with your Clisto." He nodded. "If he's on Navarys, we'll find him."

Mater's smile warmed. "That's all I ask." She looked pointedly at Nikos' hand. The marshal let it fall from Mago's shoulder. She resumed: "Excellent. And I'll take custody of my son. Thank you for fetching him for me!" The dip of her head was as regal as her voice. She placed Mago's hand on her arm and swept him downhill, leaving Nikos behind them.

"Mater, am I to board the caravel with you and Pater?"

Her smile turned saucy. "No." Why was she happy about it?

"I will board the *Subindo* with you!"

Oh. Mago felt a shrinking in his stomach. He'd not welcomed the news of the wave. Who would? But he had anticipated the two weeks free from Mater's supervision . . . buoyantly. And now, he wasn't to have it.

"Our monarch is most gracious," Mater continued. "Such a sympathetic man. He quite saw my point of view."

"But Pater –?"

"You know Zandro won't be parted from his workshop, even if it be packed in crates in the caravel's hold." She sniffed. "Your pater will be –"

"Fine," finished Mago for her.

But Mater fell silent. He turned his head. Evaia below! That was a tear track glistening on her cheek.

"Oh, Mago," she whispered. "I wish he were."

"What's wrong with him?" She'd been about to tell him earlier this afternoon when Phyllos interrupted them. Would she do so now?

"I call it *trull*-disease." She swallowed. "For obvious reasons."

The air grew entirely still, stagnant. Mago had been wrong outside Daymo Ramias' house. That dying of the breeze had been mere precursor, stirred yet by subtle movement. *This* was dead air.

He glanced at the sky. A strange yellow tinge darkened the light.

Mago shook his head. Trulls?

He delved through his sense of dread. Why was that term familiar? The view of a cage in the zoological gardens rose in his memory. Three troglodytes – *trulls* – sat behind bars, grooming one another. Mago jerked to a halt.

"No!"

Loathing pulled his voice high and thin. But Mater's label was all too plausible. He'd found that first sight of the trulls disturbing. Monkey-like creatures with long golden fur, they stood hunched and half the heighth of a man. That wasn't the disturbing part. It was their faces, so human, but with – Mago tried to stop there, but his thinking drove onward – with a dumb suffering in their eyes. If Pater's nose elongated and curved just a bit more, it would be a trull nose. And if his ears enlarged, his spine curved – Mago shuddered. "Will he become a trull?"

Mater had stopped with him. Now she drew him forward, restarting their progress down toward the aerodrome. "We don't know." Her reply was matter-of-fact.

"We? Is there a physician who knows about it? Can cure it?" He could hear the eagerness in his questions and bit his lip. *I sound like a little kid.*

"No. Your father and I have discussed it." Mater's haughtiness was creeping back. "Naturally."

"You have to *do* something," Mago insisted.

"Mago, I thought it was time you knew Pater was sick, but your father and I will handle this. You do not have the ordering of our household, and I'll not brook defiance!"

Mago hunched his shoulders, then straightened them. "You wouldn't have told me, if you had a solution in train," he pointed out. Ha! Had he ever stood up to Mater before? It felt good. Really good. Or it would if – Mago sagged again – if they were disputing about something else.

"Mater, do you know why? How did Pater contract this trull-disease? Does someone else have it?"

"It was his research," Mater replied. "And his invention. The new one."

"Making lodestones causes trull-disease?" That couldn't be right.

"Yes. Or no, not exactly."

Mago stifled impatience. His mother relayed social gossip with flawless accuracy, but give her a set of events and she garbled it every time.

"The prototypes, the small lodestones were alright. It was the big one for the ore trams that did it."

"Did what?"

His mother shook her head.

"Mater, what did it do?"

She gripped his hand where it lay on her forearm. "I'm not a fabrimancer, Mago, so I can't really understand it."

Mago tried another question. "What did Pater say?"

"That he'd drawn too much *energea* through his vertices and ripped them from their anchoring. But, Mago, I just don't understand what that means. I can't see the *energea* like Zandro does, nor feel it as you do."

Mago felt his eyes widening. He hadn't known vertices *could* be ripped. None of his lessons on *energea* – theory or practice or protocols – suggested it.

"What *is* a vertex, anyway?" Mater burst out.

"It's where *energea* enters our bodies. There are seven major vertices and fourteen minor ones." How could Mater not know this? Even though she couldn't manipulate the *energea*, it still flowed through her being. And every Navarean learned about it in school, since more had the ability to use it than did not.

"Well, your pater's are drifting from their proper spots." She sounded pettish. "And how to get them back in the right places and anchored, I'm sure I don't know!"

Mago thought that one through. The flow of *energea* between the vertices supported the physical structures of the body. Which meant – Mago was appalled. Moving vertices meant the energy flow was warped, which meant Pater's body was warping to match the deformed *energea*.

That was why Pater's nose and ears were strange.

"Mater . . . this is serious."

She released Mago's arm. "Would I have told you, else?!"

They'd reached the flat streets near the harbor. The aerodrome lay to the north in the fields beyond the city. Not far now. The breeze was picking up again. A sudden gust blew a rubbish bin against the bronze gate of a courtyard, clanging its bars. A storm cloud edged over the peak of Mount Sohlon.

Mater, her lips opening on diatribe, paused, then gripped Mago's arm afresh. "Zandro's condition will wait," she declared. "Hurry! The airships cannot lift into a storm."

Even as she spoke, Mago saw the vast magenta curve of the *Ganador* swell above the roofline of the shops and guild halls. The first of the airships was aloft, rising swiftly at an angle steeper than normal. No doubt the airmen saw the approaching weather too.

❧❦❧

Liliyah's teeth crunched through pastry, and its honey sweetness spread within her mouth along with the buttery richness of macadamia nuts. Yum! She licked her fingers and looked regretfully at the platter of desserts. *Subindo*'s pantries must be well stocked. Dinner's lavish spread filled her to bursting.

She turned to check on Neoma. The toddler slumped, eyes wrinkled shut, with her chin nodding on the napkin tied beneath it to protect her pinafore. Should Liliyah carry her up to bed?

"Take a break, sweetling," came Eirene's direction from the far end of the table. "I'll need you in the night. Don't spend it all now." Her nurse's gaze was firm and calm. She'd recovered her poise over the meal and looked ready to handle twenty infants, all colicky. A mere sixteen, some too old to be considered babies, would be a piece of cake in comparison.

Except . . . Eirene wouldn't be getting any breaks. Liliyah stood, hoisting little Neoma into her arms. Not so little Neoma – heavy Neoma!

"Liliyah," Eirene's voice chided. "There's plenty of child minding to go round. Let the others have a chance."

Liliyah blinked – what others? – then noticed a boy and two girls from the next table lining up little ones and herding them toward the stairs. She transferred Neoma to her nurse's waiting arms. Eirene smiled and nudged Liliyah toward the windows. "Sun's setting. Enjoy the sky over the harbor for a bit."

Oh! Caught up in the puppet show earlier, then the bustle of getting young ones down to the dining chamber, and then the savory tastes of her meal, she'd forgotten why she was here, aboard *Subindo*. The beacons at the harbor's outlet, brilliant like evening stars against the green and orange of the horizon, brought it all back. One of the modern caravels, powered by *energea* stones, not sails and wind, passed between the beacons, headed out to sea. Was Mama standing on its deck, gazing at the *Subindo* while Liliyah gazed back? No.

Mama's and Papa's caravel would be long gone by now. Good! Far away was safer. But Liliyah felt suddenly alone, despite the hubbub behind her.

She leaned closer to the window, checking for activity on the paving below. The ground crew were busy, transferring the tie-down ropes from the permanent stanchions to the weighted cars that would pull *Subindo* away from the air terminal before the airship launched. Lift would be soon, then.

"Liliyah!" Mago's voice shouted her name. She spun just in time to fend off his embrace. Too many clutching toddler hands and grubby toddler hugs made her resist any more touch. Dama Mytris, over by the stairs with another group of children, raised an eyebrow before turning away. Hadn't Mago said his mother was assigned a sea berth? What was she doing here, supervising youngsters? Surely she'd prefer traveling in luxury, being served, not serving.

"Liliyah!" Mago grabbed her hands, when a side step put her beyond his reaching arms. "Did *you* catch him? Clisto? Did *you* get the lodestones?"

She frowned. "How could I? Mago, I've been busy!"

"When you finished helping Dama Omys, of course."

"But –"

"Liliyah, you knew how important they were. You couldn't have forgotten!" Mago looked stricken. "Did you?" Why did he have to sound forlorn just when she was ready to get angry?

"Mago, I never agreed to help you. I told you: I *trust* Palujon."

Mago revived. "Well you shouldn't! He *is* a thief. I saw him give one of the stones to another aeromancer. So there!"

"So! Maybe his friend is helping him with his project. Didn't you hear him tell your papa that our safety depended on it?"

"Lies to fool Pater. Pater didn't believe him, and neither do I."

Subindo lurched.

Liliyah rocked back on her heels. Mago caught her elbows and steadied her. "Lili, I thought you – I hoped you – I trusted you to have my back!" As he'd held hers just now.

The ground crew was moving the airship away from the terminal, and the breeze was coming in gusts without its shelter. *Subindo* strained at her tethers. The ground crew mounted their stirrups, restraining loops in the ropes that gave the men spots to stand while the airship launched and spools above, within the framework of the dirigible, reeled the ropes and the men in.

Movement away from the focus of activity caught Liliyah's eye. *Azulinike*, emerald green with a silver horse emblazoned on her vast flank, rose into the sky at a steep pitch. Were the airmen worried, that they hurried so? Liliyah craned her neck, trying to see around the bulge of *Subindo* above her. The silk covered framework housing the gas bags blocked the view from the passenger gondola. There it was: *Ganador*, well away, the first of the fleet to embark. And there – ah! the reason for haste – storm clouds boiling up over Mount Sohlon.

"Mago –"

He nodded, his face strained. "Mater and I ran when we saw it. I hope we ran fast enough. They were waiting for me. For us. If the launch goes wrong because of –"

"Because of you searching for those seabound lodestones!" Liliyah burst out, reviving their quarrel.

"Evaia below!" Mago retorted. Except he wasn't responding to her. "It's him!"

Liliyah looked outside again.

Palujon Clisto was racing for the rearmost car. Legs pumping, robes blown by the same gusting wind that Liliyah could feel shuddering the airship, the aeromancer could barely keep his feet.

Did he intend to mount *Subindo* via her tethers, as did the ground crew? The men didn't see him. The last one set the brake on the rear car, fitted his foot into a stirrup, and loosed the massive snap hook holding the bouquet of tethers in concert with the men doing the same at the middle and forward cars.

The tethers swung out, released by the snap hook, and rose. Palujon grabbed the one that smacked into his chest, no time to use the stirrup, and wrapped his legs around it.

"Seawrack!" cursed Mago.

Liliyah didn't wait for him, but darted toward the stairs, mercifully empty of children. Up and up and up, she raced, Mago on her heels. Then down the corridor between the staterooms, and through the kitchens where cooks battened down the cabinet doors on sliding soup pots, too harried to notice the intruders.

Bursting out of the sternward door, Liliyah almost paused. The keel passageway was a sort of bridge, running the length of the airship near the bottom of the dirigible framework, but high enough to be uncomfortable. It was narrow, too. Luckily there were hand rails! Liliyah dashed into the cavernous space criss-crossed by immense girders and filled with the first of the enormous saggy gas bags that kept the *Subindo* aloft. She didn't have time to be afraid. Not for herself. Palujon was the one in danger.

The slope of the keelway grew steep as the airship lifted, and its framework thrummed from the buffeting of the wind. Short gangways connected the keelway to stations on the airship's flanks. Engine nacelles? Viewing portholes? Liliyah didn't know or care, but a few held platforms for the tether spools with fabrimancer crew activating the spools. Liliyah ran. Palujon was on one of the rear tethers, the last to be reeled in. The fabrimancers would never get there in time. Would she?

The view from the rear platform was dizzying, despite the modest size of the triangular aperture through the airship's canvas. Rails guarded the platform sides, but the outer edge where the tether rope dangled from its massive spool was open air: no glass, no barrier of any kind. And *Subindo* had climbed high, was headed higher. Liliyah clutched the righthand rail, shrinking from the fall. Navarys lay below, just as it had yesterday, yet not the same. Racing cloud shadows whipped across the island, and an ominous darkness tinged sky and sea. *Subindo*'s framework vibrated and jerked. No pleasure cruise, this.

Liliyah leaned forward. There was Palujon, tiny and tumbled on the end of the rope, snatched by gusting wind. But clinging yet.

Liliyah let go her hold to approach the tether spool.

Mago, arriving abruptly, caromed into her.

She lurched, grabbing something . . . anything . . . nothing. Where was the edge? Had she plunged over it?

"Lili!" Mago screamed.

She felt folds of his clothing in her clutching fingers, felt his grip on her arm, felt . . . firm flooring under her feet. She was safe.

"Hurry!" she gasped, reaching again for the spool.

"Not that way!" corrected Mago. His face was white. "Reach with your vertices, not your fingers."

Of course. They needed to start the *energea* stone controlling the spool, and mere physical touch wouldn't do it.

She re-anchored herself to the railing, closed her eyes, and tried to find calm enough to perform the centering ritual. *Breath in. Breath out.* And . . . *reach* with the *energea* streaming through her right hand. In her mind's perception, a bright note sang out, echoed by a deeper. That was Mago, reaching with her. A trill of notes deeper still answered them. The *energea* stone was awakening. The spool creaked. Had it begun to turn? She peeked through her eyelashes. Yes! The great drum turned over once, then picked up speed. She *reached* harder. Go, go, go! Was Palujon yet attached to the tether's end?

"You do the spool," grunted Mago. "I'll grab Clisto."

"Yes!" She closed her eyes again, poring her concentration into the spinning spool. How long could Palujon hang on? A shout arrowed through the canvas aperture. "Slower!"

Liliyah's stomach clenched. "Evaia, help!" she whispered. And *reached* in a different way, struggling now to brake the massive spool. She'd bet an airship fabrimancer practiced this move many times before taking a ground crewman's life in his hands. At least Palujon *was* attached to that tether. He hadn't fallen.

"Stop!" yelled Mago.

Liliyah's eyes flew open.

She saw Palujon gracefully perched on the small cantilevered step just outside *Subindo*'s canvas, his hand wrapped firmly around the grip at the apex of the opening. The tail end of the rope whipped past his cheek – the spool still revolving much too fast. The aeromancer stepped up to the platform, balanced despite the airship's juddering, stretched out his left hand, and . . . *ohm!* The powerful tone of his *energea* stopped the spool dead.

Liliyah's jaw dropped. How had he done that?

Mago didn't share Liliyah's amazement at Palujon's impressive fabrimancy. Or her relief that everyone was safe. In fact, Mago looked furious, standing with his arms akimbo, his body, tall and stiff.

"Wrack it!" he snarled. "They're not yours! How dare you?"

Palujon lost none of his self possession. Nor was he confused by Mago's unprefaced demand for the lodestones. Liliyah had suffered a moment of "what is he talking about?" when Mago hurled his rebuke.

Palujon stepped past Mago, answering over his shoulder. "My borrowing is, of course, a theft. But I've got five-thousand lives to save, one of them yours! Come on!" He paused a moment beside Liliyah. "Will you help me, demoselle? The fabrimancy will be tricky, and I'll need an assistant."

Liliyah lifted her chin and nodded. *I knew Mago was wrong!* "What must I do?" she asked.

Palujon traversed the short gangway between the platform and the keelway. Liliyah pattered after him. She could hear Mago thumping and puffing behind her. He was still mad, not at all persuaded or mollified by Palujon's sketchy explanation.

The aeromancer strode toward *Subindo*'s stern, instructing while he hastened. "I shall hold back the wind to protect us, but I cannot do that and affix the lodestone to the airship fin, which requires fabrimancy to activate the glue."

Mago pushed past Liliyah to grab Palujon's robes. "I don't care that you claim an errand of mercy." His voice grew pugnacious. "I don't believe you."

The aeromancer kept going despite Mago's hold on him. "Did you not see the storm?" Palujon's light tone held astonishment. "Can you not feel its force?"

The airship shuddered as though a cloud giant had tapped it with his club. Liliyah's grip on the railing kept her on her feet, but Mago went to his knees. Palujon yanked him up, reached his other hand toward Liliyah to grasp her arm, and yelled, "Hold fast!"

If a cloud giant had tapped *Subindo* a moment before, now he batted in earnest. Liliyah felt her feet leave the keelway as the airship plunged, hurled earthward by violent weather. *Subindo*'s frame groaned. Liliyah's hold on the railing broke. Evaia below! Where would a tumble through the vast girder-threaded interior land her?

But Palujon's grip remained fast, and three descending chords – more fabrimancy at work – held him on the keelway, both children anchored there with him. *Subindo*'s dive ended as abruptly as it began, and Liliyah's legs trembled under the sudden press of the metal beneath her feet.

"This is no ordinary tempest." Palujon started for the stern as soon as he saw Liliyah and Mago were steady again. "Just as Evaia shrugs and the seabed moves, so does her sister Caecia spin, and the airs swirl. This is the great wind, the *typhon*, and these love pats, a mere prelude. I must attach two lodestones to *Subindo*'s tail fins, else she perishes in the maelstrom."

Mago's face, glancing back at Liliyah, whitened. Now did he believe? His lips moved – "no" – but his eyes – horror in their depths – said "yes."

The keelway ended at a metal ladder climbing a vertical girder, one of nearly thirty radiating out from a central spoke to the perimeter of *Subindo*'s frame. Surrounding rings attached at each rung gave some protection to a climber, but Liliyah's belly shivered as she ducked inside the first when Palujon beckoned. The ladder vibrated as Mago and then Palujon hustled after her.

The platform at the top, on the level with the airship's central spoke, stretched wide enough for two triangular apertures, one to each side of the *Subindo*'s vertical rudder fin, accessing the top surfaces of the horizontal elevator fins. *Subindo* had risen into the clouds, and scurrying mists fled across Liliyah's view. She shrank against the hand rail – Evaia be thanked there were hand rails! – flinching as *Subindo* moaned. Mago joined her; then Palujon arrived in a flurry of melody. Was that why the openings in the airship's canvas funneled no wind inside to the platform? Palujon wielded his *energea* even now to protect them? He seemed to require no railing to keep his balance.

"Mago, are you willing to help?" Palujon asked. "*Subindo*'s girth dwarfs those of her sister ships. Placing both lodestones together, rather than sequentially, is safest, but I'll not constrain you."

Mago's throat worked soundlessly.

"Quickly, now. Yes or no?"

"Yes," Mago croaked.

"Good. Listen." And Palujon issued his instructions. Within his bubble of still air, Liliyah and Mago would each advance onto an elevator fin and place their lodestones against the vertical fin, using the rearmost hoof of the unicorn painted on the sheathing as a target. On the aeromancer's count, they would use *energea* to activate the glue adhering to each lodestone. "You must keep your balance," he enjoined. "I will still the wind, and I can steady you, but some effort you must make of your own."

Liliyah nodded, gulping. Her head for heights was normally good, but surely this demanded something more. Palujon's melody slowed and deepened. The cloud wisps traveling over *Subindo*'s fins lost speed and drifted, even while those outside the aeromancer's restraint blew faster.

"Go now." Palujon's bidding was quiet.

Liliyah bent to fit through the opening in the canvas . . . and didn't arise once outside. *Seawrack!* She'd never ever imagined herself standing on an airship's tail fin – its metallic surface humming amidst the violence of a hurricane. This was crazy! She crouched lower, heart pounding.

There was reason for confidence. Palujon's still air surrounded her, protecting her from the buffet of the storm. The elevator fin under her feet spread wide, wider than the parlor back home, although not as deep. If she flung herself forward, lying flat, her fingertips wouldn't quite reach the edge. But, oh! This was no place of comfort.

She sidled closer to the vertical rudder fin. Its metallic skin felt cold to her touch, cold and smooth. She couldn't grip it like a railing, but its looming solidity eased the racing chaos of cloud and wind. She inched closer to the unicorn's rear hoof. If only the beast faced to the rear instead of forward. Then she wouldn't have get so near to the drop. The elevator fin notched in there, presenting a nasty abyss of roiling mist.

Subindo jerked downward as the wind outside Palujon's control gusted and howled.

Liliyah curled, seeking a solid surface even as the fin bounced under her. *Goddess!* She came to rest right beneath the unicorn's hoof, much too close to the v-notch.

"You're there," came Palujon's calm voice. "Reach up."

She reached. *Wrack it!* Nowhere close enough to that hoof. She would have to get her feet under her and stand. It seemed impossible.

"Don't think. Just do it," Palujon urged.

Don't think, straighten up, she urged herself. Her legs felt cold and stiff, but she rearranged her feet sole down. *Now.* And pushed herself straight. Well, straighter. Could she reach the hoof now? Almost.

"Good!" Palujon approved. "Open your *energea* sense."

No difficulty there. Palujon's notes had sung to her all through her ordeal. Her ear for the *energea* was open. She *reached* to perceive Mago's lodestone on the other side of the rudder fin, to hear its faint song. Was it in place? Where? Where? Ah! There! Just a touch . . . rearward. Liliyah heard a whimper escape her lips. She would have to shift closer to that dreadful drop.

Then *Subindo* dropped and juddered again.

Stretching to reach over her head, not crouched like last time, Liliyah fought for balance, swaying left, then right, the abyss looming. No! She slung herself forward against the rudder fin and stuck, somehow, sheer will acting as glue. She flung her right hand up, lodestone clenched in her fingers, and *reached*. An arpeggio of sparkling notes shimmered. The adhesive on the lodestone melted, then hardened. She'd done it! Evaia below! She barely noticed her scramble back through the aperture to safety.

Mago tumbled onto the platform an instant later, grinning and manic. "We did it, we did it, we did it! Sea's bells!" he chanted. And grabbed her into his frantic arms, pressing his brow to hers. "Are you alright?"

She'd heard the true note of his *energea* – clear, neither sharp nor flat – as he placed his lodestone exactly right. So odd to realize that, as a kinesthetic fabrimancer, he *felt* the *energea* rather than hearing it. But he was right. They'd done it. She turned her head for Palujon's confirmation.

And didn't get it.

The aeromancer posed on the platform like a charioteer, legs straddled, arms extended to control invisible reins of *energea*, focused on completing his task, every bit as demanding as theirs had been. His energetic music swelled loud and louder, powerful notes, vigorous and fast. The crescendo peaked, hit a cymbal crash, then silenced. And *Subindo's* juddering ceased, transitioning abruptly to the quiet of smooth sailing. Liliyah's breath huffed out.

And Palujon opened his eyes.

"*Subindo* is stable and will remain unharmed by wind so long as those lodestones stay in place to channel the air. Mago, you can remove them and return them to your father when you dock in Imsterfeldt. *Energea* will release the adhesive."

Mago's arms fell from Liliyah's shoulders, and he turned to face the aeromancer. "I –, I –," he stammered.

The "I told you so!" that would have burst from Liliyah in other circumstances, didn't. She could only grin, happy Palujon had justified her faith in him, happier still that they were safe.

"I should have known," Mago blurted. "I did know! I just –"

"Trusted your father," finished Palujon. "Of course you did. Why shouldn't you?"

Mago's face acquired a stern expression. "Because – because he'd given me reason to doubt him, that's why." Good for Mago. Loyalty kept him from criticizing his pater to a stranger, but didn't keep him from owning he'd been wrong. "And I'm sorry. If I'd gotten those lodestones back from you . . ."

Liliyah shuddered. If Palujon hadn't stolen those lodestones, *Subindo* would be hurtling earthward, seaward, to be broken on the waves. Waves? *Evaia below! The* wave! Liliyah peered through the stern aperture again. The airship was climbing, tilting her bow upward, yielding a better view over her tail fins. She broke from the cloud occupying that stretch of sky to emerge under the greater cloud cover spreading above. Navarys lay at some distance, on the horizon, hurrying gray sky wrack above its mountain, pewter gray sea surging around its coastline. The tiny dots of the caravels speckled the ocean below *Subindo*, most well away from the dangerous shallows ringing the island. But not all. Liliyah could just discern two yet at anchor in the harbor, one sailing between the beacons at its outlet.

Mago hissed. What was he noticing?

Then she saw it too: a strange swelling or bulging of the salt deeps below. As she watched, a prominence formed, a ridge gaining height as it raced toward toward Navarys. "No," she whispered, and felt Mago's hand take hers. "Oh, no."

At the last, she couldn't look, couldn't bear to witness the wave lunging down on the straggling caravels, breaking over the city, foaming up the slopes of Mount Sohlon. A sob escaped Mago, and she opened her eyes. He did not weep, despite the sob, but his eyes were stricken.

"I must go," Palujon announced softly. He was securing the lodestone wallet in his belt pouch, strapping it closed, checking its buckles.

What?

"The *Belezea* and the *Magnifikat* need me."

"But how? And there's only one lodestone left!" exclaimed Mago.

"One will suffice. Provided I hasten."

"You can't!" Liliyah felt her heart thumping. "You mustn't! It's too late. They've sailed! And if they hadn't – Still it would be too late!"

Palujon smiled gently. "My aeromancy will get me to *Belezea*. I can sense her in the storm. Finding *Magnifikat* will be harder, stabilizing her, harder still. But, I *am* an aeromancer!"

"No!" Liliyah barely knew why she protested. Except she did. Palujon's words made his task sound easy. But it would not be easy, no. Desperate and dangerous and chancy. "Please!"

"Lili –" Palujon's voice grew firm. "The children on those two airships deserve life too."

She gasped and nodded.

"Be well." It was all happening too fast. His parting came even as he sprang through the aperture, sprinted across the tail fin, and leaped into the air amidst a shower of *energea* notes, limbs spread as though they were wings. And perhaps they were, for he did not fall, soaring outward and up, a scrap of silhouette in the vast gray of the sky, headed straight for the cloud fragment *Subindo* had just exited.

Liliyah burst into tears.

"Ssh, ssh." Mago's arms were around her again, enfolding her, comforting her. But she was not comforted. Palujon's goodbye had been so final.

ℰᴑℭ

Two weeks later, *Subindo* sailed into Imsterfeldt's skies. The day was bright and breezy, sunshine bringing vividness and cheer to the scene below. Liliyah stared eagerly at the tall stone houses, packed tightly shoulder to shoulder, and the many canals angling inland from the harbor. Coolness flowed through the airship's partially open casements along with the fishy scent of the wharves and faint applause from the crowd in the central square. So *this* was the mighty trading port of the continent. This was . . . home?

She glanced aside to Mago. His shoulder felt warm and solid against hers. He smiled. "We're here."

So they were, all thousand and some of them. The divans of *Subindo*'s sitting area overflowed with eight- and nine-year-olds, murmuring, poking one another, or gawking out the windows. A few older girls exchanged glances – should we restrain the unruly ones? – then shrugged and ignored the racket. The younger tots and their nurses filled the dining rooms on the level above. No one wanted to be shut away in the windowless staterooms.

The voyage had been grueling. The pantries ran low after a week's worth of tempting meals; the tureens of porridge, rice, and beans that followed grew repulsive quickly. Infants wailed, toddlers cried for their mamas, the school children played pranks or were sick or whined they were bored. And Liliyah's attempts to amuse Eirene's bunch failed more often than not after the first few days.

The storm, with its driving rain and powerful winds, affected *Subindo* not at all. She sailed serenely through the tempest. Whatever Palujon had done worked. The airship's captain and crew marveled, even as they performed the tasks normal to sailing: trimming the vessel, monitoring altitude, charting their progress. They knew, of course, about the lodestones. When Liliyah and Mago descended from the rear platform, two grim-faced sailors escorted them to the bridge where Captain Balthazar demanded explanations. And allowed himself to be mollified by what he heard. He even went so far as to offer them a complete tour of the working areas of the airship, as well as a turn manning the helm.

The storm blew itself out in three days. Liliyah found herself retreating to the crew areas whenever Eirene sent her on break. Where else could she get away from all the whiny, naughty brats infesting *Subindo*? And the crewmen welcomed her, feting her as the heroine who helped save their ship.

But now her ordeal was over. They'd be disembarking soon.

Mago nudged her. "Look," he said. "The mooring tower."

Subindo had passed over Imsterfeldt to the marshlands beyond. A series of dikes created dry meadows where cows grazed the grasses surrounding the tower. Three more towers receded in the distance. The nearer flew the magenta-striped bulk of – "*Ganador!*" exclaimed Liliyah, while Mago murmured, "*Azulinike!*" The emerald green airship, anchored at the far tower, showed damage from her passage through the hurricane, her rudder hanging askew and one elevator fin torn away entirely. Nor had *Ganador* emerged unscathed, Liliyah noted. A long gash in her canvas marred one flank, with the ragged end of a broken girder protruding. Was Palujon that much more skilled than the aeromancers who protected the damaged pair? Or was one lodestone each insufficient?

Subindo's nose cone glided closer to the mooring tower. Liliyah held her breath. The maneuver seemed tricky: the airship so large, the tower unyielding. Then the fore tether shot across the gap to be secured by ground crew. *Subindo* came gently to a halt. Sudden pandemonium erupted within the sitting area.

Liliyah found herself jumping up and down at the bow exit, holding Mago's hand while the mob of excited kids jostled behind them. The door swung open, and she darted across the gangway, feeling its metal vibrating under her thumping feet, then the solid flagging of the tower balcony. And, oh!

"Papa! Mama! Papa!" They were here. They were both here. Safe and sound and *here*! She tumbled into her father's arms.

✂

Liliyah smiled and lifted her pen. That reunion still lived in her memory, a confusion of joy and sadness, relief and anticipation. With reason. Her old life on Navarys had ended, her new one in Imsterfeldt, just begun in Papa's embrace.

A gull cried outside, its strident voice loud through the open casement over her desk. She looked up from her parchment, sniffing the seawrack on the air, surveying the pointed roofscape of Imsterfeldt beyond the dry meadows surrounding her tower. *Subindo*, a more faded blue than she'd been two decades ago, approached the tower nearest the city, preparing for dock. The two towers between the airship and Liliyah's home stood decrepit and abandoned, crumbling a little more with each winter's onslaught.

Once word of *Belezea's* crash in far Bazinthiad came north, the fourth tower – now Liliyah's home – was auctioned off to the highest bidder: Daymo Lykos, as it chanced. Three mooring stations provided adequate space for three airships and the remote chance of lost *Magnifkat* turning up. Then *Ganador* and *Azulinike* were retired after a mere five years of flight, too battered from their passage through the storm to stay air-worthy without the sophisticated repair facilities of Navarys.

Liliyah studied the ink drying on the scroll before her.

Was she right to get the story down so? The true story? She and Mago had argued about it. Mago, still remorseful from misjudging Palujon, wanted to proclaim him a hero, see him honored on gala days, and his name given to public buildings. Liliyah was not so sure.

"He cared for what he did, not for what people thought." Palujon's indifference to Mago's scorn and disdain arose so definitively in her memory. *I know I'm right about that.* "And he did what he set out to do: save the lives of all on *Ganador*, *Azulinike*, and *Subindo*."

"He deserves our remembrance."

"He has mine. Yours."

"Everyone's!" Mago was stubborn.

Then the last caravel docked at Imsterfeldt's quays – the derelict, surviving the wave against all expectation – and bringing news of lost ships. Zandro Mytris had drowned under the wave on one of them.

Pomp and and an outpouring of grief accompanied his funeral, attended by nearly all the Navarean exiles, as well as their monarch (who'd been hustled to safety against his will by friends). Daymo Mytris had been a popular and renowned figure. Mago held his tongue for his mater's sake, but chafed under his private knowledge. Had his pater prevailed, the funeral services would have commemorated the deaths of five thousand children. As it was . . .

When word of *Belezea's* crash came north, Mago reopened their disagreement.

"The airship's a wreck of twisted girders, but every last passenger on *Belezea* survived the landing accident. Because of Palujon. *Palujon!*" Mago glared. "It's not right! We have the Zandro Mytris Academy of Fabrimancy, but the only mention of Palujon Clisto is as a rogue who tried to steal the lodestones that saved us."

"But Palujon is dead."

"We don't know what happened to *Magnifikat*. And we do know that he made it away from *Belezea*. Just like he soared away from *Subindo*."

"But he's not *here*, Mago. And Ione *is*. Palujon would rather history marked him a thief than destroy your mother's happiness. She clings to your father's heroism. It's all she has left, now that he's gone."

"Clisto's already reviled," Mago grumbled, "doomed to go down in ignominy."

And it seemed he was right. Palujon's reputation had not changed for the better since Mago uttered those words. She glanced at her manuscript again. *I'm setting the record straight at last.*

Giggles on the stairs recalled Liliyah to the present.

"Is she there? Is she?" came the laughing voice of her daughter.

"Nah, Papa said she's pulling horsetail stalks out of the butterwort." That was her son, up to mischief, from the signs of it. "We'll sneak in, check behind the hangings and in the study nook, and then pull the casket out from the under the desk."

"But it's locked!" Did little Ismene sound shocked. "Mama keeps it locked."

"Pooh! My fabrimancy's up to that! I'll have it open in a trice," boasted Ismene's brother.

Liliyah swiveled, turning her back to the desk. Two tangled, curly heads popped above the tread of the last step, followed by the shoulders, torsos, and feet of her children. They stopped, appalled to see their mother, very much present in this chamber and not five floors down in the garden.

"Oh!"

"Mama!"

"So you've become a lock picker with your fabrimancy, eh?" Liliyah questioned her son.

"Er . . ."

She'd kept her tone light, but he knew he'd no business nosing through her things. Especially not *those* things. For the lodestones had proved less safe than her papa had asserted, back in the Navarean exhibition hall. It seemed that proper *energea* stones exerted some protective effect that was lacking for a practitioner using a lodestone or acting without a stone altogether. And that was a serious problem. Daymo Mytris was the first to catch the trull-disease, but unfortunately not the last.

When a fabrimancer pulled immense flows of *energea* in his or her working, a traditional stone channeled the better part of the power through its vertices. The lodestones divided the current strictly in half, and if that half were too much for the fabrimancer's vertices, he or she developed the trull symptoms. Liliyah shook her head. Imsterfeldt's physicians were working on a cure. And they needed one. There weren't enough *energea* stones to go around to all the new students of fabrimancy. No deposits of the star-stone needed to make them had yet been discovered on the continent. And practicing fabrimancy with neither *energea* stone nor lodestone was even more risky.

"The sanctum of a thaumaturge is no place for prying," she chided her son.

"Ho! *I'm* a thaumaturge," he bragged.

His sister nudged him. More prudent, perhaps?

"Are you now?" Liliyah injected amusement into her words. "What was your father telling me just last night? Something about your desk at the academy belching green phosphor?"

"Aw! Mama!"

"Liliyah? Is Alex with you?" Mago's deep voice rumbled from the floor below. The tromp of her husband's feet on the stair treads followed the called question. "His bedchamber's knee deep in mess, and I told him he needn't beg my permission to attend the mummer's play with his friends until the chamber was tidy."

Alex squirmed, and Ismene's eyes widened.

"Ah, ha!" Mago arrived, taking the last few steps in a bound. "Pestering your mother, are you?" Well, it was more serious than that. She and Mago would need to discuss more secure storage for the lodestones. But an end to this interruption by her progeny, so she could finish her record of Palujon's deeds, would be nice. "Come away, culprits!" Mago sang out, passing around the children to touch Liliyah's hand and brush her cheek with a kiss. "Another turn of the glass?" he inquired.

"Less than that. A half turning should suffice."

Mago's left brow twitched up. He knew her too well. Half a turning became three all too easily, when she grew absorbed enough. "Alright, one then," she corrected herself.

Mago nodded, grinned, and shepherded their son and daughter downstairs.

Liliyah indulged reverie for a moment. Alex and Ismene were so precious, despite their occasional naughtiness. Might a third child come to her? She and Mago both hoped for it. Eirene was getting a bit old to help with an infant, but even she had expressed a wish for another small Mytris in the nursery.

Liliyah swiveled back around to face her desk.

Should she complete her story of how Palujon saved the children of Navarys? Or would burning the scroll be the better choice?

She dipped her quill in the ink pot, wrote three more paragraphs, and then a last one.

If, perhaps, you find this scroll in an odd cranny among the bones of the ancient world, then you'll know I spared it from the flames. And you'll know that Palujon Clisto was no rogue.

There. It was done. For well or ill, done.

She sprinkled sand on the trailing curve of the parchment, shook it clean, and rolled it closed. What now?

Liliyah *reached*, hearing the merry music of her *energea* gilding the scroll with . . . blessing.

॰)෴

Resonant Bronze

Paitra knelt in meditation.

The orange wool of his cushion, traced by patterns of aqua and green, itched the bare skin of his shins. He could have donned a longer robe, but he welcomed the sensation. Mindfulness and he were old friends.

The room glowed: the deep red-orange of its rock walls and its rock floor, illuminated by the light of *energea*-lanterns in their brackets. Located high within the cliff sanctuary that was Torbellai, this chamber's window must shine like a beacon of welcome across the mountain pass.

Paitra's eyes followed the flames of the torches lining the distant track up from the lowlands.

Did straggling pilgrims climb the steep way even now, hopeful of Torbellai's hospitality and comfort?

For the mountain peoples had descended from their heights to embrace the exchange of ideas, culture, and goods with the valley dwellers. Torbellai alone remained – the last bastion of the Ghriana's ancient magics and the ease they wrought: bright lamps, warm water, cooking heat and such, all without the hazard and mess of fire. Too few Ghriana-folk dwelt within each valley hamlet to generate their traditional tribal *energea* lattice. They had traded convenience for their renaissance.

The soft air of summer's dusk breathed in through Paitra's unguarded window.

He turned his gaze from the outside world to the inside.

The cushion under his knees rested on a modest square of carpet, woven in deep blues and greens, resembling a patch of water against the warm tones of his surroundings. Below the abstract bas relief adorning one wall, a tray of edibles – morsels of candied ginger and living mint leaves – awaited him on the floor.

He inhaled.

Could he smell the scent of mint on the air?

The sparseness of the space pleased him, but it was peripheral. The heart of this inner sanctum – the heart of Torbellai's contemplative community – was the ancient gong that called the brothers to prayer.

Paitra studied its heavy, resonant bronze.

Wider than the full length of a man's arm, deeply furled along its circumference, and molded to depict fabulous beasts. Yet a hidden inner marvel eclipsed its outward beauty.

He remembered the first time he'd seen it. Partly because the thing itself was startling. Partly because of what happened after.

All those years ago, he'd run down the passage, giggling, his brother hard at his heels.

"Ssh! Ssh!" came Tohma's indignant hiss. "How can we sneak in, if you're going to be so loud?"

Did he *really* think whispers and tiptoe would work?

Paitra glanced at the *energea*-lantern bracketed to the red rock wall above him and shedding its rosy glow – one of many lighting the tunnel.

"We should go at night. When it's dark," objected Tohma.

As though it were ever dark in Torbellai or any of the strongholds of the Ghriana-folk. The lanterns brightened with the setting of the sun, then dimmed as the evening latened, but only the sleeping chambers grew truly black.

And even were every lantern to fail, the boys' presence in the tribal *energea*-lattice would spark more obviously within night time peace than in daytime bustle. They were just arrived at the threshold of their own magical practice, awkward and blatant in their lack of control.

Besides, normal bickering stood out far less than quiet creeping!

Grandfather had wished their enterprise well, even though he didn't know what they were up to. "Don't be too sneaky," he advised, a slight twinkle lighting his tired eyes. "Pretend you're fetching a special focus-crystal or a worry-stone for Sekar."

How had he guessed they were headed for the smithy? Or was he merely tossing out a random suggestion?

Paitra had bent and kissed the old man's brow, seized by sudden grief for what he was losing, while Tohma bent to touch his own brow to Grandfather's knuckles.

Did Tohma sense it too? That Grandfather was leaving them.

For Grandfather was not merely old; he was failing. He rarely left his sleeping bench, and he napped more than he woke. His skin showed yellower and yellower beneath the cinnamon hue normal among the Ghriana.

I won't think about that now. Grandfather wouldn't want me to. He knows we're in mischief. Let's make it good – just for him!

Paitra cast a merry glance over his shoulder. "Race you!" he yelled, and quickened his pace.

Tohma's scowl lightened.

"Hah!" he shouted, "I'm faster than you!" And he was. A year older and taller, his twelve-year-old stride overtook Paitra's in a laughing rush.

He tagged the corner and hurtled around it – straight into Keivas, the newest *flaumeikos* in the smithy.

"Whoa!" Keivas caught his balance, managing to steady Tohma and Paitra too. "The high adits are for racing, not the low." But he wasn't angry, just reminding the boys because he knew he should. He shook his head, smiling, and moved on with his errand.

Paitra grabbed his brother's hand, towing him forward.

The warriors, the myrmon, had returned last night bearing a prize. He'd been long asleep – he and Tohma, both – when the Torbellai warlord and his band negotiated their home gate, jubilant. By morning the mood of the entire citadel had changed from dark foreboding to optimism.

"Now we have a chance!" proclaimed their cousin Hern at breakfast.

And: "Without their cursed heart-hammer, those foul vermin – those *truldemager* – will bend to our courage." That was Breccan, Hern's brother and banner-man to their warlord.

In the long months before this unexpected victory, Paitra had planned with Tohma how together *they* would turn the years of defeat around. When they reached battle age and took up arms, their great deeds and valiancy would push back the troll horde once and for all, making Torbellai safe forever. Yes, they'd planned and boasted and resisted their mother's suggestions that their gifts fitted them better for other tasks.

"You could be a *flaumifer*, Paitra," she'd said. "And you, a *magikos*, Tohma."

These were high among the Ghriana-folk. With their magic, *flaumifers* heated the bronze to be wrought into swords and shields. *Magikosi* wielded the *energea* to shape the molten metal. While a *flaumeikos* – much rarer – did both.

But Paitra and Tohma longed for more violent pastimes.

"Ri Declan needs us!" Tohma asserted every time. "When *we* bear arms, the winds will turn."

They needed to turn.

For generations the Ghriana-folk had retreated, first to the north when death and chaos flooded the south, then to the mountains when the troll horde claimed the remaining lowlands. There were no further refuge holdings left. Here victory must come, or else final defeat.

The Ghriana were quick and nimble fighters, and their blades bore enchantments within the metals.

But the troll horde were numerous, powerful, and wielded a more terrible magic – the unrestrained *potentia* that brought them both sovereignty and their troll-disease. Despite the resources accruing to their foes, the Ghriana fought efficiently. Propelled by desperation and the harmony wrought by their unique tribal *energea*, they brought off unexpected conquests.

Or they had.

Something had changed the previous autumn in the Battle of the Falling Waters.

The Ghriana warriors poured into the valley between the lake and the cliff, high-couraged and fell, sweeping the troll horde onto the precipice, pushing them over its brink where the waters tumbled.

Victory seemed near – the next in a string of crucial victories – when a low, resonant throbbing disturbed the air and shivered the earth. The Ghriana faltered, suddenly weak at the knee and hollow at heart. The troll horde recovered and, under Regenen Carbry's command, seized the field.

The Ghrianan death toll grew grievous, and every conflict since had featured troll dominance, Ghrianan rout, all accompanied by that hideous throbbing groan on the breeze and rumble through the ground.

But, now, *now*, something had changed again. Why?

Paitra wanted to see the bounty brought in by the victorious warriors. What *was* this prize, that its capture should bend the current of the war?

As they neared the smithy, Paitra finally heeded his brother's demands for stealth. Yes, the smiths, the *magikosi*, and the *flaumifers* would sense even their surreptitious presence, but if the boys were quiet, the men wouldn't break their concentration to shoo spectators out.

He slowed and made his footsteps soft approaching the archway to the sanctum.

The lambent light of molten bronze flushed its keystone, and the deep hum of the artificers filled the hallway. Paitra felt Tohma's hand take his wrist.

They crept into the chamber.

The forging of the sword had reached its most critical point: held high by the *energea* of the smiths and red-hot, by the effort of the *flaumifers*, the blade shimmered in the intricate manipulations of the *magikosi*. Once slow-cooled, its edge would stay sharp, its blows would deal lethal damage, and its wielder would be strong and accurate. This was a weapon of might, one among the many enabling the Ghriana to hold back the troll horde.

Tohma tugged at Paitra's arm, and he started.

Right. They weren't here to gawk at blade-making, fascinating as that might be. The idea was to slide past the working smiths, men too absorbed in their demanding craft to notice that the boys departed not through the smithy's front portal, but via the side passage connecting smithy to armory.

Paitra could feel the men's essence within the tribal *energea*: weighty, warm, and intent. They sensed him too – he knew that – likely a bright, nimble, frenetic mote similar to Tohma beside him.

But they were busy, oh, so busy, and didn't look round.

Paitra reached the small passageway, stepped under its low arch, and shook Tohma's hand from his forearm.

"We did it," he whispered.

His brother's expression grew pained. "Not there yet, Pai."

No, they weren't, but the riskiest bit was done.

The armory side door lay open, unlike the locked panels of its double front portals. Paitra stole under its lintel and stopped.

He'd seen the racks of bronze swords, the piled shields, the suspended hauberks, and the shelved helmets before. The space gleamed with polished metal . . . and murmured with imbued *energea*. This was the heart of Ghrianan power: magical, derived of ancient disciplines, and unique.

Within the dark golden sheen of the tribal implements of war, the captured artifact shone like the moon – a vast, silvered disk with a black, cratered center.

Paitra felt his lips part.

So bright. So dark.

The troll shield was like nothing else in the armory.

He stepped nearer, Tohma beside him in shared fascination.

Up close, the spiraling traceries in the icy metal revealed themselves as images of fabulous beasts: dragons, gryphons, a flaming phoenix, and three noble fauves.

Paitra reached for the central boss – raised, not concave as its black hue made it seem from a distance – then withdrew his fingers without touching.

"It's not a shield," whispered Tohma.

Paitra looked at his brother, then looked back at the artifact.

Tohma was right. A harness rigged at its back enabled the bearer to strap it to his arm – and how mighty must troll thews be to support a metal circle an arm's length in diameter? But two holes near the top rim allowed it to be suspended by knotted ribands from above.

It hung from the armory ceiling now: a gong. What music might it make?

Paitra reached again, but with his *energea*-sense, not his hand.

Oh!

The gong-shield was even more interesting energetically than as gross metal.

Was the artifact a living entity? Not merely a marvel of smith-work?

Curving streams of sparkling silver light underlay the physical traceries of the fabled beasts, arresting in their resemblance to the *energea* animating his own limbs. Glittering, bending, and coiling, the brilliant network connected to a hub of aching gold beneath the central boss. Its searing intensity blurred the intricate structures within, but Paitra thought they resembled the energetic shapes within his own radices – the anchors at crown, brow, throat and so on, stepping down his torso – the roots of his own *energea*-lattice.

He stretched out his fingers again.

Stopped again.

No.

This was the warriors' prize. Not trivial. Not merely musical.

Not safe.

He turned his suddenly chilled face toward his brother. Just in time to see to see Tohma's eager hand approach the beckoning surface of the gong.

"No!"

He struck his brother's arm aside, grabbed it, and swayed under Tohma's return attack. He could hear Tohma panting, feel him straining to break free. They grappled, there before the foreign tocsin, lurching first to one side, then the other.

"Let. Me. Go!" grunted Tohma.

Paitra didn't answer. His brother was the stronger, and it took all his concentration to maintain enough leverage to hold that greater strength in check.

Tohma pushed harder, and Paitra allowed that force to turn him slightly, farther from the gong's perilous proximity. Now he could speak.

"No," he hissed. "This turned our warriors to clabber when it sounded. Leave it be!"

Tohma stopped so abruptly, Paitra nearly fell.

No! No! I mustn't!

Leaning, weaving, he grabbed for balance, frantic to avoid the gong.

"What are you doing here?" cracked Kievas' voice.

Paitra whirled.

And toppled.

Metal tapped his shoulder on the way down – such a little touch, so small.

Deep resonance bloomed, throbbing, spreading, booming.

Pain flowered in Paitra's bones, born of his radices, probing his *energea*. He was weak, limp as the dead grass of winter. He felt hands under his shoulders, under his knees. Kievas was lifting him, carrying him, removing him from danger.

He fainted.

And regained consciousness amidst hubbub.

He could hear his mother crying, his father's bass voice questioning, the master smith expounding, and at least three artificers arguing. Through it all, the scent of hot bronze coiled on the air.

He lay in the vestibule of the smithy, eyes closed. Gentle hands felt his arms, his legs, his ribs. Gentle *energea* soothed his radices and his energetic lattice. An encouraging voice murmured in his ear: "Come, lad. Thee's awake now. Hide thee not behind closed eyes."

Paitra raised his lids to Marko's concerned face.

"Didst thee see gold, lad? When the gong sounded?"

What had he seen? Paitra scrubbed a palm across his face, up into his cropped hair. What had happened? He felt blurry, disoriented.

I wanted to see the warriors' prize. Had he?

Memory of a nauseating reverberation twisted his gut. There'd been that sound like a bruise and, yes, spicules of light, sparking and racing outward, gold through silver, transferring their dread *energea* from metal into air.

That was *potentia*, he realized, the fabled troll-magic. *I did see it.*

He nodded.

"It was gold," he told the healer.

"Good thee's young, lad, since thee actually touched the infernal device." Marko looked worried. "Didst thy skin contact the metal, the arsenical bronze?"

Paitra felt his brows contract. Had he flailed and clutched as he fell? "The cloth of my caputum and of my tunic came between."

Marko sighed relief. "Up with thee, then."

Paitra swung his legs over the side of the sitting bench where he lay, only then noticing Tohma at his feet. "It's my fault," his brother blurted. "If I hadn't —"

Paitra interrupted him.

"No. It isn't. I reached for it too."

There wasn't time for more. Their mother bustled up, calmer and ready to be effective.

"Let's get you home." She pulled his arm around her waist, wrapped her own around his shoulders. "Can you walk?"

He was surprised he wasn't dizzy. Nor were his legs wobbly. He could walk just fine, but Mother refused to let go. Father swept Tohma in their wake.

Back in the family suite, Mother put him to bed.

"I'm not tired," he protested.

"Well, you should be." She pulled the sheepskin up to his chin and patted his cheek, her face softening. "Rest, sweetheart."

Lying awake, he could hear Tohma sent to bed with much less sympathy. Apparently Mother and Father both blamed him as much as he blamed himself for the whole debacle.

It's not fair. I'm the one who wanted to sneak into the armory.

Then he did sleep.

And awoke with a jolt.

Something was different yet again. Not the citadel. Not the artifact. Something closer to home. Something in the familial *energea*. There, in the most complex turnings and crossings of the lattice.

He focused his inner attention. Was the aqua light muted? The green developing a chartreuse penumbra? The energetic lace felt mushy, but with an underlying and growing tautness. The change wasn't here yet. It was coming. It was —

Grandfather!

Paitra shot up from his sleeping bench and out the archway of his nook.

Father emerged from the neighboring nook towing Tohma, who looked teary-eyed.

"It's the disrobing," blurted his brother.

Paitra glanced up, and Father nodded, his face somber. "You knew it would be soon, Paitra."

Yes, Paitra knew. But he'd hoped it would be a while longer before he sang his farewell in grandfather's bidding circle.

"There's time for you to eat. Come."

Father poured him a cup of broth in the buttery, heating it over the *energea*-brazier. He spooned mare's cheese onto a plate while Paitra sipped from his mug. The portions were small. Did he know his son's stomach felt too tight to accept much food? Tohma looked on. Had he not missed nuncheon, earlier?

Father guided both boys to the locutory. Grandfather's bench had been moved there – the largest space in their home – and the extended family clustered around him, cross-legged or kneeling on the carpet, eyelids lowered, fingers in the *zephirum* of meditation.

Paitra could feel their weight in the *energea*-lattice: heavier than usual, concentrated.

Father led him right up to Grandfather's side, threading through the seated crowd, and placed Paitra's palms on the old man's upper arms. Grandfather muttered, but didn't open his eyes. His skin felt cool.

"I love you, napah," Paitra whispered.

Then it was Tohma's turn. Paitra couldn't hear what he said, but his brother's lips moved in a long, subdued outpouring. Confession? Or merely an appreciation more comprehensive than love?

Paitra felt his father urging him to a clear spot on the floor, and he sank down on his knees, calves folded under his thighs. Tohma joined him a moment later, and the gathered clan began to hum.

"Paitra." Faint reprimand imbued Father's tone.

Paitra started his focusing ritual: breathe and breathe again. Allow the blues and aquas of *energea* to bloom in his mind's eye, follow their curves from radix to radix, his own and those of his gathered family.

Breathe and intone: ohm!

He felt his muscles relax. He felt his mind relax. *I am here. We are here. We are love.*

Ohm!

The glow of the family lattice brightened, forming a gauze of aqua mist. Grandfather's lattice brightened, too, chartreuse in a silver fog.

Blue and silver lightning sparked, darting from radix to radix, soundless, but potent.

The reach of the lattice extended, out and out again, fountaining high, probing deep. Within that sphere of cool radiance, Grandfather's *energea* whitened and blazed. Intensified. Were Paitra seeing with his physical eyes, they would have been slitted nearly shut.

"Ohm!" he intoned.

There, within the brilliance, translucent forms appeared.

Not the lacy traceries of *energea*, but beautiful women, gowned and winged. The handmaidens!

Not everyone could see them, but there were stories. These were the mythical attendants who aided the soul in its preparations for the transformation of death. There were three, and they sang, blessing Grandfather and offering him . . . everything.

Now Paitra could see Grandfather too: upright, smiling, arms and fingers flowing through the mudras of joy. He seemed to stand within a small chapel, apart from the vaulted space where the family congregated.

Paitra's perception widened.

Two guardians, vast and robed, bearing sheaves of flax in their clasped hands, rose high over the event, protecting the participants. And a majestic presence enfolded all.

Grandfather lifted his gaze, his joy shading into ecstasy.

He raised his arms.

The white light flared, a sensation of flight took Paitra's limbs, and the *energea* pulsed. Paitra *gave* . . . something. And Grandfather returned . . . something else.

Then he was gone.

And Paitra was back in the locutory, surrounded by family in various states: sobbing, singing, talking, quiet. Paitra's mother was one of the sobbing, Father one of the quiet. Tohma wanted to talk.

"Did you see them? The valkyries?"

Paitra didn't want to talk.

Yes, he'd seen them. And now he wanted to think.

He felt so sad: Grandfather was gone. But Grandfather had been so happy, there at his end, that Paitra was happy for him. How could he feel so happy and so sad at the same time?

He stood to look at the sleeping bench. Grandfather's body lay absolutely still. He was indeed gone. Completely gone. How was it that the absence of breathing could be so profound? Paitra turned to go.

"Paitra, wait!" pleaded his brother.

I can't bear to wait.

He stepped carefully, not wanting to bump his relatives, wanting solitude.

Sitting on his sleeping bench, slumped against the wall, he sighed.

Then Tohma appeared in the doorway of the nook.

"Go away." Paitra heard the flatness in his own voice and flinched. He hadn't meant to sound so unfriendly.

Ignoring his brother's prohibition, Tohma rushed into speech. "It's my fault! It's all my fault! *Please* don't say it isn't!"

What? Paitra's irritation subsided.

"Tohma, you said that before, and I don't get it. I'm the one who wanted to see the captured prize. Who came up with the smithy plan. Who struck the blasted gong with my shoulder. Why are you going on like this?"

"Because I pushed you."

"Well, yah! We were wrestling. Of course you pushed. I pushed back. And I stopped you."

"No. After that. When you were falling."

Oh.

"And it killed Grandfather."

Paitra's stomach felt abruptly chilled and sick.

"I slew Grandfather?" he whispered.

"No! *I* slew him. *Not* you," corrected Tohma.

"But if the gong killed him . . ." Paitra shook his head. "How? The smithy's in the deep adits. Grandfather was here, at home, near the high adits and on the opposite side of the citadel."

"Father says the gong's reverberation penetrated even so far as the peak meadows outside. It was everywhere. It's a *battle* gong. You can hear them fifteen leagues away."

"Then *I* killed grandfather." The sick feeling in him grew.

"You would have missed the gong. But *I* lost my balance too. I *grabbed* you, so I wouldn't fall." Tohma sounded bitter. "If I'd just taken the fall – been the hero like we both say we want to be –" Tohma gave that word hero an especially derisive twist.

Marko's voice spoke from the nook archway. "Many bear responsibility in this. Not you alone."

"Father blames me." Tohma paused. Then: "I think he's right."

Paitra didn't think so. *It's my fault. Me. I did it.*

Marko's voice stayed patient. "The warlord chose to keep the troll-shield in the armory for a time. To display his success and raise Ghriana courage with it. Even though he knew the piece was perilous. The smiths and artificers who sensed you two sneaking by them could have stopped you. Your grandfather himself" – the healer smiled slightly – "yes, he told me you were headed out on mischief and that he forbore to stop you."

"But I didn't stop Paitra," insisted his brother. "I urged him on. I *joined* him. And then I was afraid to take the fall when Kievas startled us both."

"Yes," agreed Markos.

Paitra sat up straight, surprised the healer hadn't challenged Tohma's last assertions as well.

"That is the great difficulty in this: how to take responsibility for what is yours without taking more. The extremes are easier. 'It's all my fault. It's not my fault at all.'

"But: 'I did this and not that. I did that and not this.' Those are much harder." Marko was looking at Paitra now. Paitra looked straight back and spoke.

"I decided to sneak into the armory, a place forbidden to me without adult supervision."

"Yes."

"I persuaded Tohma to join me."

"Yes."

"I knew the gong was lethal – I'd heard the myrmons' stories – and I took care. But not seriously. More as a game."

"Yes."

Paitra stiffened himself to make the last confession. "And grandfather died today, because my choices combined with other people's choices."

"Yes." Marko's assent was very low. Paitra felt his borrowed strength ebb under it.

"I want him back! Oh, I want him back!"

A sob burst from him. "He might have had months more. I could have heard the story of the champion and the giant one more time. I could have brought him pannkuja this Neracha. I could have –"

Marko stopped him. "No. He had another week, at most. More likely just a day. Or two."

"Oh." Paitra deflated.

"Paitra." Marko held his gaze a moment, then turned. "Tohma."

He had their attention.

"You are not shirking your responsibility. That is good. Your *grandfather* would be proud." The healer nodded. "Now, somehow, you must balance on that edge – especially narrow in this case – where you neither retreat from your contribution nor claim more than is yours." Marko's mouth quirked. "Likely you will wobble to one side, then to the other. But" – his voice strengthened – "always head back to the balance after the wobble. And talk to me, or someone, if you cannot. That is the only way you can atone for your misdeed." His voice deepened still more. "*Be* the grandsons he would want you to be."

Tohma's eyes were wide. Paitra could feel his own were the same.

"I will!" he chorused with his brother, then met Tohma's gaze. *"We* will." Tohma nodded.

And within him, grandfather's parting gift of *energea* swelled into certainty, celebration, into grandfather himself.

Grandfather was truly gone, but a piece of him survived within his descendants.

Fifty years later, Paitra knelt in the watch-tower beside the gong that had caused so much trouble. Its metal shone less silver now, more golden. And the beasts adorning the surface had changed: a unicorn, three pegasi. Yet the phoenix remained.

Paitra tapped the tocsin with one finger, gently, just enough to bring the pre-tuning hum that would allow its full tone to bloom when it was struck in earnest.

And with the sound, as always, came a sense of Tohma's presence: full and sturdy and strong. His brother would live forever beyond his death. Summoned by the striking of the gong – this gong reforged on the mountaintop after so much struggle and sacrifice. Reforged by *Tohma's* sacrifice.

Paitra remembered that crisis as though he'd just now stepped away from the cooling metal. Just now stepped toward his brother's lifeless body.

They hadn't come lightly to the decision to meddle with the gong. It was packed away in a deep storeroom after Grandfather's passing, triple-locked, and muffled with energetic barriers.

And Ghrianan fortunes in the long war against the troll-horde improved. The enemy retreated for a time, weakened both by their innate troll-disease and by the lack of their magical talisman: the shield-gong.

Paitra and Tohma grew up to become myrmon – warriors – as they'd desired, and *flaumeikosi* as their mother wished. That is, they surpassed her goal for her sons, each claiming both the heat-making *energea* of the *flaumifer* and the *energea* manipulations of a *magikos*.

Paitra grinned.

He and his brother had, in truth, become the heroes they'd aspired to be as children.

Tohma was stalwart in the thick of battle, unflappable, lending courage to his men, dealing certain death to their foe with his mighty arm.

Paitra was nimble, dodging the troll blows and finding leverage to move his own warriors forward to advantageous terrain. In the lulls between battles, he snuck into the troll camps, into the pavilion of Regenen Carbry himself, and listened to their councils.

Many a Ghrianan victory was born of Paitra's spying.

When the troll regenen died – not of wounds, it was said, but of his troll-disease, advanced to its ultimate end – the Ghriana-folk rejoiced. Without Carbry's inspired leadership, the horde would falter. The Ghriana would triumph. Once and for all, just as Paitra and Tohma had imagined, those decades ago.

It didn't turn out that way.

Dreben, the new troll regenen, was smaller, meaner, and more ruthless than his predecessor. Where Carbry had devised clever battle plans and inspired his warriors to bravery with tales of troll heroes, Dreben devised clever *sequences* of fiendishly clever battles and motivated the warriors with gifts of *potentia* for success and scourging for failure.

Such a strategy might sag over decades, but its short term results were impressive.

The Ghriana lost the eastern foothills they'd gained ridge by painful ridge. Once the hills were troll territory, the horde pressed upward, aiming for the central peaks of the Tahdenfialls. The battles would be lapping Torbellai's gates within weeks, if something weren't done.

Torbellai's elders turned their thoughts to defense of the citadel and commissioned massive sculptures to flank the ramp descending through rocky earth to its main portal.

The stone would take the shapes of two *undreigar*, massive faces with somber eyes and strong lips, and *energea* would thread it through, creating terror in the hearts of any trolls who approached. The smiths, the *flaumifers*, and the *magikosi* would work through the nights, as well as the days, in shifts until the gigantic artifacts were done.

Paitra and Tohma turned their own thoughts to more aggressive possibilities.

"Amarad's the wrong speaker for these times," grumbled Tohma. "He insists on consensus for everything, lets the minority voice speak for days, and won't overrule anyone. We could have won the Nissa-vale, if he'd just authorized the raid by the Guhlir brothers."

Paitra grimaced. "Their mother knew they wouldn't survive it."

"So." Tohma jutted his chin out. "They knew it too. And wanted it. Amarad should never have granted the listeners an interval for commentary. Maia believes we should send a diplomatic delegation to negotiate with the horde! She'd never let her sons go toward certain death." He snorted and muttered, "Infernal peace-mongers."

"At depth, we are a peaceful people," Paitra reminded him.

Tohma gave him a scornful look. "Surely you don't think Amarad and Maia are right?"

Paitra felt his lips curling. "No. No, I don't."

"We should do something," urged Tohma.

"I agree."

"But what? What can we do? Besides strengthening our gate and stockpiling *energea*-imbued rocks to toss down on our besiegers?" Tohma shook his head.

"Something more than criticizing Amarad." Was this the right moment to broach his idea? *If it's not, there won't be a right moment.* Wars don't wait on personal weakness, Paitra told himself.

"Like you never criticize Amarad," accused Tohma.

Paitra smiled. "I know. I'm worse than you are."

Tohma laughed, then sobered. "Paitra, what can we do? Do you have an idea? You're the one who always comes up with crazy schemes. That work. Do you have one now?"

There was a perfect lead-in, if ever there were one.

"I do."

"You do?" Despite his professed faith in his brother, Tohma looked surprised. "Say on!"

"We should use the troll-gong."

Tohma's surprise turned to shock. "Are you mad? May as well open our doors to the horde and surrender the citadel!"

He stared at his brother, scrutinizing his ears and nose, reaching out a hand to touch. Trolls sported elongated noses and enlarged, flap-like ears, but Paitra's features were normal. "You haven't contracted the troll-disease, have you?" Strong, callused fingers pinched Paitra's earlobe, then withdrew. "No, you're healthy. Human." His eyes grew puzzled.

"Of course, I'm human. I've never manipulated the *energea* solo, the way the trolls do, even once in my life. You know this. Check my radices now."

Tohma's touch through the *energea* was delicate and light, the exact opposite of his physical style. Feathery pressure grazed Paitra's crown radix and moved down through the others: throat, thymus, heart, plexus, belly, and root.

Paitra mirrored him, assessing his brother's lattice, noting the elegant scrolls of *energea* where it connected to the energies of his wife, his children, and his friends. Tohma's connections to Torbellai-tribe were strong, as were his own. No Ghriana lay vulnerable to the overdrawing of *energea* that created trolls and troll-disease.

The tribal lattice – comprised of the links between individuals – served as both overflow and regulator. Should one *magikos* attempt to pull too much through his or her radices, the needed extra would come from the tribe, leaving the *magikos* safe and unharmed. Should too much *energea* concentrate in one person, it would dissipate through the tribe.

Tohma's brief suspicion was absurd, and he knew it. Only non-Ghriana, so alone in their magic, their *potentia*, could tear their radices from the anchor points and become trolls.

Paitra watched his brother's shoulders settle. Tohma grinned sheepishly.

"So what's your idea this time? I knew it'd be crazy, but not so crazy I couldn't guess it from your first hint."

"You remember the legend of Navellys?"

"The golden age when *energea* powered great airships from one horizon to the other, Zia's handmaidens lived among us, and all mothers bestowed untold riches upon their children?" Tohma laughed shortly. "I'd ask what that has to do with the gong, except I know you're going to tell me."

"The drowning of Navellys came without warning as most tell it, but one grandmother in Segura recounts a version in which they had warning, in which they packed the airships with children and a few chosen guardians that they might escape the wave."

"And?" Tohma knew him too well, knew he'd left the pertinent detail unspoken.

"And that rogue – Palijon Clisto – stowed away in the struts containing the silken airbag of one of the ships, bearing with him the lodestones of Zandro Mytris, the master smith."

Tohma leaned forward.

Paitra nodded. "One of those lodestones is melded within the metal of the gong's central boss."

"You know this?"

"I didn't until after I took a detour from scouting Castellum Caellys."

"So that's why you were so late returning! I never did believe you'd tracked Carbry's battalions south through the fields of Hrask."

"Oh, I did. That's how I knew Carbry planned to try a feint up our western slopes. He was coordinating the attacks of the troll-lords of Hrask to distract us while he did it. But I wanted to check the ruins of the old Hamish-folk there.

"Grandmother Elihy claims her Hamish ancestor who escaped from the sack of Olluvarde passed down the tale of Palijon Clisto. Along with something else."

This time Tohma leaned back from Paitra's pause. "And?" he repeated.

"A tale of the vaults of Olluvarde where the legends of Navellys were rendered in stone."

Tohma frowned. "So?"

"Carbry visited those vaults. Visited them and disappeared for ten years."

"And reappeared with a shield! The gong-shield!" Tohma pre-empted him.

"Yes."

"But how do you know the shield's boss holds a lodestone?"

"It doesn't *hold* the lodestone, it *is* the lodestone.

"The vaults showed the entire sequence: the flight of Clisto, his capture, his escape, the taking of the lodestones, the forging of the gong, and the blending of the lodestone with meteoric iron that is the boss. And it is a gong, incidentally. Carbry adjusted it to serve as his shield."

"Why would the ancient Hamish make an artifact that strengthened trolls? They were fighting the horde, just as we are."

"I believe the gong weakened trolls, originally."

Tohma made the mental leap. "You want me to reforge it. Return it to its first purpose."

"Us," corrected Paitra. "We'll do it together."

And they had, but once again things did not go as expected.

They couldn't use Torbellai's smithy. The arsenical bronze of the gong had the same melting point as the Ghrianan tin-alloy bronze, but the iron boss would require much, much higher temperatures. And the boss, incorporating the lodestone, lay at the heart of the needed transformation. Reforging the artifact inside risked a concentration of poisonous gases from the arsenic, as well as the danger of melting the rock of the smithy itself. They must work out of doors.

Fortunately, high summer cloaked the mountains in green, not white.

Tohma selected a cupped vale higher on Torbellai's peak, reached by one of the upper adits. Its shallow dimple featured a small tarn of still water and a flat area of turf. They planned to slow-cool the gong for improved timber, but the water would be needed for the first fast cooling, and it was well to be prepared for accidents.

Persuading the speakers' circle was harder than locating work space.

The gong-shield had been locked away for a reason. Amarad and his conservative cohorts, risk-averse as always, resisted any perilous undertaking. The secluded site chosen by the brother *flaumeikosi* helped their cause, but it was the listener commentary that won the dispute. Amarad might prefer to dig in his heels; the community at large agreed with Paitra.

Once Torbellai was under siege, how would the dairy boys reach the low valleys to milk the wild mares? How would the wilding sisters hunt medicinal herbs and greens? How would the runners carry messages and light parcels between Ghrianan strongholds?

Torbellai held great stores, but it was not self-sufficient. Courting a siege conceded eventual defeat.

Paitra and Tohma received both permission and grudging support for their project.

They didn't wait on events. Dawn saw them setting up in the forging glade – form here, brick shims there, tool caddy at hand – and briefing the apprentice from the smithy proper.

Kaebor had volunteered and could be spared; his fellows remained tied to the sculpting of the great *undreigar* at the front gate.

The first stage went as planned.

Paitra, Tohma, and Kaebor lifted the silvered disc with *energea*, raising it shoulder high, hands free. Next came the heating, pulling vibration through their radices, directing it along their lattices into the metal, allowing the surge of the tribal *energea* to bolster them.

The bronze grew shiny, hot air quivering from its surface, then glowing orange-red.

Paitra moved to shape the *energea* streaming through his fingertips and from those of his companions. It was important the shield-gong retain its proper curvature. They were reforging it, not melting it down.

The black patina on the boss smoked, burned away, revealing polished metal beneath.

Paitra nodded, and the trio intensified the energy pouring through them. The encircling bronze shimmered.

This time Kaebor fielded the extra requirement, adjusting the scrolling *energea* to tag the disc's center more frequently than its perimeter, placing additional pennons to move fire through the boss and out. This was his specialty: achieving an even dispersal of heat through metal.

With Kaebor's work in place, they redoubled their labors.

Paitra felt sweat beading on his brow, sliding past his temples, down the crevice behind his jaw.

The heat grew.

The fiery structures within the brilliance of the central boss took definition, strangely open arabesques of shape, criss-crossing in lambent space, a bizarre variation on the diamonds of force within Ghrianan radices.

Ancient gods! It was a troll radix, floating, ripped from its essential *energea* lattice, shaping sound to suck life from anchored radices, channeling strength into itself, into any drifting radices – trolls – within reach of its vibration.

Paitra hissed.

"Steady," murmured Tohma. "I see it."

"Do you?" Paitra collected himself and renewed his outpouring.

"What is it?" piped Kaebor's boyish voice.

"What troubles you, brother?" came Tohma's deeper rumble.

Did they not know? Paitra reached within for his reserves, focusing yet more heat on the gong. No, Kaebor had never left the mountains, never seen a troll in the flesh. And Tohma encountered them only in battle, scarcely a moment for cultivating the relaxed inner vision needed to examine energetic arrays.

"Troll radices appear thusly," he grunted.

To match the diagrams of the Olluvarde bas reliefs, they would need to re-anchor this drifting conglomeration to its surrounding lattice.

Was such a thing possible?

Troll-disease in living creatures could not be cured. Once ripped from their foundations, radices drifted forever, moving always further from their null points.

Could this artificial radix be re-anchored?

Paitra reached deeper, pouring more of himself into the gong.

This was their last hope. It had to work.

Kaebor's fingers moved faster – flick, flick, flick – pulling heat out of the bronze, threading it into the iron boss.

Paitra removed all his attention from the outer world, concentrating on the inner one: hurtling streams of *energea*, curling and kissing and interweaving. The glittering silver sparked, bright and brighter, acquiring a faint coppery tinge.

Quivering contours of heat coalesced in his mind's eye: winged and equine, soaring through light.

A voice rang in his awareness, thunderous and bold, yet soundless. "Spare naught, brave makers, give more! Ride on toward the gallop and beyond, touch sky!"

The pegasus, all incandescence and motion – no solidity – flickered, nickering impatience.

"Yet more!"

Paitra delved, felt Tohma and Kaebor do the same.

The *energea* flashed gold, flashed silver, as the tribal lattice contributed its reserve.

"And more!" came the command.

Paitra had no more.

He opened wider, calling a potent surge from the tribe, allowing its vastness to race through him, a cataract of gleaming ice.

He saw the intersections of the open radix quiver, and he pushed, willing them to collapse into the diamonds of an anchored configuration.

He felt Kaebor and Tohma add their efforts to his.

The vibration increased.

Almost there, almost – surely now. Or now. Or now.

The open crosses juddered, but held their flaring shape.

"More still!" trumpeted the pegasus.

The *energea* glared gold limned with orange.

Tohma shouted, and Paitra realized he had given tongue as well.

He sensed Kaebor's radices stretching, felt the littlest dwellers within Torbellai – the children – at risk.

No!

Ghriana-folk couldn't become trolls. They were protected!

Tohma stretched out his energy body, arms radiant like the sun, grasped his own lattice . . . and pulled – not his radices, but the energetic connections between them – hurling the glistening web into the white-hot maelstrom of the boss.

The frenetic crosses of *energea* clicked abruptly into closed polygons – *snap* – and a searing effulgence burst outward together with an echoing explosion of sound: away, and return, and away.

Paitra felt dizzy.

Only the tribal support held him upright, working through a disorientation of *here*, *there*, and *here* again. Holding the gong's new configuration without faltering.

The lodestone's polarity had reversed.

And the little ones in Torbellai were not trolls, were safe.

As was Kaebor. Steadfast, he stitched and stitched, controlling heat, holding the gong's metal a hair below liquidity.

But Tohma was gone. Borne away on the tide of the reversal, accompanied by the pegasi, his bright energy body soared upward, sunward, leaving cold clay behind. And a trust Paitra could not betray.

Fail me not, brother. Finish it.

He would.

Stepping over Tohma's fallen body, he guided the glowing metal toward the mountain tarn, over and down, Kaebor in his wake supporting him. Together they submerged it, flinching as the roar of hissing steam fountained up in this first cooling of bronze and iron. The boss would be hardened and stabilized for a second finishing heat, the outer disc softened for hammering. Odd how the two metals responded so differently.

And there, to either side of the column of white vapor stood the guardians, tall and solemn, enrobed in a vast presiding presence. In a moment, the handmaidens – the valkyries – would come.

Paitra's body sweated and groaned, but his spirit chilled, frozen and still.

"My brother, my brother," he whispered.

Kaebor sobbed openly, but without releasing a jot of his energetic control.

Steady despite their emotion, they supported the gong beneath the water with *energea*, supported the gong's inner anatomy with the same. This bath for the metals would be brief, but must last more than an instant.

Paitra waited.

Waited, patient, for the metals to cool.

Waited, grieving, for the handmaidens to appear.

A flutter of wings drew his glance aside.

There on high they came, translucent, noble, and bearing Tohma with them! Not the valkyries, but the pegasi! Spiraling down and down, his brother's radiant energy body astride the equine king's back, flanked by two more, empresses of their kind.

"Now, my brother! Now!" cried Tohma.

And Paitra bent energetically to the gong, lifting it, turning it, placing the disc on the waiting form beside which Tohma stood, spirit and clay married once more, merry and laughing, brandishing his smith's hammer.

"Now!" he shouted again.

And Paitra and Kaebor took up their tools to work the bronze for timber and strength.

The rhythm of their blows ebbed and flowed, tapping and quick, heavy and slow, or syncopated with each forger taking his own line. Tap, boom! Boom!

And then they heated the artifact again, not so fiercely this time, enough merely to anneal it before air-cooling.

It was yet morning when they finished.

Kaebor packed away their hammers and calipers. Paitra soaked in the mountain tarn, its waters warm from the gong. Tohma watched the sun swing through the arch of the summer sky, life-giver, resplendent and benevolent.

At dusk, they tested their work.

Kaebor gave the priming tap – likely unnecessary on this instrument, so finely crafted – and Paitra followed with a solid buffet from the mallet. *Bong!* The resonance carried him away, then here, away and here.

But this time – *this* time – strength infused his limbs, his *energea*, his spirit.

Had he fifty gongs to reforge, he should forge them; fifty foes to fight, he could fight them; fifty councils to persuade, he would persuade them.

So.

There were trolls within fifteen leagues, near enough to be drained by the gong's reverberation, near enough to lend their strength to Ghriana-folk.

That was the first thing he noticed.

The second was odd, too odd to be understood for a moment.

Tohma sat there at the dell's edge, listening, energy body and corporeal body solidly together.

How was it that another energy body leapt on the waves of sound emanating from the struck bronze? He was there *and* here. Not there, *then* here.

"Tohma!" gasped Paitra.

Kaebor's eyes were shocked.

Only Tohma himself remained calm. "I died," he remarked.

"But, this? What *is* this?" Paitra dropped the mallet to touch his brother's shoulder: solid, warm, living. As the echoes of the gong faded, so too did Tohma's duplicate energy lattice, shimmering on the air.

Tohma smiled. "The pegasi bore me up into light, light so strong it acquired density. And in the light, a new lattice of *energea* burst from my radices, re-weaving itself. But the old one . . . I threw away. I suspect we just saw it, brought forth with the gong's sounding." He chuckled.

"Are you well?" demanded Paitra, running his hands down Tohma's arms, checking his heartbeat with one palm. His brother felt well, vital.

Tohma's gaze held serenity. "Yes, very."

Despite Tohma's obvious health, Paitra insisted he leave the carrying of the heavy gong to Kaebor and Paitra. Tohma humored them, and then delayed their return home to watch the stars appear.

Were all things new to him now?

Paitra gripped the flared surface at the gong's edge, Kaebor hoisted the other side and adjusted the angle of the belt around his hips holding the tool caddy. Tohma loitered in their wake.

The mountain turf felt soft under Paitra's steps, the air gentle on his cheeks.

The gong-gifted strength was ebbing from him, ushering in fatigue and lassitude.

At the entrance to the upper adits, they suffered a repulse. The gong, while yet requiring effort to hold it above the ground, simply stopped as though a boulder stood between it and the doorway. Paitra's wrists quivered.

What now?

Did some energetic repulsion act between the reforged artifact and Torbellai?

Kaebor beat him to the inner looking. Paitra felt too weary to check. What had he seen?

"Tohma, we need you," the boy called.

Tohma had fallen behind, watching the moon rise. Once he caught up, the gong's stasis ended and it came easily.

Their hero's welcome was quiet and small.

Tohma's wife kissed his cheek and led him away. Paitra's mother served dinner and didn't ask questions. Likely she knew as much as any of them did: they had succeeded, her eldest son had made the ultimate sacrifice and survived it, the morrow would demand greater effort.

The understanding and its ramifications must wait.

Paitra drew his attention back from these old memories, looking again at the gong suspended beside him.

It would always hang there, immovable, indestructible, and singing of Tohma.

He smiled.

They'd succeeded, he and his brother, in all they set out to do, but the gong bore this one odd quirk. To depart from any location, it must be accompanied by its energetic twin: Tohma. And Tohma would not be following it anymore.

The winds of the war had turned.

Bearing the gong into every battle, Tohma at its side, the Ghriana pushed the *truldemager* out of the mountains, beyond the foothills, and into the lowlands. Dreben, the troll regenen, fell to Tohma's sword, and his replacement was both less able and shorter lived. Each leader arising in succession accomplished less, until the hierarchy of power failed entirely and the troll army dispersed.

Ordinary folk emerged from hiding – a hermit here, a family there – and the Ghriana found allies. Lowland pockets of safety grew larger, more numerous, and then it was the trolls on the run. The northern ice floes received some, the vast western wilderness a few, and the rest perished under the vigilance of civilians eager to secure their future.

Never again would magic be wielded so profligately, so carelessly, so prone to rip radices asunder. Laws and limits would prevent the creation of new trolls, and the old ones must suffer execution.

Tohma settled in the lowlands, bringing his family and a large portion of Torbellai's population with him. Paitra stayed in the mountains, organizing a contemplative community that would remain to guard the gong and seek inner wisdom through prayer, meditation, simplicity, and the cultivation of awareness.

Be here now. Be here.

Paitra shifted, moving his calves beneath him, easing the ache in his knees caused by long sitting.

He thought back again to his first sighting of the gong, not immersing himself in the experience this time, but remembering who he'd been: new come to sense and enthusiastic for more. More understanding, more doing, more living.

And then later, a warrior – one of the myrmon – and a *flaumeikos*, still young without knowing it; still eager for more, and knowing *that*.

And now, five decades behind him and strangely content, carrying the boy and the youth of yesterday within him, and knowing that he would always be new come to something.

Life was like that.

Paitra smiled and tapped the gong with a priming strike. The bronze hummed, and he swung the mallet in its full arc as though the wooden tool might pass through the metal like summer air through the wild pear trees: warm and gentle and powerful.

Deep sound bloomed along with Tohma's energetic presence.

The Ghriana might depart their mountain refuge and dwindle, their culture lost in the currents of time and change and renewal. But Tohma would live forever.

Rainbow's Lodestone

At bedtime, all across the North-lands, motters and patters tuck children into bednooks, sit on the edge of the mattress, and tell the story of *The Princess and the Troll* or *The Sea-dragon's Triumph over the North Wind* or *The Griffon's Gift*.

This is the tale of the rainbow's child.

It happened in the days of Koschey the Deathless. He was a mighty troll-lord who governed a secret realm in the vast pine-hill stretches above Giralliya's north border, somewhere between the Tahdenfiall range in the east and the Iarbaston mountains in the west.

His incantors defeated the sentinels the emperador sent to vanquish him.

And his troll-heralds – his most special envoys – scoured the countryside for wealth to enrich him, for slaves to serve him, and for news of his potential enemies.

The cruelest of his heralds, one Gefnen, who had served Koschey long, was returning from Silmaren alone. His purpose there had been fulfilled, and his satisfaction in bearing news of his success might have given pleasure to a newer troll. But Gefnen was decades into his troll-disease, and nothing brought happiness to him save the deliverance of unhappiness to others.

The weather was stormy.

Gefnen cared little. His troll-blood ran hot in his veins, warding off any chill. And the sodden dampness brought by sheets of rain was merely uncomfortable, not dangerous. He hitched his woolen cloak more securely around his shoulders, tipped his high-crowned hat forward to better shield his eyes, and spurred his horse. The beast had slacked its pace due to the steep grade of the mountain path they followed.

Lightning stabbed ahead, followed by its crack of thunder.

Gefnen's horse shied, tossing its head, then obeyed his hand on the reins, settling into a faster walk. The wind gusted suddenly, flapping Gefnen's cloak out behind him. Another curtain of rain turned the path into a rushing stream, foaming around his steed's hooves.

He paid no heed. The water level would ebb between downpours, and he wanted to reach the other side of the mountain before nightfall.

The storm eventually outpaced him, driven fast into the west by its winds.

He reached the top of the pass perhaps an hour before sunset. The sun was hidden behind the massive cloud bank, but its radiance limned the thunderheads in searing white, streaming out into blue and gold above, beaming Jacob's ladders down to the rain-swept land below.

In the mountains, stillness had come. The twisted pines no longer thrashed, and the granite cliffs were drying. Soon a mist would rise from the soaked turf.

Gefnen turned his gaze from the lowlands to the spot where he paused in a bowl of ground cupped by higher peaks. The rock on one side was sheer, rising vertically to heights unseen. The ruins of a Ghriana-folk stronghold clung to the other, farther side of the mountain saddle.

Should he delay long enough to enter the ruins? Unlikely that any Ghrianan treasure remained, given the traffic this route over the Tahdenfialls saw every summer. Still, it would take only a few moments.

He knotted his mount's reins on the horse's neck. The creature would not stray from his command, even in this desolate spot, but leaving its tack hanging was not Gefnen's habit.

Just as his booted feet hit the ground, the lower edge of the sun emerged below the storm clouds ahead. Lances of golden light blinded him for an instant. He blinked, frowning, and turned away toward east-lying Silmaren behind him.

Its lands dreamt in the shadow of the mountain range, stretching away into dusk. The sky above the darkened vales was clear turquoise, and a rainbow arched across it, one foot springing from the distant horizon, the other splashing down – Gefnen followed the brilliant curve of prismatic light – a few paces away.

He growled.

There in the midst of glowing scarlet, gold, sapphire, and amethyst, the rainbow's daughter leapt and spun, dancing to a music unheard by earthly ears. Joy illumined her exultant face, grace shaped her out-flung arms, wonder informed her sweeping bows and lilting steps.

Gefnen groped in the leather wallet on his belt.

Not that, no; nor that.

There. Hard, smooth, small, and oval. He drew it out.

It looked innocuous: black, the size of a flattened quail's egg, made of matte metal.

It was anything but innocuous.

There were three like it, rumored to have been forged by the master smiths of Navellys before that island kingdom sank beneath the waves, four artifacts preserved by the renegade Palijon Clisto who fled the disaster, and collected by Koschey, one by one, from their scattered hiding places.

They were the lodestones. Each of Koschey's heralds held one.

Gefnen contemplated his, then returned his gaze to the rainbow's daughter dancing.

With the answer to her exuberance in his palm, her happiness offended him less. Indeed, prolonging the moment of her downfall gave him a perverse pleasure.

He watched.

She did not see him, but a rainbow's child might not. The sky was her realm – air and light and wind – with brief visits to earth and the creatures of earth.

She pranced and leapt and whirled. She tossed back her head, tresses swirling, and flung her arms skyward. She bent and bowed. She rejoiced in this highland dell.

He threw the lodestone.

It caught the hem of her gauzy gown of light, pinning a sapphire panel to the ground.

Pain. Terror. Shock. Her face registered all these and more.

She tried to straighten, tugging at her dress.

It dragged her downward, trapping her against the ground.

She looked up, eyes dilating, pleading in the gesture of one hand. Now she was seeing him.

She did not speak, but her face said much. *Please! Please will you help me? Please?* She did not know him as the author of her distress.

He smiled unpleasantly, taking in her strain and stress. This would be a memory to savor, later: the awkward bend of her body anchored to the earth, her powerlessness, her shocked and frightened eyes.

Her further shock as she realized he would do nothing increased his satisfaction. Sneering, he turned to his horse, mounted, and rode away.

He didn't look back.

Imagining her despair was better than seeing it. And he would return for the lodestone later. It couldn't be stolen, couldn't be moved, couldn't be lifted, until he grasped it again in his hand.

What would he find, when he returned?

Could a rainbow's child be killed? Or would she merely go mad?

He curled one lip and passed into the west.

෴

She'd been leaping across the sky in the wake of a thunderstorm, glorying in the energy of the wind and lightning before her, exulting in the rush of the earth beneath her.

Then her rainbow splashed amidst a range of peaks, their tips still snow-capped in early spring, and she slid down the curve of light, eager for the differences awaiting there: dense, moist air; firm surfaces; the flute of birds; a whole new way of moving.

She jumped the last bit, landing lightly, and snatched a handful of emerald and sapphire light to be her gown. Then she was spinning and prancing and flinging her legs into high arabesques. It was fabulous! An entirely different experience of freedom.

She lifted her arms in celebration, then swept a bow to mother earth.

Something black flashed at the periphery of her vision.

Then pain pierced her in a thousand places and weight forced her bow lower.

What was this? She struggled to straighten; couldn't. Her back strained over her collapsing legs. She tipped her face up.

A black stone pinned her skirt to the ground, and beyond it stood a dark figure, his back to the light of the sunset.

She knew little of mortals. Would he help her? *Could* he help her? She gestured with one hand. Surely he could see her plight.

He took a step toward her, away from the sun. Now she could see his face: green-white skin sagging off his bones; cracked and bleeding lips; dead, empty eyes. So this was one of the troll-children, damned by powerful magics, exiled by men and women. There was no pity in his features, no interest in *her*, despite his stare.

Please! Please will you help me?

One corner of his mouth lifted unpleasantly. His flat eyes met hers. Then he turned, mounted his horse, and rode away.

Despairing, she yielded to the pull of the black pebble on her gown, sinking into the damp turf under her limbs, feeling the tickle of the grasses against her ankles, the sharp press of a mountain rock at her elbow.

When had the troll-kind ever been generous? She had seen them before: hunting or hunted, never in harmony. But what had she done to this one, that he preferred to leave her desolate?

She strained against the weight bending her, yearning to straighten. Past a certain angle, it couldn't be done.

She closed her eyes and gave all her effort to the task, directing the energy of her sky-spanning leaps into a bid for freedom.

It made no difference. She was held in a low arc against the mountain bones, trapped like a butterfly in the strong strands of a tangle-weaver spider's web. She could go lower, but not an iota higher.

Stricken, she surrendered.

What has happened to me? How have I been exiled from my sky? I am no creature of earth, to do more than touch lightly on the soil.

She was not touching lightly now. Even her hands felt heavy, like the massive stone fists of the golems at World's End, and her feet seemed to have grown roots into the mountain itself.

She lunged upward again, quivering in her exertion, and met the same low limit. The earth had claimed her with one small fragment from its body: that smooth, black oval distorting the light of her garment was her cage. She sensed it. And reached toward it, scrabbling her weighted hands along the ground, since she could not lift them.

It was smooth, almost sueded against her fingertips. Its matte surface seemed to drink light, but was neither cool nor warm to her touch.

She cupped her hand over it, digging her fingers into the turf to get some purchase, and pulled.

She might as well have pulled against a golem's foot. The stone moved not the slightest.

She struggled futilely as the sun sank and the light dimmed. Like a butterfly in truth, she battered herself against the mountain's rigidity, striving for liberty, gaining nothing.

Darkness found her broken, huddled against dampness, spangled tears on her cheeks.

The night was long.

Her back ached in its enforced bend, her legs cramped in their crooked position, and her neck yearned for relief from the weight of her head. She couldn't stop struggling to straighten and paused only when exhaustion claimed her. She alternated between frantic exertion, depleted limpness, and a dazed delirium.

The sun rose bright and joyous next morning, and she was not free. Nor was she free when it set that evening.

She became a blur of pain – cramped limbs; pins-and-needles at every joint; bruises where the ground anchored her; and longing, *longing* to stand, to arch backward, to leap upward into the sky that was her birthright.

She lost count of the days.

There were only her pains, her agonized boredom, her panicked sense of permanent loss. Had all the millennia when she chased storms across the heavens been a dream? This earthbound existence the only reality?

She was too empty to cry.

Then one sunrise, something changed.

She hardly knew what was different, but she was no longer fighting her prison.

Her awareness crept out through the mountain bowl cupping her tortured self, out to the cliffs of its rim, noting the dew-spangled mosses, the scents of the alpine flowers, the nest built by a snowfinch in one twisted pine. At the base of one cliff, grotesque faces carved by the Ghriana people of the distant past flanked a ruined gate into their abandoned cavern fortress.

She sent her rainbow arch inside, into the darkness, as once she'd sent it plunging toward earth in her bounds across the sky. She could see, in her mind's eye, where the prismatic light glimmered amber and citron and ruby-red on dusty interior walls, carved with intricate geometries of line and shape.

The underground stronghold was empty, but the flow of its spaces soothed her. She explored for a time, ignoring her numb pain to attend to the architecture of a forgotten civilization.

At the uppermost extent of the delving, a small arched opening gave onto open air. It was a look-out, of sorts, and something more. She sensed it, there in the deeper shadows, yet could not see it clearly: something glinting, gleaming, and bearing a warm hum in its essence.

Her awareness circled around this one bright mystery, inexplicably comforted by its strangeness. She felt rested, despite the continuing pain in her body.

Her inner peace lasted all that day and the next.

She sent her rainbows everywhere after that, wondering what the folk of the valleys must think to see the flicker of prismatic light about one peak in the Tahdenfialls, day after day.

The waterfalls in the glens of her mountain were bright with clear water and scaled fish in the pools below them. The forests harbored deer and foxes and highland lynxes. Lowland meadows collected herds of wild ponies.

She roamed all over in spirit, secured by her painful anchoring, yet free.

Her diminutive realm was beautiful. She reveled in it, tasting the delights of the earthland in a more protracted way than ever before.

I missed all this and never suspected its bounty.

Yet always her rainbow-haloed sojourns began and ended with a touch on the strange, glimmering hum in the lookout of the Ghriana-folk. She found that it responded to the caress of her light with a change in pitch.

Violet induced a vibration so piercing she doubted any earth-child could hear it, while red provoked a rumble like a cloud-giant's laugh.

She began to play harmonies to charm away her loneliness. The star-dragons and the wind sprites, her usual playmates, could not visit her here. Yet she grew accepting, if never merry, in the possibilities of her prison.

Many days passed.

The air grew chill with autumn, although not so chill as the upper reaches of her sky home. And one morning she heard travelers climbing the eastern trail.

Her serenity fled.

The timber of their voices was friendly. Would the strangers help her? Could they?

Rising hope brought renewed struggle. She fought gravity as she had in the beginning, bruising herself, wrenching her limbs, flailing her gossamer light against the mountain rock.

Lost in futile fight, she didn't see the five newcomers until her paroxysm ended in familiar exhaustion. They stood in a bunch some paces away, appalled shock on their faces. One, a tall woman with curling auburn hair, stepped closer and spoke a tentative string of sounds.

The rainbow's daughter answered in her own speech: *I am meant for the sky.*

But they didn't understand her. How should they? She was a child of air, they were offspring of earth.

Still she watched them with hope intact. They weren't simply departing, leaving this puzzle in their wake. The auburn woman engaged in an animated discussion with an even taller, ice-pale man, while the others listened. What might they attempt?

The pain of her utterly fatigued legs and the ever-present cramping in her back distracted her from their activities. She pushed back against the temptations of distraction.

This is my chance. What do I want them to try?

She knew instantly: go into the ruins of the Ghriana-folk and discover the shining, humming mystery that dwelt in its topmost space. She looked up eagerly when the auburn woman approached again, drawing her companions with her this time.

They gestured at the black stone pinning the rainbow-daughter's gown and pantomimed removing it. She shook her head vigorously, laboriously touching the fingers of one hand to her other, left over right, right over left, then indicating the stone, and shaking her head a second time.

They seemed to understand, but drew back slightly in consternation.

She attempted to lift her arm in a sweeping wave that encompassed them all, but failed. Arm and hand were too heavy.

She tried again, tears starting in her eyes.

The ice-man stopped her, turning his hand palm down. Then he did an inexplicable thing: stretching his own arm to indicate himself and his friends. How did he know? Her abortive gesture could have conveyed nothing. He symbolically gathered his group again and offered them to her.

She managed a nod and then painfully turned her palm upward and outward to indicate the Ghrianan gateway.

His face lit with comprehension.

She followed them inside with her rainbow arch.

Their voices, such friendly voices, acquired awe as they observed the intricate carvings there revealed by her accompanying prismatic light.

They were slower than she wanted, testing surfaces and steps as they advanced. Perhaps there were potential hazards to an earth-child in a place of stone and age.

She danced a sliver of her light ahead to the warm dazzle of the enigma in the lookout, touched it with green and gold and then green again, sliding into ruby.

Resonant sound emanated, low and lower, back up and then lower still.

The shortest fellow – was he a young one? or were the others just so tall? – caught the arm of the man in the bear cape, and they ran up the last stairway into a scintillating halo of vividness. The auburn woman, the ice-man, and the short lady – surely *not* a child, with her white hair and lined face – swiftly joined them.

The rainbow's daughter brought all her powers of light into focus, playing the gleaming mystery as the winds sometimes played the trees.

Richness sounded forth, deep chords anchoring beauty, while a water pattern touched delicate rills and intricate descents, the music cloaked in the shifting aurora of the spectrum.

She lost herself in her symphony – as lost as when she'd drowned in pain. There was no place for coherence and design and linear deeds in this. She knew not how her freedom would be created from her art, only that it would, if these generous strangers could be moved by her hymn.

She played.

The glint of a golden hammer flashed in the periphery of her vision, as once something black had done months ago.

No! You'll break it!

The hammer smashed the center of her glory.

Its aura splintered, splattered away like rain driven by wind, and silence arrived.

Along with the absence of weight.

She sprang upright in one bound, leaping into the sky with an ecstasy beyond any she'd known before, dancing from cloud to cloud, shouting in triumph.

The airy reaches were hers!

The choice of backbend or gavotte or stretching for the stars was hers!

She was the rainbow and the child of its light, and she vaulted across her realm as was her wont.

Behind her, the bear-man and the auburn woman studied the unusual gong that hung in the Ghriana-folk's lookout, while – returning outside – the boy collected a black pebble into his pocket.

When Gefnen returned to the mountain in spring, his lodestone was gone.

Star-drake

Láidir couldn't find her anywhere. He was the strongest of the wind spirits, but still he couldn't find her.

Not in the long, hard blow from the northern seas down to the first fringe of green land.

Not in the wild updrafts along the mountains' flanks.

Not even amidst the sun-haloed thunder-battles of late summer afternoons.

At first he didn't worry. He and Geal trusted chance to rule their meetings. If he didn't chase her at sundown, then he'd dance with her at dawn.

So it had always been: the wind and the rainbow. Who could keep them apart? He blew rain into mist, and she shone within it.

He dashed ahead of himself to catch his playful companions, the erratic puffs heralding a storm.

"If you see her, tell her the sun is strong at my back!" he told them.

Léim, the littlest, somersaulted, laughed, and called, "We miss her, too, Láidir. Tell her to visit soon!"

But he didn't see her. Not then, not the next day, or the next.

He blew south to the warm and brilliant seas laving white sands to find Odhéas, the changeable zephyr. Sometimes she gusted hot and rough. Others – like now – she drifted languorously.

"Geal," she purred. "Geal."

"Have you seen her?" he pressed.

Odhéas smiled. "No."

How could she be so calm? He didn't feel calm. Nor confidant. Not anymore.

"It's been too long."

Her eyelids lowered. "Has it?"

He blew away in irritation, blasting the fronds of a palm forest, then whipping the tepid sea into vigorous waves. Somewhere mid-ocean his annoyance ebbed. Láidir sighed and paused, gliding through air so still it felt like liquid moonlight.

"It's been too long," whispered a voice.

Láidir turned mid-air, surprised. "You've noticed," he observed.

Translucent skirts flowing, gauzy curls unfurling, the gentle breeze swirled toward him. "Your speed and my serenity accord rarely," Milis agreed. "Drift with me," she invited.

"I didn't mean you," he blurted. "I meant Geal."

"The rainbow's daughter," she murmured. "I see her more rarely than I see you."

"But have you seen her?" Láidir probed, slowing his slow drift.

Milis considered. "No. I haven't. But you should have."

"Yes. I should."

Milis collected herself, twisting her trailing bannerols into a narrow tail, and inclined her languid self toward fleeter flight. "Let's search then," she offered.

He'd been searching. Alone. It felt good to have company in both his looking and his concern.

Through the golden evening they soared, and on into starlight, hunting the dark spaces between the sparking suns.

ᔓꙄᏻ

On horseback, Gefnen inhaled, long and lingeringly. He could smell them – his prey – somewhere ahead, warm and live and vibrant.

My lord Koschey will be pleased with this catch.

Pure and piercing amongst the scents of the elders came the perfume of the young one. Gefnen would secure him first, then the others as chance permitted. But Koschey's deathless essence would expand threefold on the boy's vitality alone.

Gefnen glanced at the star patterns in the black sky.

Moonrise would come before he reached the travelers' camp, but no matter. His troll blood gave him an advantage in the dimness of starshine, mapping his surroundings by smell alone, while his human foes blundered in the dark. But they were little better under lunar light. And they would not be expecting him.

He felt his lips stretch in a not-smile, their dry surfaces cracking at the center points, oozing fluid. His sweeping tongue caught the droplets before they stained his chin. Slightly salt, strongly metallic.

He frowned and urged his mount forward, slowly, for the track he followed was rough. The beast depended on his guidance by night.

ᔓꙄᏻ

Emrys woke to a hard tap on his shoulder. The bulking shoulders of the Tromme-lander shaman loomed dark against the star field above.

"Skaval time," Paavo muttered. The greasy scent of his wolverine hood stung Emrys' nose.

"I'm ready." Emrys eeled from his bed roll and pulled a seacorn-hide cloak from atop his blankets. The autumn night was cold and damp. He wrapped the heavy leather around him, fastening it with the spiraling silver of his cloak pin, then shoved his stocking-clad feet into boots.

"My wards hold," Paavo growled.

Emrys shrugged. "I can't use your murk. You know that."

"Seems a waste to place three sets of augury around our camp each time we stop."

Emrys shrugged again. "Haral's a Hammarleeding and a duoja-adept. I'm a sealord and a water-patterner."

Paavo snorted softly. "Just variations on energy manipulation."

Emrys half smiled, folding his blankets and strapping them to the lump of shadow that was his pack on the ground. They'd spoken almost these same words every night since he'd joined these travelers.

Paavo was likely right – he'd been Haral's teacher once, so some blending of disciplines was possible – but Emrys preferred setting his own trip lines anyway. He favored the lowest spots where mist gathered for his warning pattern, while the Trummer-shaman selected the higher crests.

Someone nearer the embers of their fire muttered in sleep, voice lighter than Haral's. Tor: the young one. Was he dreaming of *seolhs*?

Emrys compressed his lips, then rose to his feet.

The constellation of the goblet swung low on the horizon – Paavo's skaval – and he'd best draw his magical pattern before the shaman's wards ebbed.

He glanced across the swell of moorland he would encircle.

Dark turf on a dark slope stretching to the thinner dark of the skyline. No lingering glow from the fire's remnants. Sleepers indistinct silhouettes in the black hours before dawn.

Lilli, the grandmother, curved protectively around her grandson. Tallis, the salver, bracketed the boy's other side.

Haral stretched near Paavo's rug.

The shaman returned from his visit to the edge of their camp and began smoothing his bedding prior to turning in. He was always so tidy with physical things, in strange contrast to his wild handling of *energea*.

Emrys shook his head and moved outward to the hollow where the track curved around their hill.

He paused, centering himself with three long and slow breaths. A tracery of silver and blue sprang into being in his mind's eye, webbing his limbs, netting his core vortices, from fundus up through crown. He stretched out his hand, touching moisture, gathering it, weaving a strand of *energea* in a long arc around his slumbering companions.

ഇൻഗ്

Gefnen stiffened, raising his head.

He'd been nodding on this easier stretch of track, letting his steed plod forward unattended. Now he reined the horse in, paused a moment, and inhaled deeply.

Something had changed ahead.

The lingering musk of sheep wool was altogether gone, the peppery warmth prevalent earlier had faded, and a cool salt essence now dominated.

He exhaled.

More than one *magikos* awaited him. Three?

No matter. The strength of his troll-magic could best many wielding the lesser *energeas*.

He urged his mount onward.

‰ﬠ

There.

Emrys felt the halo of mist he'd created quiver as the ending arc joined its beginning. He let his focus soften, allowed the glimmer of *energea* to fade from his awareness. No need for such conscious vigilance now.

He would know if anything crossed, even brushed, his invisible circle.

He moved back to the hilltop just above Paavo and Haral and settled on the bare expanse of rock there. Moonrise was coming, and when it did his eyes could supplement his water-patterning ward from this vantage.

Moonlight.

Once he'd loved the moonlit nights. Neued and he would steal away from the castle to the shore, shed their nightshirts, and plunge into the waves, letting *seolh* essence shape them in the pull of the tides.

On land she was pale and lovely, belying her essential inner fire.

Asea, she was dark and liquid and warm.

Together they swam, down through chill depths, up through luminescent waves, twining in a dance more complete than any merging possible on their silken couch.

Awake, he dreamed of his wife.

‰ﬠ

"Why do we search by dark?" inquired Milis. She sounded curious, not critical. "How shall we find prism-light where no sun shines?"

Láidir smiled. "Have you never seen the pale haloes round the lamps of the cities far below? There is light, even in night's eclipse."

"This pine forest below us shelters no cities."

"Ah, but I've always hoped to see the rainbow by starlight. Geal by sunlight is vivid and impassioned. Geal by lamplight is subtle and nuanced. How might she be in the realm of the star-drake? Lit by a million suns against primordial darkness?"

He felt, rather than heard, Milis' sigh of delight. "It's well then that we of the sky need no rest as do flesh and blood creatures of earth. How if we . . . slept?"

Rest was foreign to Láidir's nature. He was the storm front, the hurricane's spiral, the tornado's funnel, the blast between rock chasm walls.

But he'd learned to slow himself in Milis' company. Just as she'd discovered speed in his.

How if he broadened his experience yet more? What was this sleep? He was huge now in his loitering. How if he expanded again?

Milis laughed, feeling the swell of his pennons within her trailing tresses.

She moved into his embrace, blending her breezes with his, slowing still more, tasting clean strength in his marrow.

&)(&

The bright disk of the moon was vast as it cleared the mountains to the east. The peaks of the range, invisible by starlight, sprang into sudden relief beneath the moon's stronger light. The moors stretching away from the foothills acquired a dappling of silver and shadow.

Emrys flinched.

By moonlight Neued had bade him farewell.

The sea-longing awoke in her without fanfare. One morning she was content to dwell on land. The next she was not. She fought it to the last, staving off her departure with daily swims, nightly swims, dampened gowns.

On her last shore-compassed evening, she told him, "No, I'll never leave you."

And then the moon rose.

Tears streaked her face, she lifted her arms in pleading, and she backed into the waves. The *seolh* form took her, and she swam away.

His brother – the king of the Tuisil-isle – said, "Follow her. I can spare you."

But the land-love gripped Emrys yet. He could no more thrive in the sea than Neued could thrive on its beach.

He hated moonlight. Despite its help during night watches and nighttime travel.

Grimly, he stared across the moors.

Was that blot of shadow moving?

He glanced up. Just a stray cloud drifting through the star field, casting darkness on the brindled land.

He glowered at the creeping shade.

❧☙

Láidir stirred, untwining himself from Milis.

"I . . . feel . . ." He couldn't articulate what he sensed. Nothing seen or heard or touched. Something with glamor, captivating.

Milis stretched, breezing from their standstill. "It's Geal!"

She sounded certain.

"But it isn't. Not quite." He felt equally certain.

"A hill she's touched then. Or a lake. A cliff face."

Láidir chuckled. "She's lighted upon every feature of this earth at one time or another."

Milis put on more speed, and he followed her.

"Then a creature, a stag rainbow-touched, or a hind."

"Ye . . . ess. Come on! Let's go!" He dashed ahead of her. Geal had vanished for so many months. This would be trouble, if it were anything. "Be ready!"

Milis giggled. "How shall I ready myself?"

It was a reasonable question. How might a gentle zephyr such as herself bring force to a fight? But Láidir had an answer. "You've learned fleetness, Milis. Blow! Blow hard!"

"Oh!" She leapt ahead of him, and they rushed across the sky.

ℬ)ℭ

Emrys turned to check the west, the north and south. Then peered eastward again. It was just a cloud's shadow, wasn't it?

The breeze was picking up.

His cohorts were waking. Tallis rekindled the fire and brewed tea. Lilli set out dried scarletberries and cheese, then heated flatbread at the edge of the coals. Haral stuffed his blankets into his pack. Paavo rolled his rugs. Only Tor slept on, undisturbed by the bustle around him.

Emrys monitored that cloud shadow, moving too steadily, until it advanced into a fold in the land.

Lilli roused Tor to eat something before they set off. The boy was groggy, unused to rising after so few hours of sleep. He perched on Lilli's pack and munched with his eyes half closed, while his grandmother tied up his bedroll.

Paavo offered to carry Tor's strapped bedding.

Haral stretched.

Tor himself visited the bush at the edge of their camp.

Tallis doused the fire with the water sack they'd filled before sleeping, and the moon slid behind that sole cloud in the sky.

Emrys' trip line of *energea* flared.

&OC3

Gefnen approached his prey's camp.

Their fire was out, the moon shrouded, and the boy adjusting his trews.

Now!

Gefnen twisted his free hand, and a sizzle of acrid orange bolted toward his target.

The boy cried out, spun, bent in pain.

Gefnen spurred his horse, closing the ground between him and the groaning young one.

Just the boy. Worth all the others combined.

He reined in Camhir and leapt from the saddle, reaching.

&OC3

Emrys stiffened.

Hooves, shadow, the scorching crackle of *incantatio*.

That cluster of darkness was no cloud gloom.

"Troll!" yelled the sealord.

And bounded toward the young one, summoning protection as he moved.

A shaft of piercing yellow brilliance met him partway, and he fell like a wave crest hitting sudden shallow waters, his ankles abruptly glued together.

The ground smacked breath from him, but failed to stop the focused release of his patterning.

Invisible to laity, but clear in his own perception, a latticed globe of ice and azure snapped around Tor, bouncing their dark foe away.

As Emrys struggled to regain his feet, Haral hurtled past, snatching Tor on the run.

A thicker bolt of sparkling purple flashed over Emrys' left shoulder to splash against a spitting net of gold and copper, the troll's *incantatic* defense. Paavo had joined the fight.

Emrys arose, arm extended and fingers stiff. Coruscating beams of aqua flared in the wake of the shaman's attack.

Paavo stepped forward, releasing another bolt of *energea*. Violet light limned by turquoise illumined the troll.

His white face was still, utterly unmoved by the possibility of peril. His eyes were flat, dead, as though all interest in living had passed. His lips thinned. Then a web of *incantatic* strands crackled around him – wine dark this time – splintering the milder patterning into a shower of glinting splinters. Thunder cracked without lightning, and a wind gusted, flaring the troll's cloak.

Emrys heard Haral behind him, urging the women and the boy toward flight. "This is no fight for swords." And Tallis was good with her blade. "Go!"

Then Haral stood at his other shoulder, silver *energea* streaming toward their foe.

₭₯

Gefnen felt the boy removed from his grasp, felt malice incoming, felt instant victory ebbing.

A twitch of his fingers wrapped *incantatio* around him, its potent gold splattering the marauding *energea*. Feeble amethystine and sapphirine.

Gefnen smiled inside.

One never knew, not for sure, when one's foe hid *incantatio* in his breast. But these were no trolls. Mere patterners all. They could not win.

Energea healed and made, might constrain. Troll-magic conferred lethal force. And Gefnen was a troll.

Gefnen jerked his arm in a wider arc, summoned wrath from his bones, and unleashed his real assault. Cracking burgundine effulgence burst from his palm – met assailing silver and spawned echoing flashes of thunderous radiance – banished night.

The patterned shields of the Hammarleeding, the shaman, and the sea-lord withstood the maelstrom of violence.

This time.

But he would not stop.

Gefnen stood tall, hand raised, a cataract of death sluicing his victims.

🙰

Emrys felt his ribs crushing inward, choking breath. He must call aggression from somewhere within. Defense wasn't enough. But defense was necessary. And all he had. All any of them had.

Beyond the cool-sparking filigree of the pattern-shield they sustained, unnatural lightning – blood-tinged – blazed and boomed.

Lungs aching, Emrys relaxed into the pain, accepted it, stopped fighting it, and strength rose through his heels. He gathered it, focused it, and directed it toward his enemy, a cerulean jet of liquid light.

Paavo's purple and Haral's silver brightened with his attack, all three of them stronger than before.

We can win this. We're three. He's only one.

❧❧❧

A star burned where no star should shine. On the land.

The pine forest was gone, far behind in the west. Moorland stretched beneath them, fuzzy, undulating. And on its dappled breast in the distance, a blaze of silver and gold flared and glared – bright, dangerous, compelling.

"Geal!" exclaimed Milis.

Láidir frowned. No rainbow shone in the mist surrounding the land-star, yet he felt Geal's trace. "Something of her," he conceded.

"Why do you wait? Let's *go!*" And Milis rushed away.

She was right. Something was wrong there, whether for Geal or for another. He paused one more small moment – tasting something dark, something ancient, something more ancient even than the wind – then gusted forward. "Now!"

❧❧❧

Emrys felt his knees buckling.

Paavo was down, curled on the ground after a lance thrust of burgundine *incantatio* shattered his ward.

Haral fought on, wounded, blood bubbling from his mouth, loosing arrow after arrow of silver *energea*.

We're losing. How is this possible? We're three. He's one.

The loremasters of the Tuisil-isle spoke of the immense power dwelling within troll-magic, but there were no trolls in Tuisil-land. And the troll Emrys encountered in southern Silmaren had been a pitiful thing, diseased and dying and weak. This foe partook of troll-disease. Emrys saw it in his dead white visage, his cracked lips, his misshapen nose. But he was not ill, despite his disease. He was potent, invincible.

Emrys' knees hit the ground.

No. If I go down, Haral cannot last alone.

But his lungs ached. Black spots danced across his vision. His arm sagged. His shield of *energea* – extended to shelter Paavo and linked with Haral's shield – flickered.

A fleeting memory of Neued grazed his awareness. *Seolh*-dark and soulful, she embraced the sea, one with the waves – beautiful – and swimming away from him.

I lost her long ago. Perhaps now was the time to lose more. Let go?

Tor's high voice, some distance behind him, flicked his ears. "They need help! We should go *back!*"

Emrys' head came up.

No. That was not my battle. I lost, but it was Neued's fight to win, and she never surrendered. The sea took her in spite of her refusal. This is my fight, my choice. I will resist. Will fight till all breath is gone.

His arm straightened, and cobalt fire burst from his hand.

∞◡◠

Wind roared around Gefnen, whipping his cloak like a maddened bat.

His foes were strong, their struggle fierce – fierce enough to disturb the airs of the world – but he was stronger. His lips stretched and cracked and wept.

My lord Koschey will smile.

Now for the killing volley.

Never mind these lesser mortals. The boy will suffice.

Gefnen swept his arm in a slow arc, gathering power, gathering malice, gathering ultimate darkness.

His arm swept forward. And darkness came: black limned by citron, thunderous and overwhelming. Like the wing of a roc it mowed his enemies down and crushed them, night from the back of the stars, a shadow blacker than black.

Gefnen cried out. *"Mine!"*

And then another darkness came.

Summoned on the winds, winged and spangled in obsidian, swifter than death, but fanged like it.

The star-drake bore down upon the troll, stygian claws outstretched.

Gefnen cried out once more, without words. And then he was taken, riven from the earth, borne skyward.

⁊❣œ

All sight was gone. Pressed to the earth and suffocating, Emrys summoned a last resistance, a last assault on his destroyer.

No *energea* answered his call – he was empty – but vision returned briefly.

He saw a vastness in the sky, dark and ominous, but living and abundant. Like mother sea, like her *seolhs*.

Then its wings passed over him, and vision failed. He felt himself caught up, his awareness tumbled, hitched to the star-drake's flight.

His thoughts whipped in psyche's wind, perceived the moorlands far below and receding, then touched something cold and terrified.

No, no, no, something whimpered. *No, no.*

Who?

Memories, not his own, bloomed in Emrys' perception. A child weighed beneath a boulder and the moment she transformed from living anguish to cold absence. A woman pierced by nine blades and begging for an end. A rainbow pinned to earth by a stone – a butterfly on a skewer – face agonized and astonished.

The images peeled away like bark from a birch tree and blazed to ash.

No, no. No, no, whimpered something.

The troll. The troll was dying, slowly. Given memory and then stripped of it. He would cease when the memories ran out. And he knew it. *No, no. No, no,* he whimpered.

Emrys shivered and fell to earth.

Wind howled around Gefnen, buffeting him, deafening him. The darkness looming above lent no shelter. Its scales gleamed, mirroring vast spaces and endless night. Its colossal claws bruised his ribs.

But Gefnen would have welcomed the hurt, had he noticed it.

The stream of memory flowed on and on. The rictus of his friend's mouth, stunned to discover Gefnen's dagger blooming from his side. His betrothed's shocked face. The beauty of the lake lilies under a springtime sun. His father, proud and tall. His mother, fond and warm. Each image from the past bright and real for one moment, then utterly gone.

One last memory held him, his mother's arms wrapped around his infant self, her lips against his infant brow.

Then that, too, passed.

He was wordless, sightless, bound by shadow and uncomprehending.

Terror filled him, crushing breath.

Where? Where? He felt the question without knowing what he felt.

He was void, surrounded by void, black and empty. Tiny glint of awareness and nothing more.

I am.

Amidst bellowing chaos. *I am.* So feeble in insignificance.

He was falling down the night, abandoned by earth and sky, lost to self and sense.

I am.

That lingered.

I am.

Uneclipsed by clamor, by vertigo, by dark.

I am.

But not enough, never enough.

Without mouth or throat he screamed, soundless. *Help me!*

Then even *I am* blinked. Blinked again. Faltered.

And pain bloomed. Igniting deep inside, it radiated outward, swallowed him. He felt himself reshaped. Terror twisted within, coiled and uncoiled, stretched.

Then was terror no more.

He was anchored in buoyancy and radiance. How could terror become this . . . this joy?

He felt himself molded anew.

No, no. No, no. He resisted.

And noticed the words, the beginnings of thought, with celebration. *I am! Yes!*

Yes.

And *I am* was enough.

Upon that moment of acquiescence, his body curved, writhed.

It should have hurt. Instead it . . . comforted? He stretched his back, felt it lengthen. Stretched his limbs, felt them gain power. Ecstasy burst from his shoulders as wings.

He flew through the night, stars blazing around his passage.

The night welcomed him, bore him up beneath his wings. He dove, spiraled, climbed.

He was vast, a boundless shadow in the sky, an eternity in time.

Yet a greater vastness mirrored his dance through the heavens. Bending low when he bent low, reaching high when he soared high. With infinite grace its wings brushed his.

Eom? Who was this companion?

A soundless gong note rang through him, vibrating deep and joyful.

Then he knew something. And nothing. *I am.*

Merely that.

ℝ℞℟

Láidir funneled round the star-drake, Milis in his wake, caught as surely by its glamor as the troll in its immense talons. Faster, faster, and faster yet. He was urgency, he was fleetness, he was speed itself.

I am the wind. I am the storm. I am the airs above the ground.

He abandoned sight, abandoned sound, abandoned self. Movement clasped him.

And yet Milis touched his heels, flanked his wings, overtook his lead.

He laughed and swept her within himself, opened wildly to her return embrace.

We are breeze. We are stillness. We are airs throughout the heavens.

Milis laughed, and they slowed, pulled along by the rush of the great drake, but calmly sheltered below his limitless belly, no longer circling his bulk in frenzy.

"Look," she said.

The troll was changing. Its dead flesh rippled, darkened, bulged. It lengthened, serpentine and scaly, dark rainbows gleaming in its mailed carapace. Becoming dragon. Becoming drake. Reborn among the stars.

"Geal!"

The rainbow-spirit was there, vivid and defined.

Dusky pinions burst from the shoulders of the star-snake, and Geal enthroned herself between them, riding the newborn beast across the night, glorying in a sky vaster than the midnight skies of earth.

Furled and released by shadow as the star-drake swept its wings, Geal glowed undimmed and sang. Song without words, deeper than the growl of molten lava, more piercing than the neigh of the pegasi, more potent than troll-magic.

Láidir! Milis! She acknowledged them while yet singing. *Join me in my delight!*

Láidir opened again, this time to melody.

᏶ᏝᏣ

I am, I am born anew! I am, I am singing!

Gefnen twisted to see the singers. He could feel them tickling his flanks. He could hear them within his beating heart. But mere nothing met his gaze.

I am, I am born anew! I am, I am singing!

He opened his being to add his music to theirs. And to wonder.

Who am I now?

No human, no troll, no beast of forest or hill, surely.

I am!

Gefnen?

Surely not.

Save for the singers, he flew alone now. In memory, he felt afresh the soundless reverberation from the drake who birthed him. *Eom!* thundered the gong of his essence.

Eomscáthaggol.

He was shadow, he was safety, he was newness born of dark. He was star-drake, he was helpmeet, he was vengeance turned to succor. He was weeping turned to joy. He was being called to being. He was beginning called to end.

I am!

And something called him.

Scáthaggol coiled his long sinuosity midair and reversed, soaring back along his length, seeking something left behind. Not himself, not an enemy, but a wrong left unrighted.

He heeded the call.

❧⃝☙

Tumbling through stars, through wind, through night, Emrys flailed.

There was time to wonder, time to fear, and no time at all.

Would it hurt when he lighted?

Then he was down, returned to flesh, returned to pain.

He opened his eyes.

Tremendous shadow crossed the wide disk of the moon, and then another, flying eastward.

Emrys blinked.

A smaller, nearer darkness occluded moon and stars. "Emrys?"

It was Tor, crouching to kneel beside him, to touch his face. The boy murmured, wordless. Then: "Tallis tried to stop me, but I knew you needed help." He paused and frowned. "Can you talk?"

Emrys wasn't sure himself. Every part of him ached.

He shifted his legs, his arms, sat up abruptly and knocked heads with Tor, who hadn't moved away fast enough. *I'm alive.* Relief rippled through him, emerging as a soft snort. "I'm . . . whole." Were the others? His eyes darted.

Paavo was hoisting himself to his feet. Haral limped to greet Lilli and Tallis, gripping their forearms in the Hamarleeding custom, anxious in concern. "Are you hurt? We could not shield you!"

"You kept him busy," answered the grandmother. "He had no leisure to do us harm."

We survived, mused Emrys. *I* survived. How was it possible?

Then he scrutinized his relief. Did he want to live? Without Neued?

The memory of his spirit-ride through the heavens, aback a stardrake's wake, invaded his thoughts. The troll died. Or had he? What was that second shadow flying east?

Yes, he died. And was reborn. *Am I?*

He sat still, uncertain of his legs, uncertain of everything.

Tallis brought him water, and he drank. Haral sank to rest at her other side, catching his breath after the initial flurry of reunion and respite, favoring bruised ribs.

Lilli fashioned a sling for Paavo's left arm.

The sky lightened, grew gray, then turquoise blue across its dome. A sliver of sun edged above the eastern mountain ridge. The morning mist on the moors flushed golden, and a rainbow arched across the firmament, vivid and sublime.

There are yet gifts, Emrys realized. Beauty to be felt. Deeds worth doing. Friends to protect and enjoy and love.

I *am* alive.

For the very first time since Neued swam to sea, Emrys laughed, belly deep.

And over the moors, the rainbow and the winds danced – ancient deities ever young – while a creature of redemption learned in the east that old wrongs at times do right themselves.

Perilous Chance

She was eleven, and she was hurt.

Her leg lay under her, knee throbbing. Her arm ached, the broken bone within sickening in its pain.

But worst of all, *worst* of all, a vast shadow loomed above her, dark wings spanning distances too great for the grotto enclosing them, razor-sharp talons sparking with the spitting blue fire of a strange power.

"No, please, no," she whispered.

How had it come to this? Her day had started so ordinarily, getting breakfast for herself and her sister, because Mama could not. She cast her thoughts desperately back to the morning.

I'm there. Not here. I'm there.

ഔൣ

That morning, Clary had stood in the front room, turning slowly.

The cloth on the table under the windows hung askew, its corner tassel dragging on the weathered pine floor. The candles had guttered in their sockets, the wicks drowning amidst congealed wax. One, burned only halfway, lay fallen under the gluey drips from the gravy boat.

Clary's fingers crept to her mouth.

Why did this morning after an impromptu party feel so different?

The murmur of conversation last night, rising to her bed chamber, growing louder as the hour latened, had seemed normal. Uncle Maury's deep laugh boomed as always. Aunt Theosia's mandolin sounded as sweet.

But it hadn't been the same.

She stared at the welter of mismatched briar-wicker chairs, one tumbled on its side.

I won't think about that. Or who knocked it over.

But she knew who. *I won't think about it,* more fiercely.

Lyrus was whimpering upstairs in the nursery. She'd ignored him on her way down, hoping her mother would see to the baby. But she wouldn't. She hadn't risen before the children for . . . how long had it been? This was Thyril. Spring.

Had it truly been eight months? Last Sanember in fall?

Clary drew her fingers away from her lips to count, but she didn't really care how long it'd been. Too long. What she wanted to know was: would it end?

Mama hadn't been this bad all that time. But this last month. This last month with Papa being . . . *I won't think about it* . . . and Mama feeling his neglect. This spring had been bad.

Clary bit her lip.

A soft footfall sounded behind her. Then Elspeth crept to her side, slipping a small hand into hers. "Clary?" she whispered. "Lyrus's crying."

Clary knew. She could still hear him, faintly.

"There's some figs in syrup left over," she told her sister. No one had spilled wine in the dish, for a miracle. The bottles were empty, and the wine glasses held only dregs. "You could have them with some bread."

Elspeth shook her head. "Will you get it?"

Clary opened her mouth to say: get it yourself. But she didn't say it. *I'm the eldest. I'm stronger.* She didn't feel strong. Not right now.

The baby's wails were growing louder. She'd better not delay any longer.

"Okay."

Elspeth followed her back through the passage to the kitchen.

"You don't have to come," Clary urged.

Elspeth merely ducked her head and reached for Clary's hand again. Maybe she just wanted company?

The morning sun flooded through the kitchen's eastern windows, casting myriad small curls of shadow from the peeling white paint on the sills. Clary's grip on Elspeth's hand tightened. They navigated around the chopping table toward the vast range, avoiding the inner aisle between the table and the pantry cabinets.

Papa lay there on the bricks, quietened from his earlier snores.

Elspeth said nothing. Clary, nothing also.

The bread box on the counter under the windows proved empty. Clary sagged.

Elspeth darted to the canister at the counter's far end. "There's crisps!" She drew out a handful and handed two to her sister. Clary sighed.

It had been crisps yesterday. And the day before. She'd really hoped that today . . .

A resonant snore erupted from the uneven floor of the inner aisle.

Clary grabbed Elspeth's offering, clutched at her sister's other elbow, and fled.

Back in the front room, the baby's wails from upstairs acquired intermittent yells. Clary cleared a spot at the far end of the table, righted the chair, and settled Elspeth there.

She needs to sit. I'm not doing it because . . . I'm not *tidying. Not –* Clary shook head and grabbed a serving spoon. Her stomach rumbled, awake at last

The crisps were still crisp, not stale. If only she weren't so tired of them. The figs were sweet and chewy. Clary licked her thumb, sticky, then nibbled the last crumbs of cheese lingering on the cheese board. Elspeth raised the empty fig platter to her face, working on its gooey surface with her tongue.

Lyrus was shrieking now.

"Clary?" Their mother's washed-out voice drifted plaintively down the stairs at the other end of the room. "Can you see to the baby?"

"Yes, Mama," she called softy, tipping her chin up toward the ceiling. That *was* what came next. Was why she'd hurried her breakfast. Why did she delay now?

The sound of a groan from the kitchen – Papa – followed by a muffled thump, then the scrape of chair legs, urged her toward the nursery. Elspeth scurried on her heels.

Lyrus had pulled himself to standing by clutching his crib bars. His face, flushed red with crying, dripped tears. He held out his pudgy arms when Clary arrived in the doorway and plopped back on his bottom.

"Kah, kah," he whimpered.

She crossed to the crib, noticing the nursery was just as untidy as the front room below, and hoisted the baby up and over to her hip. Ugh! That nappy was beyond damp; more like sodden.

"Kah, kah." Lyrus buried his running nose in her neck. Mucous smeared wetly on her skin; tangled, blond curls tickled it.

Clary felt her own nose wrinkle, but only said, "Let's get you changed, Lye-lye."

Elspeth helped, chanting: "Ladybird, ladybird, fly away home, your house is aflood, and your children will drown," to distract the baby while Clary did the dirty work. The rhyme had several verses –house afire, children burn; house amire, children choke; and so on – but Lyrus seemed almost relieved to have his soiled nappy removed and didn't really require distraction.

"I could have done it," murmured Elspeth, rolling the dirty nappy into a closed ball and placing it in the overfull pail. Clary pulled a fresh baby dress from the cupboard with one hand, keeping the other firmly on Lyrus' belly. He was kicking energetically and demanding, "Nu nu! Nu nu!"

"It was my turn," insisted Elspeth.

Clary knew it. Why hadn't she let her younger sister see to Lyrus?

Half a year ago, she'd made a mess of nappy changing. But half a year ago, so had Clary. Now they were both neat and fast. They'd had to become so, when Mama just . . . stopped. Stopped cleaning, stopped cooking, stopped getting out of bed, stopped . . . caring? Not that she'd ever been very domestic. But some dusting and sweeping had happened. And she'd never neglected meals or preserve-making or Lyrus . . . or her daughters.

Clary dragged the baby dress – stained, but clean – over Lyrus' head, buttoned up the long back opening, and abandoned the struggle to jam his fat little feet into his shoes. At least his feet *were* fat.

I'm doing a good job. The way Mama would have wanted me to before . . . before.

Mama's room smelled of stale bed linens and dust. The drapes, dragged sloppily across the windows, created shafts of sunlight glaring through gloom. The shadows under the bed canopy shrouded Mama's stringy, unwashed hair and her creased pillowcase. When presented with her hungry infant, she shook her head and sighed wearily.

"I was awake with him all night. I can't."

Somehow, Clary didn't think so, but she gentled the protest creeping toward voice. Mama's cheeks *were* pale, her eyelids dark with fatigue. If she'd slept, it hadn't rested her.

"He needs to eat, Mama."

"I know." That note of tired impatience had once been a rarity. "Give him some goat's milk."

Clary looked at Elspeth.

Elspeth looked at Clary.

Papa was awake, and neither of them wanted to encounter him.

"Go on, then." Mama's sharp tone used to be reserved for evening bickering.

"Nu nu!" insisted Lyrus, but he clung to Clary. Clary hoisted him higher on her hip. Papa wouldn't be in the scullery where the milk cans stood. She might slip by the kitchen door unnoticed. If only Lyrus could keep quiet.

The baby chanted – nu-nu-nu-nu – all the way down the stairs.

"Ssh!" Clary whispered fiercely. "Ssh!"

Papa had opened the spigot to the cistern and was dunking his head in the sink. He didn't notice his children sneaking past the kitchen doorway. The running water gushed loudly, much louder than Lyrus.

In the scullery, Elspeth twisted the lid off the first milk canister: empty. The second held a thin skimming of liquid across its bottom.

She turned dismayed eyes to her sister. "Oh, no! What'll we do?"

"Give it to him." The hard, grim sound to her own voice dismayed Clary more than the inadequate milk supply.

Collected from the wide canister into the narrow glass of a baby bottle, the milk made a better showing: it rose fully halfway toward the rubber nipple. Lyrus grabbed for the bottle eagerly, snatching it from Elspeth's hands. He'd likely finish in six gulping sucks. Clary turned toward the scullery door as grimly as she'd uttered her instruction to her little sister.

Their mother was not happy to see all three children back at her bedside.

"Can't you manage for five minutes without me?" she demanded. "Go ask your father, if you need something, and let me sleep."

Clary imagined herself simply dumping Lyrus down on the mattress and leaving. But the baby needed someone, if Mama refused him.

"He's still hungry," she stated.

Mama looked disconcerted. "He can't be."

"Aunt Mirren didn't bring the milk last night," Clary reminded her. "It's Lunday, not Wandy."

Mama sighed, and began opening the buttons of her nightgown. Lyrus went to her gladly. Over his curly head, Mama's face relaxed. She might not want to nurse her baby, but it did calm her. Her voice was kinder when she asked, "What are your plans for the morning, girls?"

"The cistern's full from all the spring rain." No working the pump till summer, likely. "Cousin Letty brought three baskets of clean clothes. Uncle Sorrelaude promised us a ham this evening. I opened a block of brunost cheese yesterday." Clary cataloged the household needs. "I thought I'd set Elspeth some spelling problems while I read history, but . . ." she faltered, then finished, "there's no bread."

Mama was nodding. "I'll bake bread later. There's a sponge ready in the pantry. But do your lessons after noon. The chervil conserve soured." Her mouth quirked. Something was wrong with the plants in their garden patch. "I want you to get me wild cabbage leaves from the old quarry instead."

Clary dipped her chin without protest and turned to go.

"No, stay." Did Mama sound apologetic? "I promised Dame Wicklander in the village . . ." Her voice trailed off.

"What did you promise?" Elspeth's voice reflected her eagerness for the errand. She liked Dame Wicklander.

Mama made a small noise of discontent. "That I'd bring her some of last year's bramble jelly. The baby dresses she's sewing for Lyrus are ready. But . . . you've missed too many lesson days already." Mama's regret became decision. "It can wait till tomorrow. I'll send word." Then she muttered, "I wish I could go myself."

Her mother's unexpected concern for her daughters melted Clary's resistance. And it would be a treat for Elspeth. "We'll go, Mama. There'll be time in the early evening for spelling and history."

Mama took some persuading, but the girls got their way and headed downstairs.

The garden trugs were stored under the counter in the kitchen, but Papa was gone. Was he even in the house? Clary wondered.

"Let's take some brunost cheese," Elspeth begged. "I didn't know we had any. And I'll get hungry before we come back."

Clary nodded. "And some dried bramble berries."

"Canteens?" added Elspeth.

"There's a spring."

"Oh. I forgot."

It didn't take long to assemble what they needed, plus the jelly jars for Dame Wicklander. Clary stepped out onto the kitchen stoop. The sunshine lay warm on her cheeks and forearms, but the chill of the old stone underfoot crept up through her boot soles. "We don't need our pelisses," she decided. "It will only get warmer, and the air lies still in the quarry."

They passed the herb garden and the berry patch on their way. None of the plants were leafing out properly, and the bramble canes featured an unnatural gray tinge to their brown bark skins. Clary shook her head. She had enough to worry about without that.

"What if Papa's at the quarry?" Elspeth voiced Clary's fear.

"He won't be. It's too early." Except today he was up earlier than normal.

"He goes there every day," persisted Elspeth. "To see that lady, I think. She's really pretty, isn't she?"

The woman spotted by the girls almost a month ago was more than pretty. Clary's memory flashed on the lovely line of her jaw, the fire in her dark eyes, her masses of dark curling hair. Who was she? They'd never seen her before, but she came every day to the quarry also.

Clary pushed down the resentment stirring inside her. Wild cabbage for Mama. Focus on that. If she got angry, then she'd have to notice why she was angry. And if she noticed why . . . everything would fall apart. *I'll just do the next thing.*

"If Papa's there, we'll hide," she told her sister.

"But how will we gather Mama's cabbage, if we're hiding?"

Clary repressed irritation. "We've always managed up to now." Papa *went* to the quarry. She knew he did. But they'd never actually met him there. "It'll be alright."

Elspeth brightened. "Maybe the lady will greet us. Maybe she's nice. Maybe she'll help Mama. She must live closer than Aunt Mirren and Aunt Theosia."

Clary shivered. "No. I think . . . we'd better hide from her also. If she's there."

They'd crouched down below the bramble stems the first time they saw her. The other times, she'd been leaving as they arrived, or they'd been leaving as she arrived. Had she even glimpsed them? Clary didn't think so. Too far.

Why don't I want her to see us?

Could she be a troll? Surely not. Trolls were old and ugly. And wicked.

But if she were a troll, she'd be dangerous. Trolls were patterners who got greedy and grabbed too much power in their magic patterning. It gave them troll-disease and made them crazy. If the stranger were a troll, maybe she'd ensorcelled Papa. Maybe that was why he roamed the bluffs instead of working in his studio on the marble horses for the fountain commissioned by the Morofane for the great square in the capital.

But she's beautiful. She can't be a troll.

₨₧

In the abandoned quarry, it was late morning. Jennifry let her trug fall and stood as upright as she could get, rubbing the small of her back.

Oof, but bending hurt.

She surveyed her gatherings. A handful of wild asparagus, thin and new-sprouted. The last good leaves of winter's rampion. A salad's worth of fresh borage. And nettles, the leaves barely unfurled and soft.

That's enough.

She could return home, start blanching the nettles, preserving the rampion and borage conserve.

But the sun felt good on her cheeks. She lifted her face to the sky and closed her eyes. Warmth soaked into her brow, her throat, her shoulders. *Mmm.* Perhaps she could spare a few moments, linger longer in the sunshine, so grateful as the days grew longer.

But not visit the *orbis* – the *orbis* and its *energea*. That was better than sun, easing the deep ache in her bones and calming her thoughts. But something about it scared her. Could something that felt so good be bad?

She bent to lift her trug full of spring greens.

The laughter of little girls – familiar little girls – met her ears when she straightened.

They were gleaning above her, choosing leaves from the brink of the cliffs and joking.

"Clary, Clary, look! It's like green rabbit ears," trilled the younger one, flaxen curls jouncing under her mop cap.

"Like a doe with three kits," agreed her older sister, nodding and smiling.

Jennifry edged toward the cleft in the limestone behind her. She didn't want them to spot her.

She'd seen the girls often, of late, but always from concealment. Her stooped posture, large ears, and sagging eyelids would scare them. They'd think her a troll. And they'd be right about that; but wrong about the danger. She suffered troll-disease, but she'd never hurt them.

I won't go inside, all the way to the grotto. I'll just hide under that lip of rock at the entrance.

The brambles screening the crack scraped her cheek, drawing three drops of blood.

Jennifry sank to her knees and plucked a leaf of the comfrey growing there. Its sap would ease the scratch.

She could no longer see the girls – and doubted they could see her – but their voices rang clear.

"Not so near the edge, Elspeth," reprimanded the elder. "The rock gets crumbly, and the wild cabbage doesn't grow there anyway."

"Does too!" insisted Elspeth. "Look at that one."

"That's plantain," corrected her sister.

Comfrey pressed to her cheek, Jennifry felt the skin stretching as she smiled, her lips curving in memory.

We were about their age – maybe a year or two older – when we discovered the orbis. Kasharan was turned thirteen. I, almost twelve.

She pressed the herb leaf harder. Being eleven was a good memory. Finding the *orbis* in the grotto . . . more ambiguous. It was beautiful, the curving surface of it gleaming in swirls of cream and ivory, looming head height like the trap to their old ice-house.

Kasharan had stepped close to it, and her eyes lit with excitement. Her hand stretched as though she might grab the opalescent marvel – despite its massive size – and take it for all her own, but she started when her fingertips touched down.

"Oh!"

"Kasharan, what is it?" Jennifry had cried, anxious even then, before she knew what it was. Before she knew how grievously her sister could choose.

"It's good," Kasharan murmured, "really good." And closed her eyes.

I wanted to leave. It was too beautiful, too alluring. If only I had.

Instead she'd stood frozen, scared by the expression on her sister's face, but curious too, tempted.

"Mmm," breathed Kasharan. "Mmm."

And Jennifry stepped toward her, not away.

Closer, then closer still.

The *orbis* was slightly warm, and she felt peaceful. Her sister reached out one hand, circled Jennifry's wrist, and touched her palm to the lambent curve.

"Oh!" she cried, just like her sister.

She was peaceful no more, but she didn't pull away. This was dazzling, fizzy, fun. She was flying like a pegasus, soaring like a phoenix, climbing and diving like a star-drake. All while standing perfectly still. It *was* good, very good. And yet . . .

She wanted to pull away. And she didn't.

They'd returned home late in the gloaming and been scolded for it.

But Kasharan visited the *orbis* the next day and the next, dragging Jennifry with her, ignoring Jennifry's protests – *there's something wrong, something wrong* – and acting on Jennifry's unspoken consent: *yes*.

Was the *orbis* a troll's enchantment, that they made pilgrimage to it every morning for a sevenday?

The wild mix of elation and terror kept Jennifry silent. And compliant.

I should tell someone. I should do something. I should. But she'd said nothing, done nothing.

They went every day, then twice a day: straightaway at dawn, and once before bed.

"Jennifry, is it changing?" probed Kasharan. "I think it's different."

Jennifry hadn't thought so. It still felt good – very good. She didn't mind the startling fizziness so much anymore. Or the sudden internal swoops. And the warmth was just good. So good. Or had it gotten less fizzy? Less swoopy?

"I think it's changing," insisted Kasharan. "I don't want it to change."

That noon, Kasharan went to the miniature hot spring in the cleft, the nook where the *orbis* rested, to check on it.

"It's not as strong," she reported, worried. "Jennifry, what'll I do?"

Jennifry didn't know that answer, but she knew her sense of a problem growing larger was right.

Kasharan tried to drag her sister to the *orbis* the next noon, but Jennifry resisted. "It's not changing. We don't need to check it," she protested.

This time she didn't give in. There *was* something wrong, and even if she wouldn't tattle, neither would she concede.

But Kasharan checked. She got up from her bed in the wee hours of that night to visit their find.

Then at dawn, after breakfast, at noon, before supper, in the gloaming, by starlight.

Jennifry lost count of her sister's trips to the cleft in the old quarry.

And she covered for her. Gathering Kasharan's strewn clothes to the laundry basket. Sewing her sampler on the sly. Practicing her pieces on the harpsichord when Mama met with their housekeeper or cook – anything that drew her from the drawing room, so she didn't realize it was Jennifry playing Kasharan's music.

Kasharan showed no gratitude. "You should come with me," she scolded. "Help me save it!"

Jennifry winced.

"There's nothing wrong with the *orbis*, but there's something wrong with *you*," she dared.

Kasharan frowned, opened her lips to scold some more, then didn't. "Really?"

Jennifry nodded. "'Shara" – how to say it? she'd not said it to herself; just felt it – "you don't skip rope or roll hoops or read or ride Greylegs or . . . or . . . anything." How could she make Kasharan see what she saw? That all her sister's usual pursuits had just . . . stopped.

Kasharan was listening, a puzzled look on her face.

"You go to it too often!" Jennifry burst out.

"If I go less, will you come?"

Jennifry hesitated.

"If I go just . . . just three times, will you come?"

It had to be better, if she went less. Didn't it?

"*Please*, Jenny."

Jennifry sighed. Then acceded: "Alright."

The *orbis* seemed just as it had always been: glimmering softly amidst its mineral spring bath, soothingly warm, and thrillingly fizzy and swoopy. Touching it felt like coming home, and that scared Jennifry all over again.

"'Shara, I think three times is too many. Two times might be. Even *one*."

"Don't you dare go back on your promise, Jennifry nin Calcinides."

She hadn't promised; Kasharan had.

And Kasharan didn't stick by her promise.

They went four times that first day, then six, then nine. Jennifry didn't bother protesting. She'd lost. Not only to her sister, but to the *orbis*. Its halo of wonder proved too strong. *I need it now. Like Kasharan.*

Kasharan began formulating plans to "save" it using the patterning *energea* she was learning from Aunt Sophy. "I did sleep-and-heal yesterday, Jenny! I could heal the *orbis*! Keep it strong!"

Jennifry made different plans. In secret. She couldn't stop her sister. She couldn't stop *herself*. But she might just stop the *orbis*. I'm going to try, she vowed.

A sevenday later, they stood ankle-deep in the spring.

"I'll start first," instructed Kasharan.

Jennifry nodded. They'd been over the sequence a dozen times.

"Then you join me." Kasharan grabbed Jennifry's left hand. "You've been practicing, right? You remember what to do."

Jennifry nodded again. She'd been practicing sleep-and-heal, yes. She'd also been practicing something else. Something darker. Harder. Something listed in the back pages of Aunt Sophy's gramarye.

Kasharan closed her eyes, and Jennifry matched her breath to her sister's. Slowly in, slowly out. Soft and easy and free.

She opened her mind's eye. Silver filigree blinked into being, tracing the *energea* of her sister's arcs and radices, tracing her own: from sole to root, through belly and plexus and heart, out via throat and brow and crown and palm. *Ahh*. This was pattern making.

Cool blue trickled from Kasharan's fingers, flowing gently round the *orbis*, laving its surface with peace.

Be healed, be whole, be well.

"Now," whispered Kasharan. "Now."

Jennifry launched . . . her attack.

It was not gentle, was not blue, was not peaceful.

Black fire erupted from her palms, blasting Kasharan's healing gift aside, engulfing the *orbis* in thunderous violence.

Jennifry's silver lattice of radix-and-arc flashed searing gold, and she heard herself shrieking.

"Glory be horror, warmth grow chill, never thrill my spirit, bring splendor to *stop!*"

"Stop!" Kasharan's cry topped hers, and her sister's trickle of *energea* raged into torrent: fierce blue, fierce flood, fierce intent.

"No!" Kasharan's lattice flared gold, flared orange, glaring hot and parlous and corrosive. Her cataract of azure turned cobalt, turned black, turned thunderous and vile as Jennifry's own.

This was not pattern making.

This was *incantatio* – bringer of troll-disease, herald of loss – the lurking danger awaiting a patterner who reached in power and greed.

Kasharan's blue-black tangled with Jennifry's ebon-black, sparking, spitting, backing up the orange conduits of the girls' arcs, drowning their radices in dark-burning fire.

The blazing inferno of eclipse intensified.

Winked out.

Jennifry found herself sitting waist-deep in water, tangled with her sprawled sister, who wept wrackingly.

ೞ)ೞ

*C*radled within the *orbis* . . . a being awoke.

I am here.

He spun in liquid warmth, kicked out, and flipped over. He felt dizzy and happy. Here was nice, here was exciting, here was *here!*

A murmur sounded in the darkness, sweet and low.

Be thou whole, be thou one, be thou Ayr.

He was whole.

He was here.

He was *Ayr*.

Time passed in his warm lagoon, an interval of bliss and experiment. He reached and waved. He bent and swam. He swooped.

Be thou mine, be thou thine, be thou one.

I am thine.

I am mine.

I am *Ayr*.

Love lapped him and enfolded him. *Be thou strong, be thou winged, be thou fierce.*

I am strong. I am fierce. I am *Ayr*!

Ayr is winged, Ayr is crowned, Ayr is might.

I am flight, I am might, I am *Ayr*!

His mother's song swelled once more, celebrating him, then hushed and ceased.

She was gone!

She was gone, and he was ready.

I am here!

He stretched, he swooped, he strengthened. He grew. And grew.

Then another murmur.

Be healed, be whole, be well.

Mother? No, this voice sounded lighter, higher, and younger. Who?

Be healed, be whole, be well. Like Mother, she was *she*. Like Mother, she meant well, but her delight felt fizzier. She was . . . fledgling.

Sister! I am here!

They could fly together, swoop together, rule together!

He awaited her response. It came brutally: black, cold, and stinging. He choked. He flailed. He drowned.

No!

Stygian ice slammed him. He stilled. *Will I cease before I start?*

Another cold blow, so cold it burned. Burned and started a flame in his heart.

I am flight, I am might, I am Ayr! He was strong, he was mythic, he was stunning. *Sister-that-was, you shall not destroy me.*

He reached a different way, not with a limb, but with his awareness.

Where?

Where?

There!

There was power, there was force, there was *counter*.

He struck.

Silver fire erupted from his core, bursting outward, engulfing all, slapping aside the black cataract that devoured him.

Peace bloomed.

Ayr sighed. He was safe.

ℰↃ℃ℬ

*A*bove the quarry, Clary and Elspeth were drawing nearer along the cliff top. Jennifry could hear them, their innocent voices light on the sunlit air.

Below, within the shadowy cleft, Jennifry tensed and dropped the comfrey leaf. Once, she'd been young like they were. Now . . . it was well the rust-stained, creamy rock of the passage hid her.

She looked out through the sharp arch of its opening and across the quarry's sloping floor. Tough greens and messy brambles – edged by the sun's brightness – fountained from cracks between slabs of white limestone. The wildness drew her. But not so strongly as what she knew lay behind her in the grotto.

I'd better move, if I don't want them to see me when I leave.

She heaved to her feet. *Do they know they have a great aunt who's a troll?* She doubted it.

The Roanmothes hid madness in their lineage; likely the current rofane of the Calcinides hid the incantatrices in *his* descent. The old rofane – her father – had reached for secrecy fast enough. His discovery that his child harbored troll-disease still formed a bitter memory.

She and Kasharan had stumbled home in the dusk, dripping and disoriented, unaware of the fell change in the *energea* of their bodies.

Rofane Parthen and his wife were hosting a gala and never missed their daughters, who got themselves to bed unseen.

The morning revealed the truth. To them, if not to their mother and father.

Jennifry woke to Kasharan's shriek as she encountered her reflection in the dressing table mirror.

"What is it? What is it?" she'd gasped, tumbling from her curtained bedstead.

Her sister could not answer, but she didn't need to.

Two trolls stared out at them from the mirror's surface. Young ones, with firm rosy skin and bright eyes, but trolls.

Kasharan buried her face in her hands, while Jennifry stared.

Crow's feet framed those youthful eyes. That young nose took the shape of a crooked thumb. And plump handles of flesh curved the jawline on either side of that stubborn chin.

Hers.

Her eyes, her nose, her chin.

"Oh, no. Oh, no. Oh, no," she whispered.

Kasharan saved them.

Aunt Sophy's patterning lessons had reached *chimerae* and illusions, and Kasharan put her learning to work that dawn. When the sisters emerged from their bedchamber, all evidence of trollism lay hidden by a magical glamor, and Kasharan's deceptive skills grew strong with persistent use.

Jennifry's exposure came later.

Footfalls above her current hiding place pulled her back to the present.

Clary and Elspeth were too close for her to start home now without being seen. And she bore considerable risk by remaining barely under the cleft's entrance arch.

I'll take just a few steps inside, not more. Not enough to see, not far enough to touch – her thoughts veered away from her temptation.

This is far enough.

ཨོༀༀ

Within the dark warmth of the *orbis*, Ayr started from sleep.

Was he safe? Was it over?

He remembered a cold and cruel attack from a fledgling he'd called friend, and his own silver repulse.

What then? Had he died?

He stretched a tentative limb. Warmth and giving fluid swirled along his feathers.

I am live.

Relief flooded him, but with worry on its heels. What came next? It might not be nice.

His first awareness of *being* had been nice. His mother's song had been nice. He'd thought all his sensations would be nice. But they hadn't.

Who had attacked him? And why?

He stretched another limb, and another.

Only warmth and more warmth and the liquid of his lagoon met his questing.

I am safe, he decided.

With safety came the impulse to move. He couldn't be still, but uncertainty curbed his exuberance.

I am hidden, I am shielded

Was he?

I am safe, he repeated, trying to shake his apprehension.

He worked his fore claws, kicked out with his hind paws, and mantled his wings. No hurt met his testing. *I am well.*

"Be thou whole, be thou well, be thou strong," spoke his memories. "Be thou puissant, be thou mighty, be thou strong."

I am strong.

And he was.

His limbs claimed vigor, and his confidence grew. *I am strong, I am well, I am Ayr!*

I am mighty.

I am fierce.

I am Ayr!

His dives grew daring; his swoops, more precipitate; and his somersaults, ebullient. Yet his joy carried fierceness in its wake. He'd recovered his courage, but not his innocence. Future friends would need to prove themselves.

❧⌘ଔ

Kasharan's magical glamor took on a life of its own. Not content with merely hiding the sisters' troll-disease, she made them beautiful.

Jennifry's flaxen curls acquired a silvery brightness, and her eyes deepened to the intense blue of the Sanember sky. The waif-like charm of her childhood became delicate loveliness as she approached womanhood. Kasharan's allure was bolder: brilliant black eyes, shining raven tresses, and a jawline where grace married strength.

Their suitors multiplied.

In time, Kasharan accepted one.

The son of Rofane Brusscente was clever, witty, and kind. If only he'd lived nearby, all could have been well.

When the carriage bearing Kasharan and her bridegroom to the Rivenpeaks crossed out of Ransea, her patterned glamor fell from Jennifry's troll-diseased body. She was short, not tall; dumpy, not slim; faded, not vibrant.

Her mother, the Rofanish, screamed.

The Rofane thundered: "What have you done to my daughter?" mistaking Jenny for a sudden-come stranger, and an enemy.

"Papa . . . it's me. Your Jenny. I'm . . . ill."

He'd understood then, all too quickly, and hustled her out of the ballroom where their guests waltzed and celebrated Kasharan's newly concluded nuptials.

In the deserted nursery – unoccupied by the handmaidens populating her bedchamber – he berated her. "How dare you steal power with *incantatio*! Were you jealous of her? Your sister? With her skill at patterning and her handsome husband?"

Jennifry shrank from him.

How could he think that? It was true she'd little gift for patterning, alas.

That first outpouring of illicit magic had been more illicit than she'd known: a perilous *incantatio* from the first flow of *energea* through her radices. And Aunt Sophy had never coaxed more than a trickle of the safe patterning from her since then. Especially because Jennifry had that dreadful black corrosive fire to conceal.

But she boasted as many suitors as her sister, and more offers of marriage. She'd dared accept none of them, given the hard truth of her disease. And her dependence on Kasharan's glamor.

Kasharan's choice to deceive her beloved had repulsed Jennifry. *How could she?* I couldn't bear doing that to . . . her thoughts shied away from his name.

With Jennifry's help, Kasharan had made many attempts to anchor her glamor in an item she could leave behind to protect her little sister. They'd tried Jenny's shoes, her prayer book, and even her own hair. Only the mirror in which they'd first witnessed their disease could hold the enchantment, and that apparently not in permanence.

The Rofane allowed Jennifry to pack her favorite gowns, her favorite books, and the trinkets from her dressing table. Its mirror still reflected her as beautiful, although the glamor clung only to its surface and no longer around her person.

A two-wheeled hand cart piled with more practical necessities awaited her behind the carriage house. Her father's farewell was brusque and instructional: "Follow the path to old Tilde's hut. It's been cleaned for old Nurse, but I'll give her the cottage by the crossroads instead. I'll send Josef to you with more food in a sevenday."

Her mother neither bade her farewell nor witnessed her departure.

❧⁊ℭ⅌

Darkness. Warmth. Safety.

The *orbis* provided all these.

Ayr's talons grew razor sharp, and his hind paws sported mighty claws.

But when the time came to shred the curving boundary of his fledgling world and emerge into a larger one, he could not. The shell resisted all his strength, all his passion, all his desire to be free. Slash of talon and buffet of paw availed nothing.

It would not crack.

Could not.

His wings outgrew the birth space first, curling down along the sphere, then under his legs and up the opposite arc. Within the carapace of his wings, his limbs lengthened and his torso gained bulk. Rigid limits cramped him, compressed him. The yolk sac supplying him with nourishment ran out. He grew hungry. Starving.

The attack in his infancy had become dim memory, but he hadn't forgotten it.

I survived its violence, but I may not survive this: its aftermath.

He felt certain his imprisonment possessed unnatural origins.

He delved deeper in memory, past the singing of his enemy into the songs of his mother, and then beyond those, beyond even the first simple awareness of *I am*. There in the darkness of non-being lay a portal into the heritage normally accessed after wings greeted air. He'd touched it unconsciously as a baby. Now he would do more than touch: he would claim it as his own.

He . . . *reached*. And surrounded and held.

This is mine.

Ribbons of silver sparkles streamed up his talons through his heart and into his great hooked beak. Jets of dazzling sapphire spurted into his hind claws and up his legs, through loins and belly and plexus.

This is *mine!*

He roared. He struck.

The shell of his prison did not break, but neither did it rebound the *energea* as it had his physical blows. His power passed out through the barrier, out through a passage, and sank deep into . . . richness, bounty, *sustenance*.

Here was food, here was healing, here was *life*.

He drew it into him to satiate his starvation, to soothe his aching limbs, to repair the damage of the old wrong dealt him by his enemy.

Some of the richness felt too new, too fresh. He learned to let it be.

Some of it felt old and fragile. He let that alone also.

And some of it was diseased. He avoided it.

But much more was scrumptious and sustaining. He fed.

His compression became density. *One day, I will emerge, and when I do my foe will know it.*

He consumed the life surrounding him, and the sapphire and silver *energea* of his heritage flowed all through his being. He lay still, poised for the moment when his density would overcome all. Poised in darkness, poised in ferocity, poised in crystallized wrath.

A whisper touched his hearing.

Be healed, be whole, be well.

His enemy!

But his density merely approached the needed threshold. He had not crossed over.

He hissed.

Very well. He would absorb this too. All bounty would be his. All *energea* would be his. All enmity would be his. He would be density upon density upon density.

He listened.

And learned it could not be his enemy. Sick, old, and frail, she was familiar, but not the same. And she meant him well. Or did she? He'd been mistaken before.

He listened.

Be healed, be whole, be well.

She visited him irregularly, but frequently, and always with a gift of *energea*.

She was friend, not foe.

ಬಂಙ

Jennifry took two more steps along the rocky passage, and then another. Gentle ripples of light reflected by water moved over the textured limestone walls, brightening as she shuffled forward.

Did she wade through a stream, pulled by its current? No, the passage remained dry, as always. 'Twas her memories that drew her reluctant feet onward. Memory and longing, both stronger than willpower.

An eggy, mineral odor arrived on moisture-laden air.

She passed around the bend and stopped.

There it lay, bathed in warm aqua waters. Wreathed in steam. Vast and round and creamy white, whorled by cinnamon traceries. Casting a warm glow on the glistening limestone walls around it.

She stood just out of range for a touch, but mere proximity felt good.

Not as good as those early days, when the *orbis* was exciting, as well as comforting. But it soothed her aching bones and smoothed her worried thoughts.

Despite the edgy tautness underlying its peaceful warmth. *That* was more recently different. What did its tension mean?

She'd avoided the *orbis* for years after Kasharan departed Ransea, blaming it for her predicament.

Tilde's cottage was lonely and out-of-the-way.

Josef brought provisions and anything else she needed, but didn't stay to talk. Her father never came at all in those first few months and then sank to his deathbed before his rage could soften. Her mother risked the Rofane's displeasure with sneaking visits on the sly. These grew easier and more frequent after he died, then ceased altogether when she remarried and changed residences to live with her new husband.

Jennifry had a lot of time in which to think. And think she did, although not to good effect for some time.

She obsessed about her sister, torn between worry and resentment. She raged at her father: why had he condemned her, not helped her? She missed her mother – her namesake – even though the Rofanish Jennifry nish Calcinades had never been a terribly motherly sort. She wondered what explanation had been given to her brother, Arteme, away in the court of the Morofane.

Eventually her brooding grew as boring as it was uncomfortable.

Josef brought her an unrequested book on herb lore, and she read it. Learning about the plants in the weedy garden surrounding the cottage proved interesting, and she began taming the weeds. (Although some of them had unexpected uses – both culinary and medicinal.)

When she finished *Flora of Ransea*, she asked Josef to bring more like it.

She discovered she liked wild gleaning as well as domestic gardening, and conserving her harvest even more. She began sending samples of her thistle jelly or nettle ferment back with Josef when he brought her word of a sick child or injured granny. She wondered what he told the recipients of her gifts, but didn't ask.

As her knowledge deepened, the books she wanted grew more esoteric. Volumes of philosophy and treatises on the marriage of mind and body hinted at other dimensions to physical healing. And reminded her of past choices. She'd let go of her sister's wrong, her father's, even her mother's. (How could a mother abandon her child? Even a child grown to womanhood and defiled by troll-disease?) But what about her own wrongs?

I stayed silent, when I should have spoken.

I said yes, when I should have said no.

And I lashed out, once all power to say no was gone.

It was that last deed that troubled her now.

She'd been a child for all three mistakes, but that didn't lessen their dire results. Her silence had led to her that "yes," which led to her violent action. The first two wrongs were truly wrong only in that they led to the last. But that last . . . her sister was a troll because of it.

(So was she, herself. Did she owe herself amends?)

And what of the *orbis*? Surely it was something live?

A dragon's egg? Or did pegasi hatch? She didn't know.

But if it were live, it must have taken some hurt.

She wished she could go back now and do things differently. But she couldn't. If she owed herself atonement, she didn't know how to make it. And her sister had forged her own solution. But the *orbis* . . . might await her succor.

I owe it, she decided. And visited its womb-cleft.

It seemed unharmed. But her experience of its aura *was* different: calmer, less frenetic. Was the change in her? Or in it? Was it the effect of time passing? Or the lingering aftermath of her *incantatio*? *It doesn't matter. I choose to give.*

Be healed, be whole, be well.

She'd visited it ever since, feeding it the small *energea* she'd learned under Aunt Sophy, guarding against the dangerous troll-magic that had overtaken her when she outstretched her patterning limits.

Be healed, be whole, be well.

For years she'd wished it well and given it healing. Could that make up for her attack?

I don't think so, but this isn't about righting wrongs. Some wrongs couldn't be fixed. This was about doing the right thing now. *I can't change the past. I can only act now.*

So she'd acted, as best she knew how.

The energy of the *orbis* had changed again last autumn, becoming imbued with a sense of fateful *waiting.* Readiness.

For what did it wait?

And now it was different again: tense, expectant, fierce.

Crack!

Jennifry stiffened. *Holy Teyo!*

More startling than the sound was the abrupt end of the warm peacefulness normal to this spot. She felt desperate, urgent, and hungry. Or, rather, she felt the desperation and urgency and hunger radiating from the *egg.*

It *was* an egg, she realized, an egg on the verge of hatching, with a hatchling poised to gobble the nearest morsel of warmblooded food available.

She fled.

ℼℽ⅃

How far away was far enough? How far away was safe? The rock walls of the twisting passage streamed by, then the shadow of the entrance arch, and Jennifry passed into sunlight.

A scream split the air.

Jennifry spun in time to see the littlest girl pitch over the brink of the cliff, dragging her sister with her when Clary refused to let go her frantic grab for Elspeth's arm.

Jennifry jerked herself back toward them – toward the bluff – fast enough to wrench her wrist when her hand tangled in Elspeth's petticoats.

Not fast enough to break the girls' tumbling fall.

The muffled thud of slight bodies on packed earth seemed almost innocuous.

The faint crack of bone – as the elder sister, slightly above the younger in their descent, landed – sounded equally meager.

How could misfortune arrive with so little fanfare? Jennifry's thoughts touched her own past disaster, more flashy, but similarly opaque upon arrival in its true meaning.

The girls' greenish white faces, shocked and afraid, told a realer truth.

Clary reared to her knees, arms rising before her face, prepared to defend her sister even now, breathless from her plummet.

☙❧

One moment they stood amidst thin sunlight, cool airs stirring about them while they picked wild greens at the edge of the quarry cliff. The next: a glimpse of the troll's slumped face and startled glance, Clary's wild grab for her sister's arm, the slide of gravel and dust beneath their shoe soles, and the abrupt plunge into the quarry.

Clary surged to her feet, hands rising to block . . . whatever came, the left arm throbbing with a sickening ache.

You won't hurt my sister. I'll hurt you first.

The troll stopped, drooping eyes . . . appalled? How could it be appalled? *It* was the appalling one.

"Don't you dare!" gasped Clary.

The troll shook its – her? it *was* wearing a dress – head.

"Please . . . I think your arm is broken." The voice, unexpectedly clear and pleasant, held pleading in its tones. "Let me help you."

Clary felt her own eyes widening. This was not how a troll should behave. Trolls were wicked and greedy. They helped no one save themselves. Everyone knew that. Was this some trick? She peered around her raised forearms.

Wrinkles framed the troll's eyes, folds of flesh rumpled its cheeks and neck, globules of fat hung from either side of its jaw. It was a troll, no question, for all that its skin flushed rosier than the pictures in Aunt Genevieve's catechism.

"Why?" Clary asked.

"And I think your sister's leg is broken. Please." The troll cradled its own arm. Had it – she – tried to soften their landing? "I won't harm you. I just want to help."

She didn't approach, waiting on Clary's permission.

Clary could hear Elspeth moaning behind her.

"What will you do?"

The troll's face softened. "I can't do much right away. I need the splints and bandages from my cottage, but I have some little skill with minor patterning. A trickle of healing *energea* right now will ease the pain and lessen the damage."

Clary stared. "Trolls don't use *energea*. You're an incantatrice, not a patterner," she accused.

The troll shook her head. "Only once, only by accident."

Clary considered.

Elspeth whimpered.

Clary nodded.

The troll wasted no time, kneeling, tracing Elspeth's pattern of radices and arcs, then closing her eyes and . . . concentrating.

Elspeth sighed and spoke in a thready tone, "Oh, Clary, it's better. Let her do your arm."

Clary did let her, and it did help. But her suspicion stayed strong.

"Why are you nice? Why are you helping us? Who *are* you?"

The troll got her knees under her, preparing to rise. "Let me go get my medicines and bandaging. You could walk home without further hurt to your arm, but Elspeth shouldn't be moved until her leg is splinted."

Clary's suspicion hardened. "How do you know Elspeth's name?"

"I heard you talking." The troll's reply was mild.

Clary could tell she was telling the truth. She could also tell there was more to it than that. Her lips compressed and her chin jutted, but her challenge remained unspoken.

The troll sighed. "I'm Jennifry nin Calcinides."

"You're not my great gran!" exclaimed Clary. "She died before I was born!"

This time the troll stayed silent.

"Oh, nin. Not nish." Clary blushed. Nish meant 'wife of the rofane.' Nin meant 'child of.' "Mama's aunt? Great gran's daughter?"

Jennifry nodded. "Will you stay here? Wait for me?"

"I never knew Great Uncle Arteme had a sister," Clary marveled.

Jennifry's smile was sad. "Don't move, alright? Especially don't move Elspeth. Or let her move herself." She hesitated, then continued, "It will take me at least half a glass to walk to my cottage and back. It will likely seem long, but please don't try to get home by yourselves."

Clary nodded, and Jennifry left.

She wasn't fast.

The sun moved past the cliff's brink, casting a sliver of new shadow before she reached the top of the path – winding up the quarry side to the rough, brambly land above it – and passed out of sight.

Clary looked at Elspeth. Her pinafore was rumpled and ripped; her dress beneath it, dusty; and her black wool stockings, loose from their moorings. But slight color had returned to her face, and she lay easily, a look of introspection upon her. "What other secrets are there, do you think?" she asked.

Clary shook her head. "Gran said Great Granfer Maxim – Rofane Roanmothe – had a brother who thought he was a wolf. But . . ." Her thoughts drifted to her nearer family. Would Papa's drunkenness of this last month become a secret? Mama's refusal to leave her bed?

Clary looked down at her own broken limb. Its sharp pain had ebbed and the throbbing lessened, but how could she manage Lyrus with a splint and a sling? How could Elspeth help, when she'd surely be on crutches?

I can't do anything about that right now.

The sun edged farther west, and the bluff's shadow crept out to shade Elspeth's eyes. How much longer would it be?

The breeze rustled the brambles above.

A lark trilled, briefly.

Footsteps sounded.

Jennifry? Great Aunt Jennifry, Clary corrected herself, craning her head to spot whoever approached. The steps were too quick to be her great aunt's. Papa?

No, not anyone familiar, but Clary had seen this woman before: the dark beauty with that hint of cruelty to her expression.

She was beautiful yet. And her mouth still curved triumphantly. But something was different.

Clary squinted, blinked. What was she seeing?

A blur? A flicker? A wink?

A . . . troll?

Holy Teyo, no! If this woman were a troll, she was not benign.

Clary scrambled to her feet, scurried around Elspeth, and – using her good arm – grabbed her sister's shoulder, twisted her fingers in the fabric of pinafore and dress, and pulled.

"Clary, what are you doing?!" Elspeth's question was a frightened whisper, thank Teyo.

"She's dangerous. We have to hide."

Had Elspeth seen the woman? The troll? (Clary was sure the intruder was a troll. Even though she was beautiful.) Would her sister argue? Resist?

Clary pulled. Dragged Elspeth closer to the cliff face, into the shallow cleft waiting there, then around a bend into a hidden passage. Had it been here this whole time? How had she and Elspeth never discovered it before? The quarry was their play ground as much as their gleaning spot.

"This is far enough," gasped Elspeth. How badly had the dragging jostled her leg?

"No. It isn't," insisted Clary. "What if she comes after us?"

"Did she see us? I don't think she saw us."

Clary kept pulling, backing farther into the cleft. Where was the light coming from? Sunshine reflecting on the limestone near the entrance shouldn't be making it around that bend. She glanced over her shoulder. Oh!

Looming head high, the massive orb of creamy rock gleamed, casting its soft glow on the water swirling through the puddle in which it rested, and along the stalactites and stalagmites fringing the small grotto.

"What is it?" whispered Elspeth.

Clary became aware that she'd frozen in place. "I don't know. It looks like a giant goose egg made of agate, but . . ."

"What?"

Elspeth faced the way they'd come. She couldn't see it. Clary shifted her sideways, which was a mistake.

"Ow! Don't," whimpered her sister.

Clary looked around for something to prop Elspeth's shoulders – nothing – then lowered herself gingerly to make her lap into a pillow for Elspeth's head. She jostled her own arm, but managed to swallow her exclamation of pain.

Elspeth's eyes were screwed shut. "Ow, ow, ow," she moaned.

Clary scrutinized her sister's leg. Dare she move it? The sideways movement had bent it ever so slightly. Surely it needed to be straight.

"Elspeth, I have to move your leg."

Elspeth's eyes flew open. "Oh, don't! Don't!" Her voice was frantic.

Clary hesitated. Getting out from under Elspeth and then back to her feet seemed daunting.

"Clary, it hurts! It hurts so much!"

Teyo! She *had* to do something.

Awkwardly, she got her feet under her, holding her broken arm still, gripping Elspeth's pinafore at the shoulder with the other hand. She pushed upward with her legs, hitching Elspeth along the grotto floor (and straightening that leg), then losing her own balance. "Ack!"

"Ow!" cried Elspeth.

"Ow!" echoed Clary, as she fell against the glowing orb.

Its curving rock caught her, but the impact jolted her arm. She slid down the slick surface, landing half-in and half-out of the water, Elspeth's head miraculously back on her lap, not dropped on hard floor or underwater. She relaxed her grip of pinafore and lowered her voice. Their cries hadn't been soft. "Are you alright?"

The water was warm, as was the stone of the orb. She felt it vibrating against her ribs and upper arm – the good arm.

"You were right," panted Elspeth, her face pale and clammy. "It's better this way, but –" She shook her head. And noticed the orb. "Oh! That's what you saw."

"I think it's alive."

Elspeth reached a tentative hand toward an ivory and cream swirl. "It's warm," she whispered. "It feels . . . dangerous. And . . . hungry!" She snatched her hand back, then reached out again.

Clary nodded. "I think it's an egg. Getting ready to hatch. Hatchlings are hungry, aren't they?"

"Clary, I don't want to be food," quavered Elspeth.

"Oh!" It hadn't occurred to her that she might be a meal to a roc or a hippogriff. "Maybe it's a pegasus egg. Pegasi are good, aren't they?"

"I don't think they're born from eggs," Elspeth faltered.

"They have wings though," urged Clary.

Firm footsteps slapped the passage floor, and the beautiful troll – Clary still thought she was a troll – rounded the bend.

They *hadn't* gone far enough.

Clary raised her broken arm, inadequate shield though it was, but the woman – the troll – ignored her.

"I knew it! Jenny never could get scrying right!" The troll's voice was edged, but refined. "And now I'm late. Likely too late!"

She strode directly to the egg, her toes stopping a finger's width from Elspeth's hip, the lace of her petticoat foaming over Elspeth's pinafore. She placed her palms against the egg's surface, and Clary felt the vibration against her ribs change: tighter, faster, urgent.

I am fit, I am full, I am Ayr! sounded in Clary's mind.

Crack! The egg rocked.

And rocked again.

The troll stiffened. Small crackles of orange lightning haloed her dress sleeves.

I am air, I am I, I am Ayr!

"I am witch, I am sybil, I am troll!" the witch declaimed.

Clary hunched away from her. *I knew she was a troll.*

Crack!

I am here, I arrive, I am here!

"Never here, only there, stay within!" Stridency limned the witch's voice.

"Elspeth, she's trying to keep it from being born!" Clary murmured.

"That's good! It can't eat us, if it stays in its egg!" Elspeth whispered back.

"It's not right. And *she's* not good. It can't be good, if she's doing it. We should stop her."

"How?" Was Elspeth agreeing?

"Can you grip her ankles when I jump up?"

Elspeth nodded. "Hurry! It's getting worse. Can you feel it?"

Clary could.

The egg buzzed and juddered. The orange sparks racing down the troll's arms turned black. The water soaking Clary's skirts chilled.

No! Eggs needed warmth!

She felt Elspeth lean forward and grab.

She sprang up, butting her head into the troll's belly.

She felt herself falling, feet tangled in her sister's pinafore, neck clamped under the witch's strangling elbow.

The grotto floor was hard, and her broken arm twisted under her weight.

She screamed, heard Elspeth screaming. What had the witch done to her sister's leg?

She shoved at the weight pinning her down, never mind the sickening wrench to her arm, and rolled over when the witch released her.

"Little brats!"

The witch slapped her face, bouncing Clary's head with the force of the blow.

Then she was up, ignoring Clary, and kicking the welter of Elspeth's petticoat free of her pointed shoes, returning her attention to the egg, but no longer unopposed.

Jennifry had returned.

"Kasharan. No."

Clary could see she was outraged, despite the evenness of her words.

"What have you done?" Jennifry's voice quavered.

"What you should have done long since, sister mine." *Sister? Was she another secret great aunt?* "How could you think we had months yet? How could I have been fool enough to trust you?" *Was that anguish in the witch's voice?* "This is why I came home! I *need* this." Her arm came up, and she *threw* dark lightning – not at the egg – but at Jennifry.

Jennifry screamed and went down.

Crack!

The egg split in two and dimmed, darkening the grotto.

Looming shadow, sleek and lithe and fierce, leaped from the shell, talons stretched, razor beak agape.

Snick! Snap!

The witch was gone, swallowed down that hungry gullet.

❧✸

Swallowing richness, swallowing his friend's *energea*, achieving density, Ayr strengthened. Soon he would be ready. Soon he would triumph. Soon he would emerge.

Ayr fed.

And woke in time to know his birth crisis had come.

Now!

He could not buffet or rap or strike. His quarters held him too close for that. But he was strong, and great, and ready.

He pushed.

Crack!

He felt the shell of his prison quiver. He pushed again, talons and paws pressed against one curving limit, back and wing humeri crushed against its opposite.

Crack!

His prison swayed.

He reached for the source of his own *energea* and felt it flood his sinews. Blue lightning crackled through his bones.

I am fit, I am full, I am Ayr!

Then an orange lightning from without answered him.

"I am witch, I am sybil, I am troll!" declaimed his foe.

My enemy! This time he knew how to dominate her evil. He . . . swallowed and grew greater.

Crack!

I arrive, I am here, I arrive!

The orange lightnings grew black and hurt him. He swallowed.

"Never here, only there, stay within!"

Ayr felt his limbs chilling, his strength ebbing. *No!*

Then came unexpected respite, a moment of peace. He *heaved.*

Crack!

The limits compressing him fell away, releasing his cramped limbs to freedom, exquisite in its sensation. He stretched: forelegs and talons extended, hind legs and paws surging, wings sweeping, great rostrum gaping.

He leaped.

And saw his enemy confront his friend. *No!*

Snick! Snap! His foe was food. Succulent and savory and moist. A food wholly different from the intangible *energea* he'd consumed for so long. Food! He wanted more and looked for it.

He found something else.

The damaged body of his friend met his searching gaze. She and her . . . hatchlings? They were small, and they were hers. He could see that. And they were broken. He was too late.

His enemy was their enemy, and she had struck before his release.

No!

He reached again for his ancestral power.

ഗ

Upon Jennifry's return to the quarry, the sun had shone lower in the sky. The light held a deeper golden tone, and a mild breeze fluttered the scruffy weeds fringing this craggy cup in the land. The smell of warm rock dust mingled with the sharpness of wild onion. Her knees hurt. She'd hurried.

But girls were gone, and somehow Jennifry knew they'd not headed home.

"Oh, no. Oh, no," she muttered. "They've gone inside, they've found it."

Would this be a second set of sisters lost to the *orbis* and troll-disease?

She hastened her steps as she followed the narrow track winding down the bluff. *I must save them.*

The shadow before the cleft entrance felt cool.

Crack!

The passage resounded with a blow, a violence, a birth.

Holy Teyo! It's hatching.

Twin screams echoed one after another, and she emerged into the grotto as Kasharan growled, "Little brats!" and slapped Clary's head against the stone floor.

"Kasharan. No."

She felt a fury ignite within her, like nothing she'd ever known before. What had her sister done to these nieces of theirs? How could she? How dared she?

Jennifry missed her sister's reply, starting forward in urgency.

Kasharan's attack did not miss.

Black lightning took Jenny full in the stomach like a whip from hell.

She fell, curling around her wound.

‮&‬C‮ʒ‬

Clary lay still while the vast shadow of the creature loomed above her, mantling its wings, filling the grotto's space.

Her leg bent beneath her, its knee twisted.

Her arm throbbed at her side.

Her voice whispered: "No, please, no."

I am here, I am Ayr, I am strong, thundered the creature in her mind.

I am mighty, I am puissant! It paused. *Gryphon regnant am I!*

Blue sparks chased down its talons and leaped to her belly.

"No!" she cried out. But it felt good. Cool relief flowed through her limbs, banishing hurt, banishing pain.

The gryphon sprang away from her to bless Elspeth, and then away from Elspeth to Jennifry.

Be thou healed, be thou whole, be thou thine.

Then it was gone, hurtling through the passage, seeking the heavens that would be its home.

Clary wished she could see it as it mounted to the air: plumage gleaming in the sun, its fierce eye dominating all, its tremendous wingspan claiming sky.

I'm glad it's born. I'm glad it's free. I'm glad I saw it.

The broken halves of the egg shell lit again, the glow illuminating the grotto again.

She pushed herself up to sitting and saw her sister doing likewise. Had the gryphon's gift healed her leg? Apparently so. They crept to Jennifry's side.

Clary gasped.

Jennifry's eyes were open, but she lay as one stunned. Or dead. And the clear gray of her eyes remained the only thing recognizable about her.

Where was her wound? Where was her age? Where was her *troll-disease*? Was this really Jennifry?

Clary shrank from her.

Were all bad things made good? How could rightness feel so wrong?

Elspeth whimpered. "Clary, I'm scared."

Clary buried her face in Elspeth's shoulder, felt Elspeth bury her own in Clary's.

"I'm scared, too," whispered Clary.

"Pull me to its shell." Jennifry's murmur came low and sweet. "Please."

Clary whipped her head around, startled. *Was* it Jennifry?

"The birth liquors will ease me," Jennifry entreated them.

Slowly, Clary nodded.

"Can you do it?" she asked her sister. "Is your leg . . . ?"

Elspeth smiled tremulously. "I'm well, Clary. As though I never fell."

They turned to their great aunt.

Why wasn't she well? Or . . . why was she healed, but somehow not?

Jennifry opened her hands, pleading.

I guess my questions must wait.

Clary bent to take her great aunt's shoulders, Elspeth right beside her, Elspeth's hands right beside Clary's, gripping the loose fabric of Jennifry's now ill-fitting gown as they dragged her across the grotto floor.

The nearer fragment of egg shell – the larger – lay clear of the mineral spring and tipped. Silver-whorled fluid puddled within it and around it.

Jennifry sighed as egg's curve cradled her. "Ah. Thank you."

Clary opened her lips to speak, then closed them.

She looked at Elspeth.

Elspeth looked at her.

As one, they bent to the birth waters of the gryphon and began to anoint Jennifry's face and hands with the moisture.

Later, much later, Clary voiced her questions.

"The gryphon anchored my radices," Jennifry told her. "You do know that's what makes a troll, don't you? When a pattern-maker draws too much *energea* through the anchor points of her own pattern, they break and she becomes a troll."

Yes, Clary knew that. Every child learned it in lessons right along with geography and history and spelling.

"I thought it couldn't be cured." There lay her true objection. "But you are cured, right? You're not a troll anymore, are you?"

"No, I'm not." Jennifry shook her head. "It feels very odd."

"But . . ."

"I know. But!" She climbed to her feet.

Clary stared at her.

Her great aunt was still short, but her once-dumpy figure was now slight and graceful under the slack folds of her clothes. Her face was young and pretty and held a dash of pixie mischief in the eyes.

"Our world is upside down." Jennifry took Elspeth's hand on one side and Clary's on the other, drawing them gently toward the outside. "A gryphon is a game changer," she continued. "It makes the rules. I suppose it can change them. But it's not a comfortable thing, is it?"

Clary clutched Jennifry's hand harder. That was it. It was scary when an impossibility became a reality. Even when the new reality was good.

"Will it come back?" Elspeth whispered.

Jennifry didn't answer for a few steps.

Would it come back? Clary half-longed for it to return, half-feared it. What else might it change?

"No," Jennifry decided at last. "The world would break, if it suffered many gifts such as this one. I don't think a gryphon can alight without giving. And yet our world hasn't broken."

"They must not visit us often," Clary mused.

"Good!" breathed Elspeth.

☙❧

It was early evening when they got home, but the sun lingered some way above the horizon, golden in a deep turquoise sky, prelude to the splash of peach and lavender that would herald its setting. A swift darted over the highest boughs of the oak in the front garden, and Clary's heart skipped a beat, fear and longing co-mingled again. No, it was bird, not gryphon.

She sighed.

The front door stood open. Elspeth darted forward, then stood astonished on the threshold. What? Clary quickened her stride, outdistancing Jennifry behind her. Had something else gone wrong while they'd been gone? Maybe the gryphon's passage had disrupted things here as much as it had in the old quarry.

Good heavens!

Clary stopped beside her sister, feet glued to the spot.

The front parlor spread tidily before her: furniture upright, hangings straight, table cleared, and Papa lifting a last chair into place while Mama swept crumbs into a dustpan. Then Mama caught sight of her daughters, and the broom slipped – *clack* – to the floorboards.

She ran to them, crying, "Tiber, Tiber, they're here!" and caught them in her arms, her face wet with tears.

Papa rushed forward an instant later, encompassing all three of them in a wild embrace, but his voice whispered – reverence gilding gratitude – "Thank God, thank god."

Their tumble of joy and thanksgiving delayed explanations for a while. And the explanations, when they came, started incoherently – from both sides.

Eventually Jennifry, hovering in the doorway until then, entered the conversation: the egg, her sister, the gryphon, the world upside down.

The tumult after that bore a more purposeful character: young Pomfrey from the cottage down the lane sent for the job carriage, Lyrus fetched from his nap, Jennifry lent clothes for their visit to the Justicar of the Peace, and the carriage ride to his manor.

And then yet more bustle.

Rofane ni Calcinides seemed just as bewildered by their account of the events at the old quarry as Mama and Papa had been. He was *more* bewildered by the sudden appearance of his aunt, magically healed and young. Despite his confusion, once he acquired the gist, he acted with dispatch. He summoned the wardens under his authority, instructed his housekeeper to make a room ready for Jennifry, consigned Clary's family to his wife's care, and set off for the quarry to investigate.

The Rofanish fed them dinner and entertained them in her parlor after it. The stars pricked out in the darkening sky outside. When the Rofane continued absent, the Rofanish served tea and pressed them to accept beds for the night.

Mama declined. "We'd really rather return home, if we may. Will Ni Calcinides . . . ?"

"Oh, heavens!" His rofanish was impatient. "It's not as though Arteme doesn't know where you live! He can ride over when he has more questions."

And so they'd come home.

Mama changed Lyrus' nappy – he didn't wake, worn out – and laid him in his crib, asleep. Mama and Papa together put the girls to bed, Mama singing lullabies, Papa stroking Elspeth's hair. It was almost as though they'd returned from a year's sea voyage and couldn't bear to be parted from their children for any reason.

Once Clary had brushed her teeth, Mama invited her into the dressing room to braid Clary's hair. She was very gentle with the tangles, and then drew her daughter onto her lap in the rocking chair after the braiding was done. Her body felt solid behind Clary's shoulders and her arms like a soft quilt on a stormy night, although this night was still.

"I'm so sorry," murmured Mama, her fingers warm on Clary's cheek. "So very sorry. I can't imagine what this year has been for you. Other than awful."

"Mmm." Clary snuggled deeper into Mama's embrace.

Papa seated himself on the footstool at Mama's knee, rested his hand on Clary's hand.

"This year will be different." Clary could hear the promise in his voice."

Mama sighed. "It can't make up for . . . all the neglect."

"No." Papa pressed Clary's fingers. "But it can heal. Will heal."

The blue sparkles of the gryphon's gift arose in Clary's memory. "I'm already healed," she murmured.

"It might take you longer to trust us again," suggested Papa.

"Maybe."

But Clary didn't think so. Her parents were back. Not from sea, but from long illness, the long draining of the gryphon's delayed birth. She knew they would not be going away again. And yet . . .

"Papa?" She heard her tone sharpen. "Why did you visit the old quarry every day?" *Had* he been visiting Kasharan? Betraying Mama?

His mouth straightened. "I never made it that far. I could feel that the wrongness, the weight on my limbs, came from that direction. But it grew heavier so rapidly that I sank to the ground before I got halfway. I had to crawl home when I came out of my faint." He shook his head. "Each day I swore I'd make it. *This* time. Find the source, find it and fix it. But I never did." His hand patted Clary's shoulder. "Like your mama, I'm sorry too. Sorry I failed you. Failed all of you." He paused. "A papa likes to protect his family himself. Not leave it to his children."

"We did help," murmured Clary, "at least a little."

Papa chuckled, leaving his grimness for the moment. "A little?" he repeated. "No, you and Elspeth were the nail that secured the horseshoe that steadied the steed that bore the knight who saved the battle. Sometimes the littlest things are the biggest."

Clary smiled. Papa was here. Mama was here. She was home.

Months of the North-lands Year

Janary winter

Falnary late winter

Nerich early spring

Thyril spring

Ponce late spring

Joiesse early summer

Labra summer

Jube late summer

Sanember early autumn

Ionaber autumn

Noulember late autumn

Bricember early winter

Timeline for the North-lands Stories

Ancient Times

Skies of Navarys...3000 years before *Perilous Chance*

The Bronze Age

Resonant Bronze...2000 years before *Perilous Chance*

Before the Steam Age

Rainbow's Lodestone...~100 years before *Perilous Chance*

Star-drake...immediately after *Rainbow's Lodestone*

The Steam Age

Crossing the Naiad...52 years before *Perilous Chance*

The Troll's Belt...contemporaneous with *Perilous Chance*

Perilous Chance...the now of this timeline

J.M. Ney-Grimm lives with her husband and children in Virginia, just east of the Blue Ridge Mountains. She's learning about permaculture gardening and debunking popular myths about food. The rest of the time she reads Robin McKinley, Diana Wynne Jones, and Lois McMaster Bujold, plays boardgames like Settlers of Catan, rears her twins, and writes stories set in her troll-infested North-lands.

Look for her novels and novellas at your favorite bookstore – online or on Main Street.

J.M. Ney-Grimm maintains a blog featuring flash fiction from her North-lands and other tidbits unearthed by her ever-active curiosity.

Visit her at http://JMNey-Grimm.com.